The Whol Sh Bang 2

A collection of crime stories

by Sisters in Crime: Canada

Edited by Janet Costello

Toronto Sisters in Crime, Publisher

Toronto Sisters in Crime, Publisher

The characters and events in this book are fictitious. Any similarity to real persons, living or dead, is coincidental and not intended by the authors.

Library and Archives Canada Cataloguing in Publication

The Whole She-Bang 2: stories by Sisters in Crime: Canada; edited by Janet Costello

ISBN 978-0-9880936-4-5

Detective and Mystery stories, Canadian (English) 2. Costello, Janet

Also issued as ISBN 978-0-9880936-2-1 (e-book)

Cover Art and Design by Antonia Gorton

Copyright Acknowledgements

Advance Praise for The Whole She-Bang 2

"Are the stories in this new collection by Sisters in Crime ingenious? Check. Well-written? Check. A delight, a surprise, and unputdownable, story after story? Check, check, and check. If ever there was an anthology worth checking out, this is it."

Scott Mackay, *Arthur Ellis Award* winner for best short mystery fiction

"The Whole She-Bang 2 is wonderful! With accomplished short stories that range from hilarious to gruesome to downright unsettling, this is a collection sure to appeal to any taste. It does Canada's female crime writers proud."

Louise Penny, *New York Times* Bestselling author

"Thoughtful, well-written and above all, entertaining, this collection of short stories by established and up-and-coming crime writers is as Canadian as a polite little murder on a winter's afternoon."

Elizabeth J. Duncan, award-winning author of the **Penny Brannigan** series.

Dedicated to Lou Allin, award-winning author, mentor and inspiration. Lou was wicked in wit and unfailingly generous—a true Sister in Crime.

We miss you.

Acknowledgements:

Thank you to the members of the Toronto Chapter of Sisters in Crime. Your volunteer work, for more than twenty years, has provided inspiration, support and motivation for so many.

Thank you to Dorothy Birtalan, Linda Cahill, Melodie Campbell, Janet Costello, Deanna Dunn, Jeannette Harrison, Nathan Hartley, Rayna Jolley, Jude Keast, Lesley Mang, Marian Misters, Helen Nelson, Jan Oddie, Trish Rees-Jones, Renate Simon, and Kay Stewart, all Sisters to this project. Your countless hours volunteered, accepting the stories, judging, proofreading, fact-checking, editing, providing legal help, formatting and marketing this anthology are very much appreciated.

Thank you to Antonia Gorton, cover artist extraordinaire, who stepped up to the plate with yet another seductive and eye-catching cover

Janet Costello

*Both entries in **The Whole She-Bang** series have been edited by **Janet Costello**. She also edited* Crime Scene, *the Toronto Chapter newsletter, for six years. Janet became active in the mystery community when Boubercon, the World Mystery Convention, was held in Toronto in 2004. In 2017, Janet, with co-chair Helen Nelson, will bring Boubercon XLVIII to Toronto. The To-Be-Read pile in Janet's home, which is not contained just within the library, is a siren constantly calling to her. She tells herself that, in 2018, she will devour these piles in short order.*

Table of Contents

Introduction

by Lesley Mang

Chapter President, Sisters in Crime Toronto

Well, we've done it again! Just as Helen Nelson, our former president, promised. We had so much fun creating *The Whole She-Bang* that we just had to produce another anthology of our talented members' work. The rules we established for our first anthology were used here. Again, we did not establish a firm number to be included and the judging was blind. The judges were asked to select the stories they thought deserved to be published.

Our new anthology holds twenty-four stories. Some of the authors appeared in *The Whole She-Bang*, but we are really pleased to include many new names. It is evident that we have a deep well to draw from should we decide to produce another anthology.

Most of the stories are set in Canada, and it's very interesting to read how much the landscape impacts the lives of the characters we encounter. You'll read stories set in the Arctic, remote northern British Columbia, Jasper National Park, Vancouver Island, Northern Ontario and Ontario cottage country. In each of these stories, the setting is crucial to the telling of the story.

You'll also read stories set in small towns, big cities and urban neighbourhoods. In each case, location helps to shape the story.

Other stories have small, specific settings: a funeral home, a hospital room, a book store, a university, an arena. Again, the details of the setting are important.

The settings are vital, but there is so much more to savour in these stories. You'll meet some splendid characters. Among them you'll find a frightened young newspaper carrier, a reluctant thief, an upright bookstore owner, vengeful women, old and young, unhappy wives, unhappy employees, a famous poet, an observant female police officer, a clever P.I., a brave student, a seemingly simple-minded small town shopkeeper, a deluded stalker and an older woman looking for love. More than one perpetrator gets away with the crime, but some of them suffer for it. There are a couple of characters who plan murder, but then discover redeeming qualities in their intended victims.

The settings and the characters are important but the quality of the story telling is wonderful. We are treated to irony and humour in the plots and the characters. And there is almost always a satisfying resolution to the situation.

Congratulations to all of the authors for their fine stories. We hope this sample of your work leads to many readers in the future.

This anthology was produced in record time (under a year) by a team of volunteers who put in hundreds of hours collecting, judging, editing, proofreading, formatting and planning a marketing strategy. A very big thank you to all of them.

And a very big thank you to Sisters in Crime, a volunteer organization devoted to promoting the recognition of female writers of crime fiction, for inspiring this collection.

Contents Known

by H. MacDonald-Archer

Heather MacDonald-Archer draws on almost forty years of experience as an editor, reporter and feature writer. As a journalist, Heather worked on a number of Thomson Newspapers, The Ottawa Journal *and* The Canadian Press *before landing at* The Toronto Star *for 29 years. She is a member of the Toronto chapter of Sisters in Crime and Sisters in Crime International. She had two short stories published in a crime anthology,* Nefarious North *(August 2013). She holds an undergraduate degree in Celtic Studies from St. Michael's College, University of Toronto and an M.A. in early medieval church history, University of Guelph. She lives in Toronto with her husband.*

Christopher Carlyle recognized the trunk the minute he saw it outside the back door to his shop. It was quite large and covered in thin, battered red leather that had once borne an intricate raised design of flowers, circles and tiny shapes. It closed with a large silver hasp that was evocative of Morocco or southern Spain. It had witnessed life, of that Christopher was quite sure, for its slashes, scratches and dents told a story of boats and train carriages, danger and excitement: if only it could talk.

Thank God it couldn't.

The first time the trunk had shown up, it was full of a brilliant little collection of eighteenth and nineteenth century tomes, some of them written by Dr. Johnson, Edmund Burke and Daniel Defoe. Nestled in its folds of scarlet silk lining were smooth leather-covered works by Dumas and Flaubert, Anne Radcliffe, Lady Morgan and Susan Ferrier, the pages trimmed in faded gilt. The trunk was purchased, contents unseen, at a large estate sale in Kent. All he was told, prior to the frantic bidding, was that it was full of books. But the sight of the trunk alone stole his heart and he was delighted when it was delivered the following day to his little Chiswick bookshop.

He sold the books, but kept the trunk. Well, why not? It was, in itself, a real treasure. It sat at the front of his shop for five years, used as a perch by the many perusers of fine old literature at Carlyle and Son Books, a musty, elongated shop tucked between a kebab take-away and a charity store. Even Gustav, his ancient orange cat, put its worn top to use in his final days, stretched out in the sun. Christopher found him late one afternoon, his limbs stiff, eyes closed in eternal contentment.

The trunk had left the shop exactly one year ago. Feeling relief and some joy, Christopher actually saw it carried off by the dust-men. "Nice old bit," one of them commented, stroking the soft leather sides, a nicotine-stained finger following the circles and designs. "If you like old stuff. A heavy bugger, though." The two men had wrestled the trunk up and into the lorry, Christopher at the back door, praying that the small lock securing the old hasp would hold.

And yet it was back, delivered by someone unknown and left at the rear of the shop. The hasp was broken and hung loosely and the red leather was peeled in a few places. Old wood peeked through rudely and marred the trunk's true beauty.

Christopher sat down abruptly on the back step when he found it, ashen, heart pounding. He poked the trunk with his toe, testing to see if it would move. Was it full or empty? He removed the pen from his breast pocket and looped it through the broken hasp to lift the heavy lid. He didn't even want to touch the damned thing now. The lid flipped back easily to reveal the scarlet silk, stained and musky. It was very empty.

First, Christopher exhaled noisily, feeling relief. Then a cold fear swept over him.

The Carlyles' bookstore had always been a busy one. Christopher and his late father, Owen, worked well together, their love of old books overcoming the polar differences in their personalities. Owen was a tubby old hippie with a huge white beard, long hair and a penchant for flashy clothes and leather gilets. He was noisy, robust and opinionated, and much given to smoking a reefer or two in the back, at the end of the day, while he read *The Diary of Samuel Pepys*—out loud, for God's sake—a glass of Glenmorangie in his hand.

But the punters loved Owen and even those who didn't care so

14

much for old books came by the shop to talk, take in the atmosphere, to soak up Owen and his old-rocker-turned-bibliophile reputation. He was a bona fide sixties hell-raising reprobate who eschewed his Oxford education to join a band, fathering five children by five different women along the way. Only Christopher, the last child born to a woman Owen claimed was his one true love, stuck by his old man. His mother, a delicate flower of a woman, died of asthma when Christopher was four, leaving the child in the care of a man any normal person would consider a complete lunatic.

God knows what happened to the other offspring, one boy and three girls. Christopher never met them. He learned several years ago through a great aunt that at least two of the girls were in America—a place he'd rather be right now.

Always clean-cut, fussy, exacting and particular, Owen's last child couldn't have been more different than his father. He hated rock music, hated anything to do with the modern world. At the end of a day, he'd lock up the store, draw the blinds and turn up the classical music he started playing after Owen died.

There was no nasty end for Owen; he died in the storeroom, glass of whisky in hand, reading Samuel Johnson's *The Life of Ascham*. His funeral, for all the noise and bluster he created while alive, was a quiet affair, attended by Christopher and a few local shopkeepers. So much for fame and notoriety, thought Christopher. Not his way.

He carried on with the business for six months or so, barely able to do the buying and organizing of shelves and the filling of Internet orders. It became clear that he would have to hire someone to help him. He just couldn't do it all.

The employment centre, four doors up the street, was more than willing to help Christopher find a suitable assistant and sent a number of highly unsuitable candidates his way. Twenty-three applicants came to be interviewed, from a blue-haired Goth with one-inch studs in his ears and a ring in his lower lip, to a morbidly obese woman who wanted to work and drink tea all day, yet keep her benefits at all costs. She couldn't lift books, she told him, couldn't climb the ladder to fetch them, either. And she never read books, anyway. "Is that okay?"

No, it wasn't.

On the day Christopher walked down the street to tell the centre to forget it, Sandra Keel, one of the employment counsellors at the back of the room, held up a slip of paper and waved it at him. "She's perfect," she hollered over the heads of her co-workers. Christopher reluctantly walked down the row of desks to the woman's cubicle and sat down.

Sandra looked at him with bright eyes and read the applicant's details. "She's perfect. She's got a degree in library science, has been in the country six months and has a work visa. She's been working as a maid at a hotel in Chelsea but wants the chance to use her education and get some experience."

Christopher scratched his ear. "Age? A new graduate?"

"Yes. She graduated last year. She's twenty-two. A very nice girl. I've met her twice. Should I send her along? Her English is very good and she's quite keen."

Christopher grimaced.

"Well, fergawdsake, at least she can read!" Sandra laughed.

"Yes, fine. Tell her to come along tomorrow after lunch. I'll give her the details and I'll let you know how it goes."

"Her name is Radka!" Sandra shouted at Christopher's retreating back. "Radka Boyonov!"

Christopher just raised a hand and kept going.

So that was how it started. Radka was tall, dark-haired and flamboyant. She spoke quickly and with an intensity that scared Christopher. She never took her eyes off someone when she was addressing them, all the while moving closer, and in the end, it was more a case of Radka hiring Christopher, instead of the other way around. "I will work every day needed. I'm not afraid of work. I work hard, you see. And I'm educated. You educated?"

"Cambridge." Christopher shuffled his feet during the interview, trying to avoid the woman perched on the red trunk. "Ahem. You are familiar with the Internet and purchasing books online? I have a lot of customers from abroad who order from me. We have to pack up the books and send them on. We also have to list them in the inventory. There's a lot of email communication between us and the customer. It's not just walk-in business we do here."

"Oh yes. I order all my books at university online. Much cheaper. Or I take from library. You like library?"

"Yes, there's one two blocks away, if you're interested."

"Okay then, I start tomorrow."

And Christopher, not the man his father was, simply said, "Fine."

Things went well for a month or so. Christopher learned she was very good with the online orders and keeping the listed inventory up-to-date. But she didn't seem to know a lot about books or publishers. She distracted customers with off-topic conversations to keep from them the fact she knew very little, and she frequently made promises of obtaining books Christopher knew he'd never be able to acquire.

More often than not, an interested buyer left baffled and upset. She sat and filed her nails and she made frequent calls on a cell phone in a language he didn't recognize. She became rude to him, talked back when asked to do something and was consistently late for work.

He spoke to her gently at first. He told her she mustn't do this, or that, as it was inappropriate and not fair to the customer. And if she didn't know something, she was to refer the customer to him, because he did know. She sulked and went into 'silent' mode whenever he pointed out these facts. But he was adamant things had to change the Thursday she arrived for work three hours late and offered no explanation. She simply threw down her bag, rolled her eyes and made her pot of tea.

She was livid with this latest rebuke and threw a fine Jonathan Swift volume across the room, knocking over a display. She screamed at him in English and fluent French, which took him by surprise, and flounced out the door, slamming it so hard the window cracked.

Christopher spent the afternoon on the phone trying to get a glazier to replace it. He was so upset he forgot to eat lunch and he forgot to check the email orders for the day. He was so upset he had to lock the front door on three occasions while he spent some time in the little toilet under the stairs at the back of the shop. Her behaviour left him shaking. How on earth did he end up hiring such a person? He'd have been better off with one of the undesirables he'd interviewed. At least he could have trained them. There was no training Radka; she knew it all. And she knew nothing.

Should he go back to Sandra at the centre? Ask about that degree Radka said she had? Or should he investigate himself? The latter would be better. He didn't want to disappoint Sandra, after all.

Christopher sat down at the computer just inside the back storeroom. He noticed that even hours later, the little teapot Radka kept constantly filled on the desk was still warm. He removed the lid and sniffed. It wasn't tea, he was sure. He pulled a clean mug from a desk drawer and poured in a little of the pot's contents, taking just a small taste. He was still cleaning up the mess he'd spit out when the bell above the shop door jingled and he had to rush out and tell a customer, a professor of music at the Royal Academy of Music, that he probably wouldn't be able to get the rare *Fragments Représentés Devant le Roi a Fontainebleau (Ballets. Librettos. Selections), Paris, 1754* his assistant had promised.

Radka didn't come back that Thursday and the shop was quiet after the professor left. Christopher, throwing his usual parsimony to the wind, looked up the phone number online and called the Old Bulgarian University. It took several transfers before he got the proper department—quite usual for academia, he thought—and talked to a woman in alumni affairs about former students. Did she, by any chance, have listed, as a recent graduate, one Radka Boyonov?

He waited another ten minutes, assuring himself the cost was worth his peace of mind. "No, no. Not this past year," the woman assured him. "No Boyonov at all. But five years ago, a Radka Boyonov did attend here."

"Oh, well that's fine, then," Christopher said with relief. "You see, she's working for me at my bookstore here in London and I had to be sure."

There was a long moment of silence and Christopher thought the woman had hung up on him. "Sir, it is a familiar name to me, to be sure. But the woman working with you could not be our Radka Boyonov."

"Why?"

"It is a well-known story here, very tragic. Radka Boyonov was murdered by a boyfriend here on campus two days before her graduation. She was to be a librarian. She was stabbed multiple times in front of other students in the little student café. It was horrendous, as you can imagine."

Christopher felt faint. "Dear God."

"You must look into this woman who calls herself this. There cannot be two Radka Boyonovs from this university who studied in our program. No. I'm so sorry."

"Thank you." He sounded weak. He felt weak. So who was this woman who had a dead woman's name? Who passed herself off as something she clearly wasn't? And would she dare to come back tomorrow?

She did. Radka Boyonov marched into the shop the next morning, placed a bag of croissants in front of Christopher as though nothing had happened and proceeded to get down to work. She said very little, was pleasant when they did exchange words and seemed more intent on doing the job and less on being obstreperous. She made three tiny pots of tea, however—Christopher kept track—and

18

he was convinced she was keeping herself high on marijuana. Why hadn't he noticed her tendency to become jolly so quickly, loud when it was inappropriate, to laugh when it wasn't called for? He kept his distance—but had no reason to reprimand her again—until she'd gone for the day—for the weekend, actually.

Christopher's habit on a Friday night was to go through all the orders from overseas customers—many in America or Canada—and to make sure the right books had been sent to the right customers. Many of the buyers were collectors, but many were academics who needed the books for research or for rare books libraries on their campuses. He sold books to some of the best universities in the world. It was a very lucrative part of his business. He went through the list more methodically than usual, matching names, order numbers and addresses.

It was a nightmare. The books had been mailed out, but she had sent every single book to the wrong person. She'd switched order numbers, names of books and entered the customers' names incorrectly into the program he had set up. He was horrified. Nothing like this had ever happened. And some of the books mailed to the wrong customers were worth thousands of pounds.

Christopher Carlyle wasn't used to this sort of thing. He liked an ordered life, things to be done well, a job to run smoothly. He headed for his little toilet under the stairs and spent the next half hour there. When he emerged, white and shaky, he calmly sat down at the computer and emailed every customer on the list. He explained that staff errors had been made and that he would personally see that the mistakes would be corrected. Would each customer who received the wrong book please return it? They would be reimbursed the cost. The correct books would then be sent as quickly as possible to the right customers. He was terribly sorry. He hoped this would not keep the customer from doing business with Carlyle and Son in the future. He was most respectfully theirs, and etcetera. He sat back in his chair, his face in his hands.

He didn't know much about women. He knew about the kind of women his father liked and who frequently visited the store before Owen's demise. He hadn't liked them one bit. They drank Owen's Glenmorangie, smoked, were loud and liked to party.

He did like Sandra at the employment centre. She was nice, kind and polite. She was a married woman, he knew, but if he had the chance, she was the kind of woman he'd like to get to know better. This Radka creature was like nothing he'd ever met. How he let himself be taken in he would never know. He felt humiliated and embarrassed. The bookshop was his life, part of his being and now it seemed sullied, his reputation threatened.

Should he call the police? Would she return Monday morning? No. He didn't want the police involved. He didn't want the other business people in the street, some of whom he'd caught watching Radka coming and going, to see the police there at the shop.

Would she come back? He believed so.

So just over a year ago, Christopher had spent an anxious weekend planning and plotting a way to deal with Radka, without her causing a scene or tearing his shop apart. She was more than capable of that, he felt sure. He'd be ready for her on Monday morning. He would deal with her quickly and she would leave without putting up an argument.

Christopher's plans went off without a hitch. Radka left the bookshop Monday evening and never returned. When Sandra asked, two days later, how things were going, he'd just shrugged and said, "She just up and quit. Left me in the lurch. And I'm terribly busy with orders at the moment."

"Oh, Christopher. I'm so, so sorry. And I thought, with her background, she'd be perfect for you. You just let me know when you're ready to find another person for the shop."

"Will do."

The only thing Christopher regretted about getting rid of Radka was the fact his red trunk went with her. Or rather, she went with the trunk. In the trunk, actually, wrapped up in a double canvas bag tied with a triple length of twine, along with the slim steel garrotte he used to dispatch her. It was so much easier than he had expected.

And life at the bookshop, after two months of horror, quickly returned to normal. Sandra sent him the incredibly talented and intelligent, stud-bedecked blue-haired Goth, an expert on rare books who worked quietly alongside Christopher, seeking out deals, obtaining fine books, keeping immaculate records, unafraid of working long hours because the shop was, after all, like being in heaven. Christopher was able to take more days away from the shop, venture into the countryside and purchase books at various auctions. He even bought a little van so he could ferry his purchases back to the shop himself.

Life was very good for Christopher and his new assistant, Ivan.

Christopher was happy.

But that happiness was threatened by the empty trunk, its silk lining exposed to the sun, its exterior the worse for wear. Where had it been? Where was Radka's body?

Christopher just couldn't get up. He felt weak and his stomach was churning, even though he hadn't had breakfast yet. His assistant would be arriving for work soon. What on earth was he to do? Where could he put this trunk? Who knew about Radka? Who had taken her body? Worst of all, it now looked as if someone knew what he'd done to her.

Christopher got to his feet and was just about to shut the back door when a gruff greeting stopped him cold. He turned slowly to see a man in work clothes standing by the trunk. "You weren't here when I come by earlier."

"Oh?"

"How about this, huh? Remember it?" He pointed to the trunk.

Christopher didn't know what to do so he shook his head.

"Course you do. It was heavy as hell when we picked 'er up a year ago. Don't you remember? I loved 'er even then, I have to admit."

Christopher's head reeled. He was speechless.

"Listen, I loved 'er so much, I binned that lot of old books that were in that sack and I took'er home. I loved 'er, but my wife couldn't abide the thing and the kids kept kickin' and nickin' 'er. So here she is. Kept'er as good as I could. I've brought 'er back. Some of her red coverin' is scuffed, like ... but she ain't too bad, is she? Should have asked you if I could have it, but that's what dustmen do if we sees something nice thrown out."

Christopher stared at the man, a warm wave of relief flooding his entire being.

"Here, let me help you get 'er back inside."

Christmas in Paradise

by Lou Allin

Lou Allin was the author of the Belle Palmer mysteries set in Northern Ontario, and the RCMP Corporal Holly Martin series set on Vancouver Island. Lou also wrote That Dog Won't Hunt *in Orca's Rapid Reads editions for adults with literacy issues, and in 2013 won Canada's Arthur Ellis Best Novella Award for* Contingency Plan. *She authored two stand-alones for Cengage,* A Little Learning is a Murderous Thing *and* Man Corn Murders, *set respectively in the Michigan Upper Peninsula and in Utah. A former BC-Yukon VP for the Crime Writers of Canada, she lived across from Washington State on the Juan de Fuca Strait with her border collies and mini-poodle. Lou passed away in July of 2014. This collection is dedicated to her.*

Paul Fleischer lined the plastic honey bucket in the downstairs bathroom with two black garbage bags. Then he lugged in more crappy fir from the frosty deck and placed it by the large stove in the foyer. Beneath a tuque, long underwear, woolen pants, ski socks, and two sweaters, he was frozen to the bone. It was their first Christmas Eve on Vancouver Island.

"Welcome to Paradise," the realtor, storekeepers and even the neighbours had said when they arrived from Edmonton and bought the house in sunny September. In cheaper Otter Point, west of Victoria, the attractive green and white Greek villa with a hot tub out front overlooked the Strait of Juan de Fuca where fishing boats bobbed and freighters lined the shipping lanes. The tropical banana plants, palm-like dracaenas and kiwi vines had seduced them faster than a pitcher of margaritas. The true isles of Ulysses rarely saw -7C.

From habit, when he had spied the massive woodstove, Paul ordered up two cords of dry Douglas fir. When the wood was delivered, they discovered they had a pile of logs three times the size it would have been back home. Then they trundled it by wheelbarrow into the massive woodhouse. "You promised that we'd never have to haul wood again," Fran had said, massaging her lower back. "Just a bit for the *chill*."

"It's money in the bank. Probably last us for years," Paul replied, chunking the last piece into place and wincing at a splinter. "And of course I left behind my work gloves. At a dollar a pound to move, that wasn't smart. The snowblower, on the other hand, we will never need."

When they went for a daily walk that autumn, their neighbour Les, a retired faller, often met them by his stone wall etched with the names of his three former dogs: Pinky, Rose, and Betsy. He gestured with his cigar. "Now your place always puzzled me. Build for spec, build cheap; build to live there, spare no expense. But that Todd, he smacked her up in a month, then moved in with his family. Got most of the materials for free. Used timber. Wholesale tiles. You'll be colder than a brass monkey over there with those fool baseboards. Wired some in backward. You'll find out fast enough. *Zap zap*. And 2x4 framing's a fool's savings. Heat's gonna flow out like a donkey's butt after a dose of castor oil."

A raucous Steller's jay on the hydro wires echoed his chuckles. They made an excuse to move on down the road to the turnaround. Where had he been hiding when they were looking at the place? Should they have canvassed the block for opinions? "Don't listen to him," Paul said. "Gossip's a hobby out here. Look at his place. Square and unimaginative. Probably a fixed-up cabin."

They had been coasting into a mild fall, almost blessing the tardy rains for resurrecting the brown grass, still unpacking and rearranging furniture at the end of November. Then one morning an eerie light wakened them. Silent as a nun slipping off to vespers, a foot of snow had fallen "where the rain forest meets the sea." And it didn't melt into a dew like the realtor's jolly promises. A four-day power outage pushed them back to the Stone Age, and they wondered why they had left Alberta.

In Edmonton they had built a house designed for -35C. 2x6 construction. R2000 insulation. A woodstove warmed the house like a bakery. They sweated inside, even in t-shirts. Power outages were rare, and short. Sure, they retired a bit young, at fifty-five, but Fran's second breakdown had made up their minds. English teaching wasn't like it used to be. She'd had the guts to fail students and paid the price.

In blissful optimism, they had left winter's tools behind for the new owner. The lanterns, the plow truck, two massive snowblowers, five shovels, two scoops, car scrapers, and an ice chipper for the driveway. Only the camp stove and flashlights rode along with the $12,000 moving bill. Fran would write that children's book, and Paul would do volunteer work for seniors.

As the nights grew colder and the sun surrendered to record levels of rain, they asked themselves how much insulation lay within the flimsy walls. "Chipped newspaper, for all we know," Fran said with a whimper, then scratched at her recurrent eczema. With its span of high windows to accommodate the hundred-thousand-dollar view and pink glass-brick inserts, the magical solarium grew chilly and unwelcoming, a mere repository for endless pieces of cardboard from the packing boxes. The ice palace in *Dr. Zhivago* was little better.

Now they had minimal heat, no water and no plumbing. The house, fast becoming a living entity on life support, operated on a shallow well with an electric pump. And where they could have flushed at home by gravity, given a bucket of melted snow, here a distribution pump to the field bed blocked the possibility. Darkness came early. They spent each day huddling around the woodstove and making quick and salty dinners out of instant mashed potatoes, gravy mix and a can of flaked turkey. Then they went to bed by six and stayed there until the sun came up. They did get to town on the second day when the plow came, but only for essentials and more antidepressants for Fran. "I have a reason to be depressed," she repeated as she doubled the dosage.

Les's generator stuttered into action at dawn and roared on like a diesel locomotive for the next twelve hours, bracketing the short day. Her long silver-blonde hair braided like a fairy child's, Fran pounded her pillow, then adjusted her ear plugs. Paul lay awake far into the night. He'd thought moving out west would shackle her depressive, post-menopausal demons. A fresh start in a new climate. "Honey," he said as he heard her sniff. "Do you want to buy a generator?"

"Even if we could find one, and I doubt we could, we don't have the money. And I don't care to play that game. Even if we did lose the freezer meat."

Paul felt his stomach tighten. With a thirty-five per cent increase in real estate prices that year, they'd had to cash in over $200,000 in mutual funds to make up the difference in house costs. Come March, the taxes on those gains would be brutal. His pension was adequate, but hers wouldn't start until next year. Too humiliated to apply for a disability, she'd taken a stress leave from her job for the last two years at half pay.

On the third day, the coldest at -11C, Paul had visited the pump house. He hoped the pipes wouldn't freeze, because the system was cheap and illogical. Due to summer water shortages with the shallow well, the last owner had installed an ugly black plastic storage tank. Problem was, the unprotected lines snaked up and down the outside of the monster.

One of the five traps was sprung. "Caught another rat," he called to his wife, who was using a rake to chip at the hardened snow on the deck. "Cashew butter appeals to upscale west-coast rodents."

With no words, she brought out a plastic bag and handed it to him. He deposited the third Norway rat into the garbage pail. Females gave birth to sixty offspring a year. Rats had not been a problem in the frozen bush. He wondered if Les's peacock feed attracted them. Poisoning would be too dangerous with all the wells nearby.

They had barely recovered from the first outage when Christmas was upon them. Too dispirited and shell-shocked to buy even nominal presents, they made an effort to hunt up their artificial tree. The base was broken. "The movers again," Fran said with a bitter sigh. They had sent a report charging over $2,500 in lost and damaged property, but it would be a long time before they recovered anything. With a broom, she propped it up. Then they decorated it with prized ornaments from their thirty-year marriage. "Remember this one?" she asked as she touched a plastic moose fishing through a piece of acrylic ice. Paul moved closer and put his arm around her. She sounded more like herself. Less medication? He plugged in the lights and a host of red and green bulbs lit up the room.

One lone parcel had arrived from friends back east. It sat there like a reproach, but the postage had been significant. Fly-fishing tackle for him. A book on growing roses for her. They managed a laugh despite themselves.

That night they took a walk, trying to admire their jeweled tree, despite its precarious lean. Their neighbour's house was decorated with thousands of lights, a sleigh on the lawn, and a five-foot Santa nodded by the front door, a tape loop as he waved his arms bleeping *ho ho ho*.

Les strode down the driveway, thumbs in his suspenders. "Hear the weather? Another storm from the Pacific. Could be a typhoon. That's like a hurricane for youse. We had a doozie here in the sixties.

Freda, they called her."

"It's Christmas Eve. Let's hope for the best," Paul said. His anger toward the man had eased when the power had returned, but it seemed like Les was goading them. He could feel Fran's arm tightening around his.

"*Brumm brumm.* She's all fired up and ready to go. Forewarned is forearmed, my old daddy used to say." Les gave his cigar another pull, then spiraled it into the holly bush. "Oughta get one yourselves. Maybe a thousand and you can rig it yourself."

"I don't think so," Paul said. "I'd want an electrician to wire it in... if I got one."

"Haw!" Les said. "Cost the earth, that. What kinda work you say you did afore you retired?"

Paul answered, "College professor. History."

"Tits on a bull." Les grunted and turned up his drive. Through the kitchen window, they could see his wife Myrna at the stove, stirring a pot. Drifts of savory stew met their noses. They hadn't bought any more meat. Pasta and rice had become safe staples. Maybe get a roast Boxing Day if all went well.

That night the power checked out at midnight as lights flew around the strait in demented fireworks. Their back door blew open, and Paul charged downstairs in his pajamas. The wind howled, tossing the blackberry bushes like tumbleweeds. Down the street four massive Douglas firs shook their savage curls and groaned. At least they didn't have any large trees on the property, though he wasn't confident about the cedar-shake roof. Was that Les's peacock screaming? Or was it the wind? He slipped back into the warm bed, and they huddled together in the blackness, as significant as flies in a tornado.

"Maybe it'll be just a short one," Paul said in the dark of the morning. He saw Fran bite her lip, but at least she got out of bed and put on her headlamp before slipping into a robe. As long as she keeps moving, he thought, and talking...

He went into the bathroom. They could risk one flush, a luxury. How long before the next? Did they have enough garbage bags? At home they could have used the old outhouse. Their lakefront property was remote enough. This house was too civilized... and too barbaric.

Paul used newspaper crumples and cardboard to start a fire. The coals were dead. Fir didn't last overnight like the boreal maple or oak. Then he took down the camp stove from the top of the laundry cabinet and set it up in the kitchen for Fran. He attached a propane canister and filled the kettle from the water cooler. He noted the two full five-gallon jugs on the floor.

"We can shift the fridge contents to the BBQ—just in case," he said when she finally poured the coffee. They'd had an omelet last night. Cheese and eggs kept well enough without refrigeration. He stifled an ironic laugh. Ten feet from the woodstove on its cold ceramic floor, the whole house was a refrigerator.

"Wind's still up, but it's dropping," Paul said as he surveyed the street. Except for the undulating lines and some stray plastic garbage cans, everything seemed undamaged. It was 5C. The lawn looked green even if the banana plants had turned brown and fallen over after the heavy snowfall.

Fran poured orange juice and set out bread to toast on racks on the woodstove. "Let's try the battery radio. It's nearly eight," he said, and his heart lurched as he watched her programmed movements.

The local station gave the bad news. "Massive storm pummels island." Over 150,000 people were without power, from Victoria up to Nanaimo and across to Vancouver. Race Rocks had recorded record 157 kph winds. Stanley Park was a giant's game of pick-up sticks. The fabled West Coast Trail up to Port Renfrew had thousands of deadfalls, might be closed to tourists for a year. "I'm telling you, there were starfish in the trees," a hiker reported after a reconnaissance of French Beach.

The BC Hydro line said only that a large number of calls prevented any local information and that many routes were closed. No bulletins would be issued until crews assessed the situation. Then the generator went on next door, and the dial tone went dead.

Paul's hair felt greasy already. Another four or five days without a bath? Motels and B and B's with power would be jammed for a hundred miles. The Salvation Army was feeding the elderly in downtown Sooke, using camp stoves. At Whiffen Spit at the harbour, houses had been demolished. Cars were crushed.

If it's not on, he told himself, if it's not on by four, we'll drive to Victoria, take the ferry to Vancouver, go all the way to Calgary, for God's sake. Anywhere we can get a room. Fran can't take much more.

In the few hours of precious daylight, they walked to the turnaround. Two heavy firs had crashed across the power lines. Paul whistled at the enormity of the destruction, like a fascination with a train wreck. The trees were over five feet wide at the bases. Record rains in November had loosened their roots, allowing the wind to take the whole trees, not just the branches. Convergence of the twain. What had Hardy said about "twin halves of one august event?"

The road looked clear to the left. "Let's take a drive," Paul said.

But when they headed for town on the oceanside highway, they were stopped in seconds by roadblocks. An orange-vested man said through their window, "Gotta be a hundred trees down. Poles are snapped like toothpicks. Can't even see some of the beach houses buried in branches. Good thing they're summer cottages. No one hurt."

Paul heard Fran give a small gasp. Now they couldn't get more emergency supplies. What was in their cupboard? Why hadn't they stocked up after the first storm? "What about Otter Point Road?" That was the only other artery.

"She's blocked the same. Lines down all over. Power's dead as a doornail. Good old boys got their chainsaws out at first light. Free wood." Guttural roars from all directions far and near met their ears.

They drove home in silence. Cell phones never did work out here. If they needed an ambulance, what then? Light a signal fire? Wait for the air ambulance? Fran was dead silent as they pulled into the drive. Next door, Les was tossing fresh fir rounds from his pickup to his woodpile.

Supper that night was powdered-milk noodles along with a can of green beans and the last of the Hallowe'en candy. "I'll take care of the dinner. You rest," he said, and she made herself a nest on the pasha chair, bundled in blankets. She seemed to be humming a children's song. "We all fall down." She was examining her hands as if they had a mind of their own.

"Fran, stay under the covers. I can rig you a pallet by the wood stove, using the sofa cushions. How would that be?"

Her answer was to pull the blanket over her head. Was that laughter?

He splurged by using their drinking water to cook the pasta. The ditchwater's leeches had turned him away. Good enough for bathing, but suppose they had to drink it? Would ten minutes on the boil be enough?

His great-great-grandparents on a Bowmanville farm went to bed and got up with the sun and probably bathed in a tin washtub once a week, same as his father as a boy in Toronto. Life was simple and straightforward. Folks also died in childbirth and were lucky to live to sixty. Clinical depression sent them to the local asylum or to the barn with a rope.

And the generator droned on. He could see lights next door when it got dark at five. Paul called Fran to the window. "Look, television. The bastard. There's no antenna stuff anymore. Must be a DVD." He remembered that he was going to subscribe to the movie channels on their cable account as a belated Christmas present. Someone was singing over the din of the generator, "There's no place like home for the holidays."

"I hate that man. So smug." A runnel of tears had dried on her wan face. She mustered a small fist. "I'd like to kill him."

Paul hugged her to him. "Honey, you don't mean that." The smells of roast turkey met their nose. Les had a huge freezer.

On the fourth evening, they were reduced to eating instant rice, canned tuna and chestnuts she had bought for dressing. The bread had gone mouldy. Out came the powdered non-dairy creamer. "God knows what's in this," Paul said. "But we're probably so full of chemicals that it doesn't matter."

Fran refused to get out of bed the next morning. He brought her dry cereal with the last of the coffee.

"Think the road's finally open? The chainsaws have been quieter." He waited for a reply, tried to find the slightest expression of response.

She closed her eyes and turned her head to the wall. In the bathroom, as he cleaned his face with a wet wipe before scraping it with the razor, he noticed that her pill bottle was empty.

At noon, he was loading the stove. A beep sounded, and the power came on. Paul waited, hesitantly, as if they were the centre of a cosmic joke. Surely if they tried anything, a bath, maybe, if the system still worked, the power gods would cut them off again. Half an hour later, he started emptying the pee buckets on the sheltered side of the house, doing dishes, making a grocery list and turning on the baseboards.

He took Fran some tea. Her eyelids fluttered open. "If you believe, clap your hands. Clap louder. Clap," she said over and over with a giggle that could have urged tears. The tea grew cold as he waited with her. The phone was on at last. He could call 911 for help. Let them figure out how to reach them. Air ambulance maybe.

The generator droned on like a rabid animal. Fran covered her ears and started shrieking.

"Doesn't he know that the power is back? Is he doing this on purpose? I'll fix him." Paul felt a pulse beat in his temple, and he clenched his fists until they hurt. "I'm going over there. Enough is enough. They never offered us anything. For all they know, we could be starving. Even an egg from his damned chickens was too much."

Grabbing a heavy maul from the woodhouse, he charged down the driveway, his hair matted, reeking of sweat. Dots of toilet paper marked his bloodied face, bitten by his soapless razor. Les's house was alive with lights, from the bobbing deer on the lawn to the giant pulsating star up top. The peacock in the shed screeched. The wind had stopped at last. He pounded on the door. To his right, the muffled generator was closed up in the garage under the living room. "The power's on, you... asshole. Turn off that damn machine, or I'll do it for you with this!"

He broke into the garage and smashed the generator to bits with the flat side of the maul. For good measure, he knocked down the fridge. It was full of individually packed meals. They had so much. Canned good and staples lined the shelves. Those, too, he knocked down. Just let the old man come in. Jail time would be worth it.

Strange that Les hadn't appeared. Was he drunk, too? Finally he shoved open the house door. Heavy fumes assaulted his nose as he entered the foyer and turned, holding onto the door jamb for support. His knees weakened, and his eyes watered in the acrid air. On a game show, the host posed the question: "In what novel by Charles Dickens does a young boy come to the aid of a convict?" *Great Expectations*, Paul whispered to himself. Les and Myrna lay slumped and silent on the sofa, their faces cherry red, their eyes wide and unseeing. It was stifling. And all the lamps were on. "Merry Christmas," the coloured lights in their window read. On the lawn, a bobbing Santa *ho ho ho*'d.

Plan D

by Judy Penz Sheluk

Judy Penz Sheluk's debut mystery novel, The Hanged Man's Noose, *is scheduled for publication in July 2015 by Barking Rain Press (www.barkingrainpress.org). In her less mysterious pursuits, Judy works as a freelance writer, specializing in art, antiques and the residential housing industry; her articles have appeared regularly in dozens of U.S. and Canadian consumer and trade publications. She is currently the editor of* Home BUILDER Magazine, *and the senior editor for* New England Antiques Journal. *Judy is also a member of Sisters in Crime International, Toronto and Guppies, and Crime Writers of Canada.*

Jenny wasn't sure when she first got the idea. Maybe it was the big ice storm back in the winter of 2012. One day there were icicles hanging from the eaves, glistening in the pale moonlit night like giant teardrops. The next day, as the temperature soared and the sun shone, the icicles had slowly melted, drip by drip, until they had vanished without a trace.

"Ted got laid off again," Jenny said. She was sitting in the Coffee Klatch Café with her sister, Stephanie.

Stephanie raised a well-groomed eyebrow, then shrugged. "I'm not surprised. Can't be a lot of demand for an appliance repairman's helper these days. We live in such a disposable society."

Jenny concentrated on her vanilla bean non-fat-extra-foam latte, took a sip, grimaced slightly at the too sweet taste. She'd have to remember to order half the syrup next time. They always overdid the syrup.

"So is Ted finally willing to admit it's time to get some retraining?" Stephanie asked. "Or would that take too much initiative on his part?"

"Ted has initiative; he's just had a string of bad luck," Jenny said, although she knew it wasn't true. She could picture her husband sprawled out on the battered brown sofa, a TV remote in his left hand, a scotch on the rocks in the other. When it came to watching television, Ted was ambidextrous. And ambitious. He could channel surf with the best of them.

"Maybe it's time for you to stop making excuses for him, Jenny, and start making him accountable. Lord knows he's been dead weight since the day you two got married. Retraining just might be the answer. Unless you have another plan."

Dead weight. That had to be a sign to confide in her sister.

"As a matter of fact," Jenny said, "I do."

Naturally, Jenny didn't implement her plan straight away. She was cautious if nothing else, and besides, part of her still loved Ted. Still remembered the way things had been, in the beginning. Before the endless stream of minimum wage jobs and broken promises. There might even be a chance to save him, save their marriage, save her sanity.

There was also the added complication of Stephanie. Jenny made a mistake confiding in her that day at the Coffee Klatch Café. She misread the sign. She thought her sister would understand.

She hadn't. Instead she went all holier-than-thou on her. In the end, Jenny had assured Stephanie that she'd just been kidding around. "Icicles," she had said, forcing a laugh. "C'mon, Steph, what do you take me for?"

And yet, despite all of that, the idea continued to niggle at her. Niggled through the first daffodils of spring, and another two lost jobs, one "too junior" and one "too senior" for Ted's skill set. It niggled through the hot, sticky nights of summer—the air conditioning turned off to save on hydro—Ted lying snoring and slack-jawed by her side, a thin stream of drool finding its way down his stubbly chin and onto the freshly washed cotton sheets.

It kept on niggling right through the cool, crisp days of autumn, especially when Jenny found herself doing 99.9 per cent of the leaf raking while an apparently "allergic to leaf mould" Ted stayed indoors to watch football. What if, she thought, cramming another mound of leaves into the oversized paper yard waste bag, what if the icicle became an ice pick?

For the first time since she was a kid, Jenny looked forward to winter.

It turned out the icicle wouldn't cut it. All those months of thinking and waiting and the idea turned out to be a big, fat, watery bust. Repeated attempts on Teddy—a stuffed bear, not her husband—had only served to prove it over and over and over again. The tip either broke or melted before it could do the job, leaving Teddy wet and wounded, but decidedly alive. Well, as alive as a stuffed bear could be, although Jenny was convinced that at one point his big black button eyes had begged her to stop.

Jenny could have taken it as a sign to give up. She believed in signs, in omens. Like the time she couldn't find her car keys. As it turned out, she'd put the keys in the mailbox by mistake, and a good thing, too. She'd managed to avoid getting into a major league pile-up on the highway. Folks had been stuck on there for hours while the emergency responders and tow trucks tried to clean up the mess.

But she couldn't let it go. The thought of another ten years of marriage, of another decade of defending Ted to Stephanie, left her feeling sucked dry and semi-suicidal.

She'd checked with a lawyer—under an assumed name, of course—and a divorce meant splitting everything with Ted, right down the middle. Well screw that. She'd already given Ted the better part of her adult life, the part with cellulite-free thighs and size zero jeans. She'd be damned if she'd give him half the house and half the money too. It was her that made sure the mortgage got paid, her that kept the refrigerator stocked with food, her that managed to save a few measly dollars for retirement.

Her, her, her. It was always all on her.

What Jenny needed was a Plan B. Only this time, she wouldn't share it with Stephanie. She wouldn't share it with anyone.

The idea came to Jenny when she was filling up the ice cube trays. She rarely used ice, rarely drank cold beverages, her drink of choice being coffee. But today she'd felt like a diet cola, and as usual Ted had used up all the ice for his after-dinner cocktails.

Recently, coming off a two-day marathon of back-to-back episodes of *Mad Men*, he'd switched from scotch to Manhattans, which turned out to be a blend of whiskey, sweet vermouth, bitters and a maraschino cherry. As if they had money for such nonsense.

Always a dreamer, Ted was, as if an alcoholic beverage would transform him from an unemployed loser into a bigwig in the advertising business.

Nevertheless, for once Ted had managed to make her life easier. Jenny had been reading about a Georgia woman who'd killed off two men by poisoning them with antifreeze. Apparently antifreeze had two distinct advantages as a murder weapon: it was odourless, and the sweet taste was easily disguised in liquids. Not that Jenny was about to try any herself.

Further research revealed that the ethylene glycol in antifreeze was deadly when consumed and absorbed into the bloodstream. Even better, it could take a few days to bring on death by a combination of kidney failure, heart attack and coma.

In the case of the Georgia woman's husband, and a few years later, her boyfriend, the men had exhibited severe flu-like symptoms before being taken to the emergency room. Both died less than twenty-four hours after they left the hospital, with heart failure initially being identified as the cause.

Where the Georgia woman had made her mistake, Jenny decided after reading everything she could on the case, was that she'd used the same method for both men. It was only after the boyfriend died that the police decided to exhume the body of her first husband.

Which meant the Georgia woman would have gotten away with murder, if she had thought things out a little bit better.

Jenny acknowledged that her own plan was not without its faults. It seemed antifreeze didn't freeze until -40C or so, roughly twenty-five degrees colder than a typical freezer. Which made sense, when you thought about the name. Why else call it antifreeze?

Then there was the problem of the colour, which manufacturers added so it was instantly recognizable. She'd found green, pink, reddish-orange and blue at the automotive supply store, and bought all four. But even diluted with water, the colour remained problematic, at least until all that was left was a mere drop. By that point, it might have looked clear, and it just might have frozen, but Jenny doubted there'd be enough poison left to do the job—unless she continued to make the ice cube concoction for weeks on end.

As much as she was tired of Ted, Jenny didn't think she had the stomach to poison him in dribs and drabs. And the last thing she needed was Ted getting sick enough to see a doctor, but not sick enough to die. With her luck, he'd be an invalid, and she'd be at his beck and call for the rest of her days.

Simply put, making ice cubes out of antifreeze just wouldn't work. Jenny toyed with the idea of adding antifreeze to the sweet vermouth, which had a brownish-red color, but by the time she thought of it Ted had abandoned Manhattans and gone back to his scotch on the rocks. It was just like him not to stick with something. Even an imaginary work cocktail was too much of a commitment.

What Jenny needed was a Plan C. The next door neighbour was always filling his front yard skating rink, eyesore that it was. If that water somehow flooded their driveway one night, if she sent Ted out to go get milk, if he slipped and fell on the ice, hit his head...

"I'm just glad that Ted's found a job," Jenny said, trying to insert a note of pride in her voice. She was sitting in the Coffee Klatch Café with her sister, Stephanie. Ted waved at them from behind the counter. He was wearing the brown-and-white striped apron that all the baristas wore, though admittedly he was a few years older than the rest of the staff.

"Ted does seem pleased with himself," Stephanie said. "But a barista, Jenny. Seriously, what sort of career is that for a forty-five-year-old man?"

"So maybe this isn't his dream job, but after his fall in the driveway a couple of weeks ago, I'm just glad he's able to work at all."

"You've got a point there. Lucky that the down parka with the fur-lined hood softened his fall."

"Yes that was lucky," Jenny said, staring down at her latte. "Actually I'm impressed with how seriously Ted seems to be taking this. He even managed to get the foam on my latte just right."

"Well, as long as you're happy, I'm happy," Stephanie said. "You are happy, aren't you? I mean you've abandoned that ridiculous idea with the icicles? Because Ted mentioned that he found you stabbing a stuffed teddy bear, and I have to admit I was more than a little bit worried."

This was news to Jenny. She had no idea Ted had known about her experiments with Teddy, never mind that he had mentioned it to Stephanie.

"I was just releasing some frustrations. It was all perfectly harmless. Even the bear came out unscathed. A gentle wash in the laundry and he was as good as new."

"It's just that we both know how obsessive you can be when you get an idea in your head."

Jenny thought about the half empty jugs of antifreeze in the garage. She probably should have thrown them out. In the wrong light, folks might consider an antifreeze collection obsessive. And flooding the driveway just around Ted's car had been a bit sloppy.

"What are you trying to say, Stephanie?"

"Just be careful, that's all I'm saying, Jenny. Just be careful. Who knows what Ted will do if he suspects...

"There's nothing to suspect," Jenny said. "And even if there was, Ted would be the last guy on the block to figure it out." She took a sip of her vanilla bean non-fat latte, grimaced at the too sweet taste. She'd made of point of telling Ted to give her half the syrup, and instead, he must have given her double. It was just like him to screw up the simplest of jobs. Before long, he'd be fired from this one too. She was about to take it back when she saw the look on his face.

"Made it especially for you, baby," Ted said, smiling. The way he used to smile at her, back when things were good between them. Before the minimum wage jobs and all the broken promises.

Jenny took another sip of her vanilla bean latte and decided to finish it, for Ted's sake.

After all, a little bit of extra syrup wouldn't kill her.

Jumping the Bags

by Coleen Steele

Coleen Steele, originally from Toronto, writes mystery and suspense fiction from her home in Bowmanville, Ontario. Her short stories have won the Bony Pete, the Phil Harper Award (best radio script) and twice been short-listed for an Arthur Ellis. She has also won the Crime Writers of Canada's Unhanged Arthur for Best Unpublished First Crime Novel.

Even with half his face bandaged up like some Oriental mummy, I knew it was him. I watched dumbfounded as they wheeled Wilf Bolton in and plunked him down two beds from mine. I'd thought for sure he'd been left behind in Belgium, buried in one of those godforsaken trenches or left rotting in no-man's land, his body riddled with bullets courtesy of Fritz. It was ironic: not once, in all the hospitals I'd been shuffled around in across the Atlantic, had our paths ever crossed, yet now that I was safely at home convalescing in the new Toronto Military Hospital on Christie Street, we were to be practically bedmates. My stomach turned at the thought of it.

"What's wrong with him?" I mouthed the words to the lovely nurse Edna as she came by to fill up my water glass once they'd got Bolton settled in. She'd promised me a date when I got out of here and I was counting the days.

"It's all right; he can't hear you, poor man. He's lost the use of his ears as well as his eyes."

I should have felt sympathy for Bolton, but at that moment I couldn't muster it.

"The doctors are still hopeful of saving his sight though," she said. "That's why they've sent him here rather than closer to home—we've got a specialist."

Bolton came from out west—I remembered that—though the name of the town escaped me—Crooked *Something* or *Something*

39

Bend. I was so busy trying to conjure up the name I almost missed what she said next.

"The bandages will come off in a couple of weeks and then we'll see."

My gaze swung speculatively to the subject of our discussion and I tried not to let my feelings show.

"Another hero!" Edna announced with a smile before sashaying off in her starched uniform and giving me an eyeful.

Yes, we were all heroes to Edna. She believed that as long as you weren't a white-feather man and hadn't backed out when your name was called to make the trip over, then you'd done your duty fighting for king and country and were therefore a hero. And if you were unlucky enough to get yourself wounded and come back less than whole, doubly so. If only she knew!

Not every fellow that went over was a hero, not by a long-shot. For some, one day in the trenches with shells exploding all around them and snipers' bullets whizzing past, and they were begging for the soft jobs at HQ or anywhere but on the front lines. Funny thing was, they were usually the same guys who had bragged the loudest at training camp about what they'd do to the Huns once they were let at them, like they'd win the war single-handed given the chance.

Then there were those that slunk along for months, some even years, before their gutlessness spilled out for all to see. One night they'd get that call, you know, the one to "go over the top," just like they had so many times before, only this time they'd just stand there quaking in their boots, leaving their buddies a man short in the charge. They were rewarded with a last cigarette and a blindfold at dawn.

And then there were those that did much worse... and got away with it. Or thought they had.

I glanced over at Bolton sitting quietly in his bed and felt my innards twist.

At the first opportunity that afternoon I got the hell out of there, as far away from Bolton as I was able to manage with a missing leg. I had an orderly drop me off in the recreation room down the hall, figuring it would provide some diversion and keep me from harping on my new roommate's arrival. I played five games of gin rummy with a fella who was crummy at cards and got trounced every hand. I just couldn't seem to keep my mind on the game. Frustrated and in a sour mood, my humour lightened a little when I saw it was Edna that had come to collect me.

"Too bad the new patient won't be able to play cards with you," she said as she turned my chair around and wheeled me back towards the ward. "But we'll have to think of some way to entertain him. He can't see right now and his hearing isn't too good, but there must be something he can do to help pass the time. Perhaps you can help with that, Peter."

My sour mood quickly returned. "I'd rather not, Edna."

"Why forever not? He'll need—oh," she exclaimed as it suddenly occurred to her why I might be reluctant. She stopped the wheelchair in the middle of the corridor and swung around to face me. "You know him, don't you?"

My gaze shifted away. "I did."

Edna must have seen by my expression I didn't want to talk about it—my mother used to call it my "steel door" look, claiming it looked just like a steel door had shut closed and nothing or no one was going to get in—because she took up the handles of my chair and starting guiding me down the hall again.

We went the rest of the way in silence and by the time Edna parked me beside my bed I was starting to feel a little churlish for being so abrupt with her. I let her help me into bed even though I could have managed it by myself. Sometimes when she wasn't around, I got up on my own and borrowed my neighbour's crutches to move about a bit—a man could only take so much lying in bed or sitting in a chair. But when I had the opportunity to have a pretty girl put her arms around me, I wasn't going to throw it away. Soon, once my stump was better healed, I'd be fitted with one of those new prosthetic limbs they were making here in the hospital. Edna had told me then I'd be able to take her dancing.

"Edna?"

"Yes, Peter?" she replied, not looking at me as she straightened the covers over my lap.

I noted that my ward-mates were either absent from the room or otherwise occupied but I lowered my voice anyway. "What would you think of a fella who didn't shoot the enemy when he was faced with him, but just let Fritz waltz in and catch his battalion off guard because he couldn't pull the darn trigger? Would he still be a hero to you?"

Edna's brown eyes widened and she was silent for a moment. "No. No, of course not," she said more firmly as she stepped back from the bed, her task finished.

I watched as her gaze slid in Bolton's direction. Her red lips tightened.

"I bet you wouldn't go dancing with *him*."

41

"No," she said as she turned back to me. "I wouldn't have time for someone like that." She patted my arm, gave me a tight little smile and went off about her duties.

The nightmares came back that night. I woke up screaming, thrashing against the pillows, with my entire body shaking and breaking out in a cold sweat. It took two orderlies to keep me in my bed and settle me down again. To my shame, my dear Edna was still on shift and witness to my outburst. The pity in her eyes cut me deeply. After I finally quieted and calm had been restored to the ward, I rolled over and looked in Bolton's direction—even in the faint light I could see his face, the white bandages making it impossible for him to hide. The slow peaceful rise and fall of his chest as if he didn't have a care in the world made me seethe with impotent rage—why the hell did he have to come here?

I tossed and turned until dawn and by then I'd come to the conclusion that I wasn't going to get another good night's sleep until I'd done something about Bolton. If there had been any chance of them shipping him out any time soon, maybe I could have waited it out, but he wasn't going anywhere, not with his specialist here, and nor was I.

For the next few days I thought of little else. From my vantage point two beds down, I studied Bolton, thankful his affliction spared me from having to participate in any sort of conversation with him— I don't think I could have handled that. Most of the time Bolton appeared just locked in his own little world but I quickly noticed that when Edna stopped by his bed to fluff pillows or change dressings, he always had a smile for her. The bloody fella couldn't see a damn thing but he obviously knew a pretty girl when she brushed against him. And even though Edna didn't smile back, every time he grinned that stupid grin, I wanted to go over there and smash his face in—what remained of it.

I had to get rid of him, that's all there was to it. But how? There was always someone around. I spent hours agonizing over it and just when I was beginning to fear I never would find the means, an opportunity presented itself, and on a royal platter too.

"Did you hear the news, Peter?" Edna asked one afternoon, her face all flush with excitement. "Prince Edward's coming. The Prince is actually coming *here*, to the hospital. Isn't it thrilling?"

I had to agree that a visit by the Prince of Wales was indeed an honour—a once in a lifetime event.

"Too bad poor Bolton won't be able to see him," she said, although she didn't sound too shook up over it. "The Prince is

42

coming on Wednesday and the doctor says his bandages can't be removed before Friday. Peter? Peter, did you hear me?"

"Hmm? Oh, yes, sorry Edna. That is rotten luck," I said, but I was beginning to think it was just the opposite—for me anyway.

A couple more days passed as I watched and waited, certain that the approaching royal visit and all the commotion surrounding it, would provide me with the chance I was hoping for. And on the big day itself, less than an hour before the Prince and his entourage were expected, it finally did.

To prepare for the event the nurses and orderlies had been working double-time, scrubbing the floors to a shine, polishing instruments, changing the linens, ensuring we all had clean pajamas, arranging flowers and tidying nightstands. And now with the Prince's arrival imminent, the orderlies were off shining their shoes and the nurses were off, well, dolling themselves up. I couldn't blame them, especially the girls. Prince Edward was a young eligible bachelor with a reputation for the ladies, and as Edna would remind us, he was also a war hero.

With the staff all occupied elsewhere, I just had my ward-mates to contend with.

"If you hope to sneak in a last smoke before all the fuss starts, you'd better go now," I said. To keep the wards spic-and-span for the royal visit the hospital staff had gone to the extreme of passing a temporary edict banning smoking everywhere except in the recreation room for the day, at least until His Highness had gone.

Jenkins pounced on the idea immediately. "Come on, men."

MacBride and Taylor eagerly accepted the offer. "Aren't you coming?" Taylor asked me, as he balanced himself on a pair of crutches.

"Nah. Nurse Edna's promised to come by to help me spruce up." I winked and he laughed.

"That's why you're so eager to see the backs of us. Lucky dog."

With those three gone, only Dekker, Bolton and I remained, and Dekker was dead to the world, snoring up a storm.

I slid the covers back and swung my leg over the side. I reached across and grabbed Dekker's crutches and hoisted myself upright. I was getting pretty handy with the sticks now so I had no trouble hobbling and swinging my way over to Bolton's bed.

At first I couldn't tell if he was asleep or awake. It didn't matter though as he couldn't see or hear me. Balanced on my good leg with the crutches jammed under my armpits, I turned and grabbed a pillow from MacBride's bed. I lifted it and began to lean towards

Bolton. This was going to be easy. No one would see or hear anything and when they found Bolton dead, there would be a mad scramble to remove his body before the Prince made the rounds of the wards. Afterwards of course, they would look into the matter, but by that time it would be a cursory inquest at best. And since a lot of us suffer from weak lungs because of the mustard gas the Huns threw at us, I wouldn't be surprised if the doctors rushed to the conclusion Bolton's lungs simply gave out.

I stared down on Bolton's bandaged visage, ravaged by warfare. It had been recently wrapped with clean gauze and strips of cotton but I could see the outline and knew every plane and bump of his face. When you lived side-by-side with a fellow for months on end, you didn't easily forget.

Bolton's head turned a fraction.

I jerked back, my heart catching in my throat. The bugger couldn't hear or see—not yet anyway—how did he know I was there? I took a deep breath as quietly as I could and tried to settle my nerves. I shifted forward again, the pillow grasped firmly in both hands. I began to lower it over Bolton's face. My hands started to shake. The room had suddenly gotten damnably hot. I reminded myself I had to hurry; I was running out of time. I brought the pillow closer.

"Hello? Is someone there?"

I practically jumped out of my skin. I froze, trying not to breathe or make a sound.

"If you're there, just touch my hand."

Bolton started to raise his hand from where it lay on the sheets.

I clutched the pillow back, out of his reach.

Bolton held his hand up expectantly and I felt an almost uncontrollable urge to reach out and grasp it. I glanced around wildly, not knowing what to do. My gaze fell on the photo framed and sitting on his nightstand. It was a picture of Bolton, in uniform, with a woman and a young boy, all looking as proud as punch—a family shot. How ludicrous—Bolton couldn't see it! A hysterical laugh gurgled out of me.

Bolton lowered his hand again but still seemed alert, like he knew I was there.

I had to hurry. Someone would come soon.

I reached out with the pillow again, bringing it closer and closer to his face. When I got within a hand's width, I stopped. My hands started to tremble. Oh God, not again! I hardened my resolve, determined to go those last couple of inches. To bring that pillow

44

down on Bolton's face and steal the breath from him. To make sure he never opened his eyes again. To make sure he never saw me again.

A strangled cry erupted from deep in my throat. I hurled the pillow back on MacBride's bed, almost bouncing it off the other side. I twisted around. One crutch clattered to the floor. In a panic to get back to my bed, I considered leaving it there. But I forced myself to stop and pick it up—nothing could be left behind to give me away. I manoeuvred my way back, half bounding, half skidding and then falling into bed. Lying on my back, I heaved the crutches over my chest and set them back in position between my bed and Dekker's. I then lay with the sheets yanked up to my chin, gasping and quivering like a little girl who'd just seen the bogey man.

Edna thought we were all heroes. But some of us weren't. Some of us lost our nerve when it was needed most. Some of us couldn't pull the trigger when a German soldier, looking all of thirteen, came over the ramparts from out of nowhere. Just one pull of the damn trigger would have roused the men from their sleep before the rest of the cursed Huns came swarming over, and before that kid could chuck a tickler down one of the dugouts, blasting some of our mob to bits.

I don't know how Bolton came out of that alive—I had believed myself to be the only survivor. The only witness to my cravenness.

A cheer erupted in the distance. The Prince had arrived to a hero's welcome. Dekker let out a snort in his sleep. In a moment Jenkins, MacBride, and Taylor would be back, and the nurses, orderlies, and doctors would be flocking to their posts, ready for inspection.

I threw a glance back in Bolton's direction. I immediately noticed the family photo was missing from the nightstand. Had I knocked it in my haste? My stomach clenched. Then I saw it. It was lying in Bolton's lap. And he was sitting there stroking it, as if he could somehow feel the images there—his wife, his son.

I couldn't pull the trigger on that awful day in Kemmel when a freckle-faced kid stared me in the eye. And I couldn't lower a pillow today.

I didn't know what I was going to do if Bolton regained his sight and upon spotting me, called me out for my act of cowardice.

But as I sat there watching Bolton smile at a photo he couldn't see, I considered how, just maybe, being a coward wasn't always such a bad thing.

Written in the Snow

by Ann R. Loverock

Ann R. Loverock attended the University of Toronto, where she studied English literature, and then Sheridan College for Journalism. She spent ten years working as a print journalist, writing for various newspapers and magazines. She has been trying her hand at fiction writing.

She lives in Yellowknife with her husband and daughter.

The body was as solid as a block of ice. All the coroner could do was put it in a warm room and let it melt. The walls were lined with space heaters to help speed up the process. The floor was covered in a thin layer of water.

"I'll have to wait until he is fully melted to get a better idea of what happened. It'll be at least a couple of days," said Rufus Tillerman. Rufus was the community coroner, meaning he had no medical certification of any kind. It was a volunteer position. He ran the local Arctic Mart grocery store and acted as coroner when needed, which was rarely.

He stood in the back of his store with Leroy Johnston, who had found the dead man. The corpse was inside a small storage room on top of a wooden table. Rufus poked at it.

"I found him outside the snow fence. I was tracking a wolf that's been showing up in town. I almost didn't notice it," Leroy said. "There was no trail of blood leading from anywhere. No footsteps that I could see neither."

"It sure is bizarre. There hasn't been anyone in town go missing. I wonder where they came from."

"Are you sure it's OK to have a dead body in the back of the

47

grocery store?"

"Sure it is. Just don't tell anybody," Rufus said. He ushered Leroy out into the hallway, closing the door behind him. He shoved a towel into the crack between the floor and the door to keep the water from coming out.

"Have the police been called?" Leroy asked.

"Of course. They're having an officer come in on the next flight."

RCMP officer Victoria Hunt steadied herself against the wall of the one-room terminal. She hated flying, especially on small planes. The aircraft she had taken to Colville Lake was almost as small as they came. She was rubbing her nauseous stomach when a short, stout man with red hair and an oversized parka approached her.

"Officer Hunt? I'm Rufus Tillerman. Welcome to Colville Lake."

Rufus had a wide grin on his face that annoyed Victoria. "I'm the local coroner and I also run the Arctic Mart grocery store."

"Nice to meet you."

"I told the detachment in Yellowknife that I would pick you up at the airport. I hope the flight was OK."

"A little bumpy."

Rufus giggled, annoying Victoria further. She gathered her bags and followed him to a large truck outside.

"I'm sure they told you there's no motel or anything here, so you can stay at my place. Well, it's really my mom's place, but she's pretty quiet. You'll hardly notice her."

They drove through the darkness without speaking. It was the late afternoon, but this time of year the sun barely poked above the horizon before disappearing again. Underneath the snow the roads were unpaved. The rectangular houses appeared to be scattered randomly across the landscape.

"Where you from originally?" Rufus asked, desperate to break the awkward silence.

"Windsor."

"Have you ever been this far north before?"

"No. Yellowknife is the furthest I've been. Before that it was Sudbury."

Colville Lake is fifty kilometres above the Arctic Circle. With no local police, anything illegal was reported to the RCMP and an officer was sent if it was deemed serious enough. The discovery of a dead body was serious.

Rufus's house was painted a bright yellow. Inside, it was

cramped, with oversized furniture shoved into small rooms. It smelled like musk. Dog hair coated nearly everything. As soon as Victoria entered, a husky with a missing eye jumped up, licking at her face. She shoved the animal aside.

"That's Butch. He's harmless. I rescued him from dog jail last year."

"Dog jail?"

"Any stray dogs are put in a cage near the community centre. If nobody claims them they get put down. Butch was just so cute, I had to save him."

Rufus kneeled down, letting the dog lick his face and hands. An elderly woman came around the corner. She was so thin her skin was nearly see-through. She was wearing a mint green nightgown that looked more like a curtain.

"Rufus, you have to take that animal for a walk. He's driving me crazy," the old woman said.

"Mom, I told you to just tie him up outside."

"You know I can't manage things like that with my arthritis."

Victoria cleared her throat.

"I'm so rude. Mom, this is Officer Hunt. She'll be staying here a while," Rufus said. He was still on the floor, wrestling with his dog. His mother, Enid, looked Victoria up and down.

"It's nice to meet you," Victoria said.

"You're so pretty. You can't be a police officer."

Victoria heard these types of comments a lot. She was blonde, blue-eyed, tall and thin. Her good looks often worked against her as a cop. Most people didn't take her seriously. She ignored Enid's remark.

"I'd like you to take me to the body," Victoria said to Rufus.

"You just got here. Don't you want some tea first?" Enid said.

"No thank you, ma'am."

"Of course you do. You need something to warm you up. Sit, please."

Enid made her way into the kitchen. Rufus pushed aside a pile of mail to clear a place for Victoria at the table.

"We have time for a cup of tea. The dead guy isn't going anywhere," he said.

Victoria sat down and took out her notepad.

"What do you think happened to this guy?"

Rufus took a deep breath and shrugged.

"I can't really say. I mean this isn't some big city down south. We've got a really harsh climate, little in the way of infrastructure or emergency response. People die on the land. Lose your way while hunting, a blizzard comes in while you're out on your snowmobile, you can easily be killed."

"But that's not what you think happened with this man?"

"There's only ninety-eight people in town. Don't you think we would know if this was one of our own?"

Victoria nodded in agreement. Enid emerged with a large tray carrying a tea pot and cups with small red roses on them. She sat down at the table. Her hands shaking, she poured tea for each of them. Most of it spilled onto the table.

"Why don't you tell me how a pretty girl like you ended up as a policeman," Enid said.

"Well, it's not a very interesting story I'm afraid. I wasn't any good at math and I really didn't want to be stuck behind a desk all day. Police work just seemed like it would be a good fit for me."

"I had hoped my Rufus would go into law enforcement. But he had his own ideas."

"Mom, please," he said.

"I'm not saying there's anything wrong with running a grocery store. It keeps you busy and all. It's too bad you never seem to meet any nice ladies though."

Rufus blushed.

"Mom, Officer Hunt and I really have to be going. We have serious work to do, you know," Rufus said.

"You barely finished your tea. And bingo is coming on the radio in half an hour."

"I never have any luck with bingo. We'll be back soon," he said, kissing his mother on the head before ushering Victoria out the door.

The Arctic Mart was closed to the public, so Rufus took them in the back. Inside the hallway was flooded.

"Damn!" Rufus said. "I'll have to get some paper towels."

He disappeared down the hallway. Victoria opened the door to access the body. She looked over him closely for clues, and scribbled in her note pad. The back of his head appeared to have been subject to brute force. He was wearing clothes that were not at all suitable for the arctic environment: jeans, black leather boots and a spring jacket.

"Watch your step," Rufus said. He was standing in the doorway with a handful of towels. Instead of wiping up all the water on the floor he approached the dead man. He took a pen out of his pocket and prodded at the corpse's face.

"You really shouldn't do that," Victoria said.

"Sorry."

Rufus tucked the pen away and stepped back

"We're going to need him wrapped up. His body is being shipped to Edmonton for autopsy."

"No problem. I got a bunch of plastic wrap."

Victoria rolled her eyes.

"No, in a body bag. I brought one with me. He'll be sent out on the morning flight."

"Of course. I was just joking about the plastic wrap."

"I'm also going to need to talk to the man who found him."

"That's Leroy Johnston. It's too late to talk to him tonight. We'll go to his place tomorrow morning."

Victoria woke up with her legs being crushed. Butch had climbed up while she was sleeping, making himself at home on top of her. She kicked the dog off. Rubbing her eyes she felt awake, but it was hard to tell the time in constant darkness. Before Rufus got up, Victoria was dressed and drinking coffee.

Leroy's house was nicer than the rest. Most homes were one-story trailers, easy to ship up on the barge and put together. He had a two-story house with white panelling. His snowmobile was parked in front. He didn't appear as Victoria had imagined. He was about sixty-five, his skin worn and leathery and he was missing at least two teeth.

"You the cop?" Leroy said when Victoria appeared at his door.

"Can I ask you a few questions about your discovery?"

"I guess you mean the dead man. Sure."

"How did you find him?"

"I was hunting. I had gone out past the snow fence. I was following wolf tracks and almost missed him. At first I thought he was a dead animal. There was blood around the body, but no trail leading to it."

"How much blood?" Victoria asked.

"A lot."

"Could you take me to the spot?"

Leroy nodded. "Hop in my truck."

He drove Victoria to the spot where the man was discovered. Rufus tagged along in the backseat. Leroy parked the truck without a word, got out and started walking. Victoria followed closely. The wind was fierce. She pulled her scarf up around her face so that only her eyes were visible. Her hands were warm in seal skin mittens she had picked up in Iqaluit.

Leroy walked into the vast tundra, a flashlight lighting the way. Victoria struggled to keep up until he stopped suddenly.

"It was about here," he said.

"You sure?"

"As sure as I can be."

He handed Victoria another flashlight. She stood quietly, examining the scene. Eventually she kneeled down, sifting through the snow with her hand.

"Officer Hunt?" Rufus shouted.

"What, Rufus?"

"I'm just not sure what we're doing here."

"Often clues are written in the snow," she said.

"Leroy, you told me there was no trail of blood leading to the man."

"That's the truth. There weren't no tracks either."

"Kinda like he was dropped here." Victoria peered up at the sky. "I'll question the airport employees next. This guy didn't just walk here. The only way in or out is by plane, correct?"

"Yup," Leroy said.

The terminal of the Colville Lake airport was a little larger than a bachelor apartment, with only a handful of employees. Victoria approached the short woman standing behind the counter.

"Hi, I'm Officer Victoria Hunt. Can I ask you a few questions?"

"I remember you," the woman said. "You came in on the afternoon flight yesterday."

"That's right."

"You're in town about the body, right? Everybody's talking about it. Who is he and where did he come from?"

"I'm still working on figuring that out," Victoria said. "What's your name?"

The woman pointed to her name tag. It said "Rhoda."

"Have you lived in Colville Lake long?"

Rhoda laughed. "All my life."

"How long have you worked at the airport?"

"On and off for a few years now. If a stranger had come in and never left, I would remember. Anybody that comes into the community, we know about it. This place isn't big, you know."

That evening at Rufus's house, Victoria sat at the table with Enid. She felt like the universe was playing a joke on her. There seemed to be no answer to how the dead man ended up here. In an effort to clear her head she had agreed to play radio bingo. The game had barely begun when her phone rang.

"Officer Hunt speaking."

"It's Detective Michael Reeves in Iqaluit. I have some information I thought might be of interest to you."

Victoria got out her note pad.

"Go ahead."

"There was a small private plane that came into Pangnirtung last week. We got a tip that it was carrying narcotics. We searched it upon arrival and found large amounts of cocaine hidden in the cabin and under the seats, along with over a hundred thousand in cash."

"OK. While I do find this interesting, I'm not sure why you're telling me."

"When I checked with the company that leased the airplane in Calgary, where the flight departed from, I found that three men were recorded to have been on board. Only two arrived."

The next morning, Victoria was on another tiny plane that gave her a heart attack with every little bump and thud. Enid had packed her some sandwiches. Dried white fish with pickles and onion.

"Country food," Enid had said. She had forced the sandwiches into Victoria's bag. "It'll keep you healthy and regular."

Rufus had been surprisingly emotional at the airport. She felt weird that she would miss him, a man she barely knew. She would miss Enid too. She bit into the sandwich but quickly spit it back into a napkin.

James Gray sat in a cell at the Baffin Correctional Institute in Iqaluit. He was charged with a number of offences, including possession with intent to traffic. Victoria quietly took the seat in front of him.

"Hello, Mr. Gray. I'm RCMP Officer Victoria Hunt. I wanted to ask you a few questions about this man," she pushed the photo of the dead man across the table. James glanced at it, a hint of recognition in his eyes.

"Do you know this man?"

"Nope." He crossed his arms over his chest.

"Three of you departed in Calgary, isn't that right? Your friend, David Kingston, who is in the cell next to yours, and Jason Hudson. Where is Jason? I don't suppose you 'lost' anyone along your way," Victoria said.

"What does that mean?"

"I'll be blunt. Did anyone accidentally, or not so accidentally, fall out of the aircraft?"

James shrugged. His arms were covered in tattoos and his face had multiple piercings.

"Just tell me what happened. If you don't I'm sure Mr. Kingston will. And he'll get the better deal in the end."

"It was an accident," he almost whispered. "The plane was faulty. The door swung open and Jason just fell."

Victoria knew she wasn't getting the truth. But at least the dead man had a name, Jason Hudson. And an explanation for the people of Colville Lake. She phoned Rufus to tell him the story.

The Goldstone House

by Jill Downie

Jill Downie is the author of plays, short stories, historical fiction and biographies. She currently writes the Guernsey-based Moretti and Falla mystery series, published by Dundurn. Daggers and Men's Smiles *was published in 2011,* A Grave Waiting *in 2012. The third in the series,* Blood Will Out, *was released in September 2014.*

When I was in my teens, and my parents had a cottage in Grand Bend, on the shores of Lake Huron in southern Ontario, I fell in love with houses of yellow brick. Not because of emotional attachment to the family cottage, which was more of a cabin, with siding in constant need of repair after winters facing the storms of Lake Huron while we hunkered down in Toronto, but because of the journey through southwestern Ontario to get there.

I could never decide which was my favourite; I just loved them all. There were simple one-story homes with the typical Gothic arch above the front door of so many nineteenth-century Ontario cottages; there were elegant two-story almost-mansions with clean Georgian lines; there were slightly crazy ones that had towers built over the front door, with spacious curved verandas echoing the lines of the turret above. On some of them, the towers were like miniature church steeples, or minarets, on the roof. One of the communities we passed through was actually called Goldstone. Sometimes the brick was a deep honey in colour, sometimes a creamy pale buff. My father told me that the yellow clay had less iron in it than the clay that became red brick, for instance, and local builders would use whatever came to hand.

All that—the Grand Bend cottage, and the family vacations— happened a long time ago, and after the property was sold, I didn't expect to return to that part of the world. I was busy being a successful career woman, taking my vacations in places like the

Muskokas in the summer, Europe in the fall, and the Caribbean in the winter. Then my life fell apart. For various reasons, and none of them matter for this story.

Except that, in a way, they do, because that is why I found myself standing at a house of yellow brick, with a set of keys in my hand. As I swam through what seemed like the wreckage of my life, my head held above water, my bucket list pushed ahead of me through the waves, I realized that there was still one unfulfilled childhood goal: to own a house of gold stone.

So, keys in hand, I waved goodbye to the realtor, until she and her car were out of sight between the tall firs that lined the long driveway.

The house that had spoken to me was within walking distance of a charming village just outside Grand Bend, with little more than one main street—called Main Street—but a host of equally appealing homes. This one, however, was actually for sale, and was not one I had seen in my childhood, not being on our route. It had no turret, but it had a veranda, a Gothic arch over the central upper-storey window and, around that window, the architectural feature that won my heart: a balcony, looking over the lawn and trees below.

"Like a Widow's Walk!" I said to the realtor, "Only for that you'd need a view of the sea."

"Is that right?" she said, looking at her watch, clearly not interested in what I meant.

I stroked the sun-warmed honey-coloured brick, and let myself in the front door.

A month or so later, and my house and I are happy together, a perfect fit. For a more-than-century-old house I am pleased that there is no sense of previous occupants. The house and I are a blank page, starting again together, and at the beginning of our relationship I have no curiosity about who might have lived there.

"Is there a ghost?" I am asked by my Toronto friends.

"No," I answer. "Probably because I don't believe in ghosts, and any resident ghost has realized that haunting me is a waste of time."

"Won't you be lonely? What are you going to do with yourself?"

"Keep good company—my own—keep myself to myself, keep chickens—who knows? Take up knitting. Or crocheting. Cultivate my mind, cultivate my garden."

The goldstone house is on a large lot, and the previous owners had been there long enough to have done quite a make-over, particularly on the back yard. They have left the front of the property just a bit wild, which I like—bushes and rocks and lots of trees that I, the city-dweller, must learn to identify—but they have tamed and manicured the back yard into an unhappy horticultural marriage between life in the suburbs and an all-inclusive tourist resort, which does not suit the house. I particularly dislike the fake lake, with a large concrete woman in the centre, holding a pitcher that no longer pours.

To be fair, this shortcoming was already disclosed by the realtor, who gave me the name of a local contractor who could fix it. "Mr. Weeks is completely reliable, has been in business here for years."

I phone Mr. Weeks, and introduce myself.

"Oh, right. You bought the Delancey home," he says.

"The Delancey home?" I reply. "Never heard of them."

"The original owners. Everyone around here calls it the Delancey home."

I feel quite put out, to my surprise. My realtor never mentioned the Delanceys, but she was from out of town.

"Do you want me to fix that fountain?"

"No. I want to replace the lake with a sunken garden."

"You mean the ornamental pond? My dad put in that pond. It's where the Delanceys had a vegetable garden. You want the whole thing removed?"

"I want the whole thing removed."

Mr. Weeks, the businessman, swiftly gets over the shock, and we agree on the day he will come and give me an estimate.

Beneath the eaves protected by the Gothic arch is an attic. It does not stretch across the width of the house, but is about as big as the room beneath with the Widow's Walk, as I always think of it. The previous owners did mercifully not continue their backyard mindset into the house, but kept very much in the spirit of the late nineteen-century building, repairing panelling, plastering and other original features. But they didn't touch the attic, which lay empty. By midsummer, when the mass of tiger lilies on the front lawn are in their orange glory, I have the place pretty well furnished, and decide to make a start on the attic.

It's not as if I need the space, but I have plans for the attic. This is going to be my sacred place, where I pick up a pen, literally, and put on paper all the joy and sadness and anger of a life I had thought well-lived until it fell apart. This is where I am going to write my magnum opus, and I will not transfer any of it to the computer in the dining-room until I have written every word, longhand. Doing this will be the therapy my Toronto friends say I need. It is part of my goldstone dream.

But I can't live with the wallpaper. It looks like it goes back to the early days of the house, its cabbage rose pattern faded and yellowed. Who lived up here, I wonder. Probably a servant, because under the roof the heat is unbearable, and it must be cold in winter. I will have to put in one of those portable air-conditioners, and a heater.

I have never removed wallpaper—there was always someone to do that for me—but I go into the local hardware store, and the owner, a cheerful, chubby woman in her late fifties, helps me put together what I will need.

"You're the lady who bought the Delancey home, right?" she says. "Bill Weeks says you're taking out the pond."

"I am," I reply, keeping the information to a minimum, unwilling to feed the local gossip grapevine. She gets the message, and the cheerful chubbiness changes to chilly courtesy. As I am about to go out the door, she says, suddenly, "Mrs. Sands says she sees you out on the upstairs balcony, when she walks her dog. Gave her quite a turn, the first time."

She's got me. I have to know why I gave the unknown Mrs. Sands a turn.

"Why is that?" I ask. "Is the balcony unsafe? I had it checked before I moved in."

"Oh no!" She chuckles, cheeriness returning. "Mrs. Sands is old enough to remember Maisie Delancey, from when she was a kid and used to walk by on her way to school, seeing her standing up there. She says you look just like her. Spitting image, she says."

I, the realist, feel my heart do a strange thump. *Turn away*, I tell myself. *You don't need to hear any more.*

"Is that right?" I say, borrowing from my realtor's sign-off phrasebook, and leave the store with my purchases.

Back at my goldstone hideaway, I try to forget about Maisie Delancey and, after a while, I succeed.

Removing the attic wallpaper is a nightmare, but I enjoy every minute of it, scraping and pulling it away with my bare hands, as if I were in a fight to the death. I guess I hadn't realised how much pent-up rage there still was in me. The sooner my attic sanctuary is ready, the better.

One area near the baseboard is damaged, presumably where a bed, or a chair had bumped up against it. It comes off easily in my hands, and I can see the wall behind, and a piece of what looks like cardboard. I pull it out.

It is not cardboard, but the back of a photograph, much the worse for wear. I turn it over.

The photograph is black and white, a group of about a dozen people, some sitting, most standing, outside the goldstone house. They have that solemn look which suggests this is an occasion of importance, marking one of life's major milestones. In the front row, seated, are what look like the matriarch and patriarch, with family members around them. From the clothes they are wearing the likely date seems to be somewhere around the 1930s or 40s. In the midst of the solemnity one figure's body language is positively giddy with happiness, dancing on her high heels, both her arms around the neck of the good-looking young man beside her. He is not smiling, or looking at her, apparently overwhelmed with the formality of the occasion, like the others.

That is, apart from the giddy young woman, and it is impossible to tell what she looks like, because her face has been cut out of the photograph. It has been carefully done, so that it is a perfect oval, not snipped in from the edge of the picture. But I am as sure as if it were written on the back of the picture that this is Maisie Delancey, who stood day after day on the Widow's Walk, and who looked like me. If I wanted, I could dig out an old photo of myself, and stick it in the neatly-excised oval. I shudder at the thought, start to tear up the photograph, and then I stop. In my jeans pocket my phone is vibrating, and it is Mr. Weeks, reminding me of our arrangement, and that he is already here, waiting for me. I put the photo down on the floor and go downstairs.

Keep myself to myself. My goldstone mantra. But now I actually have a need to communicate. I join Mr. Weeks by the fake lake with its brooding concrete maiden and her empty amphora and engage in the first lengthy conversation I have had in weeks.

"So your dad put this in? For the Delanceys?"

"That's right. For Maisie Delancey, poor soul."

"Poor soul?"

"Looked like she got everything she wanted, and first the baby died, and then that Delancey son of a bitch walked out on her. She was just a farm girl, hooked the son of one of the richest families around here with her looks. Saying was that Maisie knew more about forking hay on the farm than peas on her plate. What a looker she was, my dad said. Won some beauty contest at the Fall Fair, and won herself Garrett Delancey. Shotgun wedding it was, because she was in the family way. No way he would have married her otherwise. Then she loses the kid."

"What happened?"

"Crib death, my mom said. Maisie spent some time on the funny farm afterwards." Bill Weeks gave an apologetic laugh.

"Another local saying?" I ask.

"I guess. Anyways, she was never quite right in the head after that. Spent a lot of time outside, gardening like a crazy thing. Then Garrett Delancey walks out on her."

"So she was on her own here? Did he never come back?"

"Never. She had to have him officially declared dead after two years, or whatever it is, I dunno. Story around here was that he'd gone back to the States. The family was from the U.S., I believe. This was their summer home, and they gave it to Garrett and Maisie when they got married."

"So he just disappeared off the face of the earth?"

"Right." Bill Weeks turns his attention to the matter in hand. "Lucky for you, cost-wise, that she didn't want to keep goldfish or them big ones, koi, or whatever, because this is quite shallow. Won't be such a problem, draining it and getting the lining out. Biggest job may be moving that statue. Here's what you're looking at."

We agree on the cost and when Mr. Weeks and his son will be available. Bill Weeks and I are now on first name terms.

I finish scraping off the old wallpaper, wondering what else I will find, but there is nothing more. The attic is now like a furnace, so I decide to stop work until the cooler weather arrives, and I bring the photo downstairs with me, and prop it up on the sideboard in the dining-room.

I don't believe in ghosts, but the photograph haunts me. Gradually, I realise that Maisie's story has hit me hard because of my own sense of loss and betrayal, and that I am now transferring my own heartache on to someone else's pain. I find myself talking to Maisie Delancey and, if I ever believed that a trouble shared is a trouble halved, I now know that is a crock. *This is not good*, I tell myself, often out loud. *Throw the damn thing away.*

But I cannot. Then, about two weeks later, Bill Weeks and his son—also called Bill—arrive to drain the lake and start work on my sunken garden. I have photos, taken in happier times, of the kind of thing I want, and hand them over to the Weekses.

"Hmm," says Bill Senior, "We're going to have to dig down a bit. Right, son?"

"Right, dad," says Bill Junior.

They are a cheerful team, whistling and singing and having the occasional father-son disagreement. First, they drain the lake, then they bring in extra muscle to remove the lady of the lake, and there is much groaning and swearing. She lies on her side on the grass, like a beached mermaid, no visible legs, awaiting my decision as to her fate. The next day, father and son start deepening the base of the lake bed, leaving the supporting walls until later, apart from a gap through which they have driven a small backhoe. Bill Junior is up in it, gouging out the earth, with his father yelling instructions at him.

So I don't overreact when I hear the backhoe stop, and exclamations of what at first sound like exasperation and anger. I look out the kitchen window and see Bill Junior jump down from the backhoe and come running towards the house, stumbling over his heavy work boots in his haste. His father is down in the excavation, kneeling, repeating over and over, "Oh my God, oh my God." Loudly. Clearly not in prayer, but in shock. I open the kitchen window to hear what Bill Junior is saying.

"Miss, you'd better come! We've dug up a fucking body!"

He says it again, for his own benefit as much as mine, apologizing for the profanity.

I feel shock, briefly, then I turn and go into the dining room and pick up the photograph.

"They've found him, Maisie," I say.

The fucking body is, of course, that son of a bitch, Garrett Delancey.

The back of his skull was caved in, according to the Detective Sergeant who takes charge of the investigation. After nearly three-quarters of a century there is not much of him left, but enough to know that he died a violent death before being put in the ground, before Maisie had Bill Weeks's dad build her a lake. The news spreads like wildfire, and I cannot avoid speculation and discussion in the small supermarket, the liquor store, the post office. Most of the questions are the "why did she do it?" variety.

I know why; I have been so close to doing it myself.

Also, "How did she do it? All on her own!"

For me, "how did she do it" is the really interesting one, and its corollary: was it a spur of the moment thing, or did she plan it so she could get away with it?

But there is also a part of the "why" question that fascinates me. I know how quickly love can turn to hate but—if she planned it—was there another reason?

One of my favourite places in the little town is the local library, one of many built in the early twentieth century with money from the Carnegie Foundation. I like its simple, solid architecture, the sense of permanence in an uncertain universe, and I also like its Head Librarian. We talk about books, the weather, occasionally politics, but she has never once said to me anything about the Delancey home, or asked what I am doing here. I like that. So it is unusual when she, too, says something about the body in my back yard.

"No surprise to hear Maisie did what it looks like she did," she says. "My mother always wondered about that baby."

"Your mother?"

"Yes. She was the District Nurse, was called in when it happened." The Head Librarian pauses, looks up at me from behind her desk. "I've never spoken about this before, because my mother only told me in old age, when she was wandering in her mind. It disturbed her. She said that Maisie was hysterical, as you might expect, and that she was screaming over and over at Garrett Delancey something about his hatred—yes, that was the word she used—his hatred for the baby. Of course, back in those days, it was more difficult to establish what was crib death and what was not, and even recently people have been accused of terrible crimes they did not commit, but..." she did not complete her sentence.

So, here was the other reason.

"Your mother said nothing at the time?"

The Head Librarian looks down, sighs.

"The Delanceys were local aristocracy. No, she said nothing, and it troubled her."

"Where is Maisie buried? Did she die a natural death?"

"Oh yes, she lived to a great age. She is buried in the cemetery just outside the town, in her family plot. The Morgans, on the right as you go in. You should pay her a visit, tell her they've found him—and that they cannot touch her." She gives an embarrassed laugh.

"I've already told her," I say.

62

The cemetery is within walking distance, along a country road with small houses in large lots, past the little river that runs through the village. The early nineteenth-century villagers had chosen a beautiful place to end their days, on the top of a hill overlooking rolling countryside. In the distance I can hear the sound of a mower, maintaining the impeccable appearance of the grass around each gravestone and plot, but, apart from the unseen caretaker, I am on my own. I turn to the right, as instructed by the Head Librarian, and find the Morgan plot without difficulty, because it is sizeable. There are a lot of Morgans, and it takes a while to find Maisie.

In fact, I find her baby first.

Stella Marie. Aged 3 months. He shall gather the lambs with His arm.

And there, alongside her, is her mother. *Maisie Jean Morgan. Together at last.*

Mother and baby share a fine granite monument of the Madonna and Child.

No sign or acknowledgement of that son of a bitch, Garrett Delancey, or his role, in either of these two lives.

There is a secluded area in the middle of the cemetery with curved stone benches beneath tall scotch firs, planted with hostas and small evergreen shrubs, and I sit there a while, looking at the photograph I have brought with me.

The why is clear. The how takes shape in my mind...

It must be planned perfectly. He has already had her shut up for months, and he has threatened to have her committed, put her away for ever, if she keeps on saying the crazy things she is saying.

She knows how she will do it, where she will do it, and when. Friday night, when he comes back after his night out with the boys, drunk, as always. First he will jeer at her, drawing on his collection of favourite insults. *Farm girl, you'd do it with anyone, never knew if it was my kid, did I.*

It. He never says the baby's name, and now she's glad about that. If she's lucky, he'll be too drunk to demand his conjugal rights. It amuses him to call them that. *Conjugal, d'you know that word, Maisie farm girl? Ignorant as one of your dad's cows, course you don't.*

She knows how, and where, and when. Now she must get into training, like they do in the army, or for the Olympics, get those strong farm-girl muscles of hers in shape again. Day after day throughout that long summer, she digs great holes in the ground for trees, bushes, new flowerbeds. First, in the front of the house, where everyone can see her, sometimes at dusk, when she has only mosquitos and moths and the occasional bat for company. Gradually, she rediscovers the pleasure of physical effort, the sweet rhythm of turning over the soil, smelling it as it cascades to the ground around her. What started as necessity becomes an escape in itself. Then she moves to the back yard.

"I am planting red currant bushes this year," she tells him.

"Whatever," he says.

No one plants red currant bushes at this time of year, Garret Delancey.

The laughter bubbles up inside her, and she keeps it there.

She has found a massive wooden mallet in the shed, and has already practiced swinging it high above her head, splitting vegetable marrows in half. It is too early yet for pumpkins. She brings the mallet into the kitchen, standing it between the stove and the fridge. She is ready.

Friday night finally comes, the night she usually dreads. He reels in the back door of the kitchen, as always, drunk as a lord. Lord Delancey. The insults start, and finish with one of his favourites.

"Stop snivelling—go back up to that attic you like so much, skivvy, go back where you belong, Maisie Morgan!"

He turns away, she picks up the mallet and swings it up above her head. It is not too hard, because she is a tall woman, almost as tall as he is.

Crack. The sound startles her, is much louder than the sound of a vegetable marrow being split in half, and he drops to the floor. Carefully, she places the mallet in the sink. She'll clean it off later, when she mops the easy-care tiles beneath him. She bends over him, to make sure he is dead. His eyes are closed, his mouth open. Best to be sure. She unties a seat cushion from one of the kitchen chairs, holds it over his face, so he can know what it feels like to have the breath stopped, life leaving your body.

Quick now, no time to celebrate. She'll do that later. She has a shroud ready for him, a blanket from their bed. It will make it easier to drag him across the kitchen floor, out the door and into the back-yard and the grave she has prepared for him. It is dark, and the leaves are still on the trees, so it will only be the mosquitos, the moths and the occasional bat who will see her and accompany the funeral cortège, hover around her as she fills in the earth, stomping it down with her old farm boots.

Well, that's that. Give it a week or so, then make a phone call.
"My husband has gone missing. I am really worried about him."

She stands there a moment, thinking of how she once loved him. Money or no money, just crazy loved him. Leaning on her shovel, she laughs at her own stupidity...

I have started seeing Maisie in my dreams, her face a smooth, clear oval of white, so I cannot tell if she is crying, laughing, happy or sad. I wake up one morning and make a decision. I find a black and white photo of myself, from the time before my life fell apart. Carefully, I snip around my face and glue it into place on Maisie's dancing body. I take it up into the attic, where I now have a cosy chair and a footstool, so I can prop my papers on my lap while I write, longhand, my crocheted afghan wrapped snugly around me.

She has destroyed all evidence of a life with Garrett Delancey, and kept just one, to remind herself of the foolish young girl who gave her heart and her body to him, the face removed because she cannot bear to see such happiness. She will keep it hidden forever, like a talisman, to remind herself never to allow love to betray her again. And every day people like Mrs. Sands will see her on her Widow's Walk and say to each other, "There she is, Maisie Delancey, poor soul, waiting for him to come home."

I am the ending you wanted to your story, aren't I, Maisie? You needed me for the big reveal, so the world would know what you had done.

Leaning over my shoulder, Maisie laughs.

First Impressions

by Madona Skaff

With a degree in biology, then a lot of imagination, Madona worked for many years in mining research. This interest in science has always inspired her SF stories, not to mention occasionally sneaking into her mysteries. She was assistant editor for the first anthology of The Ladies Killing Circle. *Her story* "Night Out" *can be found in their third collection,* Menopause is Murder. *Short stories,* "Hideaway" *and* "The Bouquet" *appear in* The Whole She-Bang. *She's a member of Capital Crime Writers, and was past President for the Ottawa Chapter of Sisters in Crime. She has a mystery novel out in the world looking for a home.*

So this bleak countryside was Horseshoe Gold Mine.

Tight lipped, Carol Nilstrom turned away from the tiny window of the twin turbo-prop. Damn, she was the last one off the company plane. Grabbing her small backpack she hurried to catch up to the other passengers.

A blast of frigid air smacked her in the face, stopping her at the door. If it was this cold in June...

This was one of the remotest regions of British Columbia. No roads reached this far north. At her last job, in northern Ontario, they were a few hours' drive from a small town. Here, you were a hostage until the weekly plane rescued you.

Depressed by what her life had degenerated to, she trailed after the employees who trudged zombie-like across the tarmac, past a garden shed of a terminal to a yellow school bus.

"Carol Nilstrom!"

She spun around at the sharp voice, only to come nose to nose with a Native woman whose short cropped black hair had lost the battle with a home perm. A definite contrast to Carol's long neatly braided blonde hair. She was amazed to see the woman, wearing a loud Hawaiian shirt and khaki shorts, who didn't even have the decency to shiver.

"Yes." Carol painted on a smile and extended her hand in greeting.

"Welcome to Horseshoe Mine. I'm Gladys King, your shift supervisor." The woman ignored the offered hand and turned to walk back towards the terminal as she called over her shoulder, "Leave your luggage, it'll get taken to the camp for you. We have to get all that new employee paperwork taken care of."

What a warm reception, Carol thought as she trudged behind.

She hated bosses that were younger than her, who thought they knew more than she did. With over thirty years of work experience, she knew more about the gold milling process than most of the scientists. The woman might be younger, maybe in her early thirties, but luckily not too pretty, so no competition at least. A couple of years shy of fifty, Carol was definitely in better shape. She followed the Native woman to a bright red pickup truck parked on the other side of the building.

Carol had barely sat down before Gladys floored it, leaving a dust cloud behind as they bounced along the washboard dirt road. The wide road could handle the larger mine trucks, whose wheels were at least three times her height. The rutted road turned the journey into a teeth jarring ride. Despite the bumps, she relaxed and allowed herself a smile. She was in the clear.

"You're coming from Big Moose," Gladys stated.

Carol's smile vanished at the sudden comment. Her heart pounded as she realized that maybe she hadn't covered her tracks as well as she'd thought. She'd set up Sneaky Pete perfectly. Right? Reaching for the door handle she wondered which direction to roll when she jumped out of the truck. She wondered if she could catch the plane before it took off. She wondered...

"It's a good place," Gladys said, with a quick nod. "So, I'll expect more out of you."

Carol slumped back into her seat with a sigh and a tiny chuckle at her paranoia. She really had to calm down.

The day blurred into an endless stream of meetings with personnel, signing the contract and release forms, tolerating the obligatory safety video and briefing. She'd been looking forward to a tour of the processing plant. But Gladys zipped through it so fast, introducing her to countless, and eventually faceless, people, that it turned from a treat to another hazy experience. Grateful the shift ended, Gladys drove her back for supper at 7:00 p.m.

Base camp consisted of a series of modular pre-fab structures. Three two-storey buildings, serving as living quarters, radiated out from a central hub which contained the cafeteria, gym, and most importantly, the bar. Big Moose had been a dry camp, so this would be a nice change from smuggling in booze.

As they stood in line for the cafeteria, Gladys pointed to the door off the main hub labelled "Women's Quarters".

"After we eat, I'll show you your room," Gladys promised, then continued her monologue.

She reminded Carol of one of those tour guides that kept talking no matter what. Someone falls down, the guide picks them up. Someone loses a limb, duct tape works wonders.

"Cafeteria's open twenty-four hours, but hot food is available only at meal times. Coffee break is at the plant so remember to take snacks with you. And the bar, over there, is open right after shift at 7:00, til 11:00. That's a.m. and p.m. for both shifts."

At Big Moose fresh food was trucked in once a week. With Horseshoe's isolation, Carol dreaded the worst: frozen pizzas and stale sandwiches. She was relieved to see a great variety of food. One place she'd definitely be visiting was the huge ice cream freezer just inside the door. Maybe being here wouldn't be as painful as she'd thought. Carol chose the lasagna, while Gladys selected the cabbage rolls, and found a table next to the large windows. Not much of a view except for a tiny parking lot and trees beyond.

Carol caught a movement out the corner of her eye. She turned in her seat expecting to see one of the other workers walking by outside. With a loud gasp, she stood and backed away, knocking her chair over. A black bear stood upright and placed dinner plate paws on the glass. He peered in, then stared down at her with disturbingly intelligent eyes. Distantly she heard laughter.

"Don't worry," Gladys said, with a smile.

"What if the glass breaks?" She whispered, irrationally believing her voice would anger the animal.

"Reinforced glass. Relax, bears wander into camp all the time. Guess you didn't get many bears at Big Moose."

"Sometimes. In the distance. Never in camp."

"Yeah. Here, this is their land. Don't bother them and they'll leave you alone."

"They're not aggressive?"

"Nah. But don't make no sudden moves. If you startle them, they're likely to slap you before they take off."

Carol shuddered at the thought of a slap from one of those

massive paws. She was amazed that any amount of reinforcement could hold his weight. Some of the younger guys were snapping pictures and laughing. They had to be students, or new employees fresh out of school. After a few moments, the bear gave up, leaving behind his paw prints. Just as daunting as the real thing.

"Come on," Gladys chided, "don't be such a baby."

"I'll try." Anger replaced fear.

Gladys continued to fill her in on more camp rules. Carol tuned her out, deciding to figure them out as needed.

Finally Gladys stopped talking and inhaled her food, an obviously ingrained habit, then patiently waited for Carol to finish. Most of the people ate and left in about fifteen minutes and that included waiting in line. Guess with twelve hour shifts, if you wanted to do more than work and sleep, you didn't waste time eating, she thought. Gladys fidgeted with the cutlery and napkin, obviously not used to sitting still so long. Carol picked at her food, delighting in the control she had over her boss.

After a few minutes, she got bored with her game and cleaned her plate. Gladys led her into the women's wing—one floor out of six. Carol always liked the high male to female ratios at mining camps, since it made the nights pass more quickly. Of course, most places discouraged that sort of thing. It was a dumb rule, but she was always discreet.

"At Moose you had three shifts, right? So, it'll be a change for you to go to two. And we all work seven days in and seven out," Gladys began conversationally. "Guess they told you space is limited here, so, everyone splits a room."

"What do you mean?" Carol asked. No way would she ever tolerate a roommate.

"You have the room to yourself for your week in, and then Marnie's here during your week out." Gladys continued walking as Carol followed. "There are two cupboards. Yours is the one with the key."

Gladys stopped outside a door with a poster of a naked male torso. The picture started just above the chin, revealing a sensuous neck, but unfortunately stopped just barely below the hips. Carol admired the decor and looked forward to seeing inside.

Gladys handed her the room key. "See you in the morning. Remember the bus leaves for the mill at 6:45." Carol watched her continue down the hall to the last room on the left. Thank God they weren't neighbours.

Carol opened the door and stopped mid-step at the sight of the room. Posters of heavy metal bands and motorcycles lined the walls *and* ceiling. While Carol had taken a modest apartment in Prince Rupert for her week off, she could only assume this Marnie woman spent her free time with a motorcycle gang. Living in cheap motels, shoplifting her change of clothes. Carol resisted the urge to tear down the posters only because she was too tired.

Locking the door behind her, she picked her bag up from the floor and threw it on the bed. She opened the curtains to let in some light and was startled to find the window covered with foil paper. About to pull it off, she realized that it would help to keep the light out when she took her turn at night shift. Instead, she carefully folded back a palm-size opening in the corner to peek at her view. More bloody trees.

What the hell was she doing here? Enduring this self-imposed exile?

She could have stayed at Big Moose Mine and taken her chances. It wasn't that long ago that she'd discovered the ultimate "get rich quick" scheme.

Poor mixing had resulted in a tiny percentage of gold particles settling out in various parts of the processing circuit. While the company's so called genius engineers had played with their calculators, she'd figured it out through hands-on experience and found the particles first. By the time the engineers checked the area, they found only a trace amount—which she always left for them to find. Then off they went struggling to balance their little equations and calculate where the rest of the missing gold had gone. Sometimes she did feel bad for all the headaches she was causing, especially for this one female engineer who was always nice to her. But she made a hell of a lot more money than Carol did, and the company could afford the loss. Smuggling the grains out of the processing plant in her shoes hadn't been a problem either. Security only ever spot checked pockets and bags.

Yawning, she turned to her suitcase. Tomorrow she'd unpack properly. She pulled out her pyjamas, changed and got into bed. She'd brush her teeth tomorrow. Despite the time zone change and exhaustion, insomnia hit.

She'd always known that her moonlighting wouldn't last forever. After nine months, Big Moose hired a new engineer with a reputation as a real bloodhound, who never gave up till he got his answers. She had no choice but to give two weeks' notice and keep a low profile. She'd made sure all clues would lead straight to Sneaky Pete. So what if he got blamed for the one thing he *didn't* do?

But now, lying sleepless in this northern wilderness, she wondered if maybe she'd overreacted. She should have stayed at Big Moose and taken her chances. She considered getting on that company plane when it returned next week and not coming back. She watched the sky through the opening in the foil, amazed that it still looked like dusk at 3:00 a.m. She gradually blinked out the ceiling adornment of a hairy guy on a Harley staring down at her. Her eyes snapped open as the alarm buzzed. Heart pounding, she rolled over on her side to shut off the alarm clock.

"Damn!" It was 6:30 a.m.!

That meant fifteen minutes to shower, dress, eat and catch the bus. Why hadn't she checked the setting last night? She fell out of bed, tangled up in the blankets. Kicking free, she dressed in yesterday's clothes. No time to shower. Furious, she tore a poster from the wall as she raced out the door. She'd deal with the rest of them after shift.

She ran into the cafeteria. Grabbed an apple. Held it in her mouth, wishing she'd brushed her teeth last night. She opened a paper bag. Shoved in a muffin, banana and a bottle of some kind of red juice. She rushed outside just as the last person was getting on the bus.

Taking the only empty seat in the last row, she sat with a thump and tried to catch her breath. One of the few things she remembered from Gladys's endless speeches was that the processing mill was a twenty-minute quick walk up the hill. She could imagine Gladys's reaction if she'd missed the bus and arrived late for her first shift. Itching in yesterday's clothes, she again cursed not having checked the alarm. How the hell did Marnie wake up at 6:30 and manage to get ready on time? Obviously personal hygiene wasn't an issue for her.

By the time she'd finished the apple and thrown the core out of the window, the day shift bus arrived at the plant's main entrance. Gladys greeted her, already dressed in coveralls, hard-hat and steel-toe boots, looking more serious than yesterday.

"You can change in the 'dry,' through here," Gladys said, leading her inside. "Your locker number is twenty-eight." She walked away adding, "We're efficient operators here. So, change fast. Don't want to waste no more time."

"I'll hurry." Carol forced a smile. What a witch! She'd arrived on the bus with everyone else. Why single her out? Make it sound like she was late? Well, the day could only get better.

Wrong. Things went steadily downhill. Gladys kept after her all day long as though she was some moron fresh out of school. After thirty-two years of experience, Carol was confident in her skills as a technician. She could handle the most complicated equipment, could pick up on new processes faster than most people.

"Why aren't you checking the cyanide levels?" Gladys snapped as she passed by Carol for the third time that hour.

"I just did," Carol said. "I'm about to go on to the next section."

"And what about the pH readings? Don't know how you did things at your last job, but here we don't let the tanks get acidic. Generating cyanide gas isn't gonna be healthy for your shift-mates, you know."

"I'll check them again," Carol said. The levels couldn't have dropped in the last ten minutes. What she *would* like to do was drop Gladys into one of the large tanks and give her a quick cyanide bath.

The entire twelve-hour shift was one long criticism. At one point Carol considered offering to split the hidden gold cache with her, just to be left alone. Even for a day. But Carol doubted she'd accept, because the main thrill in Gladys's life seemed to be tormenting her.

At lunch Carol gobbled up her food and managed to get a sorely needed shower. As she dressed, she considered the posters. Still angry about the alarm clock, she ripped off one more poster. The rest she'd leave alone until the next time Marnie pissed her off.

At the end of the day, exhausted, discouraged and disgusted, Carol rushed through dinner to seek out the solitude of her room. After a half hour, she decided to stop all this self-pity and accept her team's invitation to meet in the bar.

She searched the predominantly male bar for a familiar face. Through the dim lights she spotted a lanky man with shoulder length blonde hair waving her over to a table in the corner. It was Marty something or other, with Frank and Sid from her group. And Angelo with his warm, dark eyes that had watched her all day. At Big Moose she'd spent a lot of her free time with Tony. She'd always had a thing for Italian men. Here, she decided it would be Angelo. But she was too tired to flirt now. Maybe tomorrow.

Carol ordered wine, glad they stocked more than just beer. "Too bad Gladys isn't here," she lied smoothly. "I was hoping to get to know her better."

"You know," Angelo said, "Gladys has a brother that works at Big Moose. Did you know him?"

"A brother?" She took her attention from his eyes and fought to remain calm. Glad for the dim lighting, she felt blood colour her cheeks. Why hadn't the woman mentioned him before?

"Yeah," Marty said happily, nodding so hard that his jowls kept moving long after his head stopped. "Name's Fred Trebilcock."

Bloodhound! "Uh, no, I didn't know him. He was probably in another section."

"We told Gladys you'd be here tonight and I hoped maybe she'd drop by," Angelo added, looking at the bar entrance.

As the conversation turned to Angelo's newest niece, Carol's thoughts turned inward. Now that she'd left Big Moose, Bloodhound's calculations would miraculously balance. He'd soon realize Sneaky Pete wasn't smart enough to figure out his own postal code. He'd think that maybe the thief had been scared off by his arrival and stopped. Or he might suspect Carol because she'd quit so soon after a promotion. But without proof, what could he do? It would be a mystery for everyone, until Trebilcock spoke with his sister. She could just imagine the two of them talking about her every single day and coming up with little schemes to trap her or trick her into confessing.

No, she couldn't keep worrying about what might happen. All the things she should have done, or ways she could have covered her tracks better. She'd go crazy or get an ulcer. She could almost feel one growing now.

"Sorry, what did you say?" Carol said. "I guess I'm tired. My mind keeps wandering."

"First day, always tough," Angelo said. "We were saying, since you were so interested in the bear that came through camp yesterday, we thought that we'd take you out to the dump."

"Yeah, get a closer look. They all hang out there," Marty said.

"Sure, why not?" Her voice projected an excitement she didn't feel. He was right. It was just her first day and she was exhausted. Her mind was playing tricks. She was free. After all, what was the real harm in taking a few dollars from a company that made millions?

"We'll go after supper tomorrow," Angelo said giving her a smile that convinced her everything would be fine.

On the second day Gladys's relentless nagging got worse. Grateful the shift ended, supper was an inhaled event, ten minutes. Carol had no memory of what she'd eaten. She wanted to hide in her room, but the guys were expecting her. Also, the thought of sitting next to sexy Angelo, driving along a very bumpy road, thrilled her.

She stopped mid-step at the sight of Gladys, dressed in yet another Hawaiian shirt and shorts, standing by the pickup truck.

Carol struggled against the queasy feeling that punched her in the stomach.

"Look who we got to join us!" Marty said, practically bouncing with excitement.

"Great!" Carol said with a cardboard smile.

With a "Let's go then!" from Marty they piled into the vehicle.

Instead of snuggling against Angelo's warm thigh, Carol found herself sandwiched between Marty and Gladys in the front seat. Angelo, Sid and Frank sat in the back. The drive was accented with a running commentary on the sights from Marty: the tailings pond with its colourful surface, a great lake for fishing in that direction over the hill, new tree growth after the big fire last year.

The dump was a giant pit with piles of garbage and sections of large rusty sewer pipes. After some encouragement from Frank, via a couple of thrown rocks, two bears came out of one of the larger pipes. One bear went up the opposite side of the pit and sat down just out of reach of any more rocks, while the smaller one stayed close to the pipe entrance. Carol could have sworn the far one sat down with a sigh.

"They look scared," Carol commented, surprised that such powerful animals were so easily intimidated. The closer bear was a golden brown colour, with a skinny body and long legs. Not the usual "bear shape." It must be still very young.

"Gotta show 'em who's boss," Marty said, "Otherwise we could start having problems. Remember that bear that kept getting too friendly, Gladys?"

Gladys nodded.

"Yeah, kept coming into camp," Marty added. "He learned to get over the barbed wire at the top of the kitchen fence to get at the garbage. Yup. Climb it fast, grab a bag then get back over, bag and everything, then take off fast."

"And Frank here," Gladys said. "Remember when he left the truck window open with our snacks inside? Bear got in, ate our food and left. They finally caught and shipped him out."

"Where?" Carol asked.

"Few hundred miles north." Angelo said. "They mark him and if he finds his way back here, then they shoot him. Never had to shoot one yet though. But," Angelo picked up a rock, "we still have to be careful and keep them afraid of us." He pitched it at the side of the pipe. The bears ignored the "clank!"

"There's usually more than two here," Marty said. "We'll take a look around. You girls wait here, but keep your eyes open. Don't let a bear get between you and the truck. They look slow but they can move damn fast when they want to."

Carol turned to Gladys after the men started over a hill. "Is he just trying to scare me?"

"No, they're dangerous. Stupid fool, Frank. Don't want them to figure out those little brown paper bags mean free food. We gotta live with them. We can keep them afraid of us, but you saw how calmly they walk in camp with us just a few steps away."

"Uh," Carol couldn't think of anything to say. She did think about insisting they leave.

"Look here, the small one's settled down." She pointed at the bear, hardly twenty metres below them. Then nodding towards the adult, she said, "We don't think she's the mother, but she cares for him. My brother works at Big Moose. Fred Trebilcock. Do you know him?"

"No." Carol felt a lump in her throat at the sudden shift in topic. "It, it's a big mine."

"Yeah, I guess so," Gladys said. "I heard they got problems with their gold production there. Got any ideas?"

"No, not really." Carol could barely force the words out. This was it. The moment of reckoning.

Gladys had hated her from the time that she'd got off the plane. Now, she was fishing for information. She had to be working with Bloodhound to get her. Carol could pretend to play along until she could get away next week when the plane came back. But where would she go?

Mining was all she knew. She never finished high school. Now, almost fifty, where *could* she go?

What if Carol tried to buy her silence? That would mean trusting Gladys to keep quiet.

But she only had enough gold for an extra retirement bonus; she hadn't had time to take more. She refused to go to jail. Not for pilfering a few grains of gold through the virtue of her own intelligence.

Carol glanced behind her. They were alone. She raised her arms to push Gladys over the side. But it was only about twenty metres. There was a good chance Gladys would survive the fall. She couldn't be sure what the bears would do. They'd probably get scared off. Carol couldn't risk a charge of attempted murder.

Not murder. An accident. Carol looked all around. The men were still out of sight. Before she could she could change her mind, she took a deep breath, and yelled...

"Bear behind us!" as she rammed her shoulder into Gladys's back. Too much force. They both went over. Carol clawed at the edge. Her feet scrambling on the side of the ditch. Somehow she stopped her own fall.

Gladys must have landed on the young bear, because she heard the unmistakable yelp of an animal through the shrill screams. Carol watched in wide-eyed shock as the larger bear growled once then charged with sickening speed, dirt rising in mini tornados under each massive paw. Carol's nails dug deeper into the dirt as the beast reached the woman. And silenced her.

Somewhere through the distance she heard shouts and yells as the men ran back. Frank grabbed a rifle from under the front seat. Fired a shot into the air as he ran to the edge of the pit. He took aim but the animals had already bolted. While he stood guard, Angelo pulled Carol up to safety. The other men slid down the steep side to Gladys.

The following night in the bar, Carol listened as the men relived Gladys's life. There was no shortage of friends or admirers and she knew she wasn't one of them. If only she could make some excuse and leave.

"At least Gladys will rest easy," Frank said, "They shot all the bears."

"They killed all of them?" Carol was stunned. "Even the little scrawny one?" If she'd known that would happen to the bears, she might have considered another way of dealing with Gladys. She was surprised to find that she felt any remorse for the animals at all. She'd never been one of those bleeding-heart tree huggers. But she couldn't seem to get the image of the young bear out of her mind.

"Too bad Gladys and her brother never made up," Angelo said.

"What?" Carol suddenly paid full attention.

"They had some kind of fight two years ago and never talked to each other since." Frank added. "We kinda hoped with you coming from Big Moose, it might get Gladys to make a first move and call Fred."

She sat bolt upright. Was it possible that Gladys hadn't known anything? But then why had she been after her from the start? If she'd been nicer she wouldn't have made Carol kill her. Carol smiled inwardly thinking of how they might have become friends. Maybe together they could have found some weakness in Horseshoe's gold milling process. But, no. Gladys had hated her, probably just jealous of her looks and her knowledge.

"You know, Carol," Angelo said, "Gladys really liked you. She only picked on people she felt had potential."

Carol sat in silence, finding no words. Or thoughts.

"You'll be okay." Angelo patted her hand. "I know that even after only a couple of days, you liked her too."

The Fifth Digit

by Carol Newhouse

Carol Newhouse is a law clerk and part-time writer who enjoys straddling the worlds of mystery and romance. She currently lives in Newmarket and when she isn't dreaming of dead bodies or matchmaking, she is walking her dogs or chilling in yoga classes.

Tributes to Gabriel Digit were everywhere. Sue Harriston squeezed past a group of people clustered around the "Name that Tune" booth and headed toward the front of the arena. A large purple banner with gold foil letters proclaiming "Long Live the King" spanned the stage. The atmosphere of celebration included streamers decorating the metal struts spanning the ceiling and posters adorning the walls. The Festival Committee had left its mark.

Aunt Edith Pillar and Aunt Adele Schmidt had already arrived. Unbridled ambition distinguished the two aunts from the other festival volunteers. Working with them was always difficult, even for family. This year they were vying for the Festival's I'm For Order Prize, awarded to the person deemed to have the most organizational savvy. A win in that category was an important predictor of political success in Ollingbrae and Sue knew both her aunts toyed with the idea of running for Town Council.

Aunt Edith shushed Aunt Adele and waved to Sue.

"Thanks for coming," Aunt Edith said.

"Right on time," Aunt Adele added, "Not like some people." Her green eyes narrowed as she glared at Aunt Edith.

"I soiled my blouse and decided to take time to change." Aunt Edith sniffed. "Are you familiar with the dress for success edict?"

"My outfit is a MacNeil, as you well know," Aunt Adele said. "Sophisticated colour coordination is worth the higher price tag, wouldn't you agree?"

79

Sue suppressed a smile. In her opinion, Aunt Edith's blue blouse coordinated perfectly with her pale yellow suit, whereas Aunt Adele's red hair looked slightly disheveled compared with her tailored grey outfit. She ignored the bickering and pointed at the throne. "Looks great so far."

"There's still work to be done," Aunt Edith said, "Starting with distributing the programs, one per chair. You've got younger legs. Do you mind?"

"Have you heard of ushers, Edith?" Aunt Adele stepped between Sue and the stacks of programs neatly arranged on a table pushed against the left wall. "Surely they can hand out programs as our guests arrive." She pointed to the back curtain. "We can put her legs to better use. The disco ball needs installing." The mirrored disco ball was as much a tradition as the throne, adding even more sparkle to the already glittering Digit mystique.

The women sighed. No one was eager to tackle the eighteen-foot extension ladder required for the installation or to balance the twelve-pound ball and hang it on the wire suspended from the ceiling, but at twenty-three Sue was steadier than Aunt Adele or Aunt Edith.

The monster ladder rested against the wall. The disco ball was in the prop trunk that should have been beside the ladder, but all Sue could see was a dusting of green sequins trailing from the feet of the ladder to the curtain and backstage. She followed the path of sequins to the edge of the side stage door, then looked back at Aunts Edith and Adele.

"Where's the prop trunk?"

"I haven't seen it," Aunt Adele said.

"Nor I," Aunt Edith said.

Although it was unimaginable that anyone had moved the trunk outside the building, Sue picked up a painted wooden sword leaning against a wall and wedged it under the stage door. Then she stepped outside and walked the perimeter of the building, even opening the lid of the giant green garbage dumpster to peer inside. Zero.

Sue went back empty-handed. The Crowning of the King contest was slated to start in thirty minutes. A line of perspiration formed over her eyebrows.

Four Gabriel Digit impersonators stood in front of the stage talking quietly. Digit lives, Sue thought, looking at the group decked out in the traditional white jumpsuits accented with gold and white sequins. Bright red scarves completed their outfits.

She continued searching for the trunk, even scanning the floor area where the vendors peddled their wares. From her vantage point she could see people milling freely around the displays and along the aisles. She finally turned back, faced upstage and spied the tip of the squared metal edge of the prop trunk peeking from behind the curtain of the right wing. What was it doing over there? No matter.

Sue hurried over, got behind it and pushed. It didn't budge. How much could a disco ball and a few other props weigh?

"Hey folks, I need help to move the prop trunk across the stage."

The four impersonators reacted immediately. "You want us to push or carry it?" they asked.

"I'd rather not have the floor scratched," Sue answered. "Is it too heavy to carry?"

"No problem, Ma'am." Each man picked up a side, hoisted the trunk and started moving across the stage.

"What's in this, lead?" one Digit asked.

"I feel like a pallbearer," another Digit said.

"Should be a disco ball," Sue said. "The trunk wasn't where it's supposed to be and I don't know why it weighs so much, but I'm guessing we'll find out."

The Digits set the trunk down beside the ladder. Sue unlatched its clasp and lifted the lid. Staring at her was a fifth impersonator, but this one was different. He looked like Digit. He too wore a white jumpsuit decorated with gold and white sequins. However a red apple gagged his mouth and the bright red scarf that should have adorned his neck was wound round his head. The disco ball had been jammed against his crotch. Sue stared in disbelief. A dead Digit was shocking, but this wasn't just any dead Digit. It was her ex-boyfriend Pierre.

"We'll have to relocate the 'Crowning the King' contest," she said at last.

An ambulance removed Pierre's body, everyone was questioned and the police left. Sue stood in the doorway of the emptied arena overwhelmed by the surrealness of Digit songs drifting from the kiosks on the sidewalks. The festival continued even though a man had been murdered.

"Sue! Sue!" She looked up to see Aunts Adele and Edith waving frantically. She walked over slowly. "It's been a busy day for all of us," they said. "The Festival can take care of itself for at least an hour. Everyone back to the house for tea!"

While Aunt Edith busied herself in the kitchen, Aunt Adele put her hand on Sue's arm. "Are you a suspect? The police spent a long time talking to you."

"I don't think so." Although she was sure the police knew of her history with Pierre, Sue didn't want that information to become a topic of this discussion or broadcast throughout the festival. "They told me everyone is a suspect."

"They say that all the time. I watch those TV shows. They're hoping you let down your guard so something incriminating can come sliding out."

"Adele, you've got that wrong, as usual," Aunt Edith said. She began placing teacups in front of everyone. "Things don't slide out. They spill out, as in beans."

"Listen," Sue said, "I don't think the police were setting me up or leading me on or whatever. I imagine they spent so much time with me because I found the body."

"You did open the trunk," Aunt Edith agreed. Almost as an afterthought she added, "And had it moved as well."

"Oh my, I think they call that tampering with evidence," Aunt Adele said. "Is that going to be a problem?"

"I doubt it." Sue added milk and sugar to her tea. "The police are sensible people. If I'd really murdered someone, would I draw attention to the crime or myself by opening the prop trunk?"

"They might think you're trying to throw people off the scent," Aunt Adele said. "I'll bet that Detective Smith considers all the angles. He continually shifted his eyes when he spoke to me."

"When I had the prop trunk moved I had no idea Pierre was inside. Besides, you both wanted me to put up the disco ball. To do that, I needed the prop trunk." Sue took a long sip of her tea.

"I didn't make that suggestion," Aunt Edith said. "You did, Adele."

"Did I? I seem to recall it being a group decision. But that is so like you, Edith. Point your finger and shift the blame if it looks like the water's getting hot."

Sue looked at her aunts. "The police have gone. Let's stop the squabbling. Of course I'm upset. My ex-boyfriend is dead."

Aunt Edith took Sue's hand. "I'm sorry about all this," she said. "You're the one who's getting hurt. First Pierre breaks your heart, then he's dead, and now the police seem to suspect you."

"I really don't think they suspect me," Sue said.

"They grilled you," both aunts said. "What a bunch of bullies."

"No." Sue shook her head. "They're just doing their job. There are connections between me and Pierre. We had a relationship. The police asked if I thought the disco ball was deliberately put where it

82

was put to be suggestive. Apparently some murderers stage bodies."

"So the police link a disco ball in the crotch to romantic sentiment?" Aunt Edith's eyes widened.

"Perverts," Aunt Adele said.

"Calm down," Sue said. "On top of everything, my fingerprints were on the murder weapon. I handled that painted wooden sword when I used it to hold the stage door open and whoever killed Pierre used it too."

Aunt Edith began to wring her hands. "I'm getting frightened. What if they come back, Sue? Oh." Her left hand had nudged the teacup. Tea ran over the table, spilling onto her lap. Aunt Adele righted the teacup and Aunt Edith began sopping up the spill with napkins while Sue raced to the bathroom for a towel. On the bathroom floor, in front of the clothes hamper, a green blouse spattered with sequins lay in a heap. Sue stopped.

Sue spread the green blouse on the kitchen table. Some sequins were hanging by a thread. There was a small tear by the buttons and a reddish-brown stain marred the material.

"This is the reason you had to change your clothes, isn't it?" Sue and Adele looked at Edith.

Aunt Edith covered her face with her hands. "I did it for you, Sue," she said. "I heard you crying that night after Pierre left. He broke your heart. So when I saw him backstage at the festival with the wooden sword an arm's length away, I couldn't help myself. I picked it up, closed my eyes and aimed for his head. He slumped forward and I wasn't sure if he was coming for me, so I gave him a good poke in the chest with the handle. But that's all. I swear."

"She's telling the truth," Aunt Adele said. "When I went backstage, Pierre was laid out on the floor. I checked his pulse. He was breathing. But as I stood there looking at him, all I could see was the louse that hurt my niece. To make matters worse, I overheard him the day before, talking to Blakey Bishop. He had the gall to say that he didn't think Edith or I deserved the I'm For Order Prize. I was livid and when I looked at him spread out, almost lounging, it all flooded back."

"I had no idea he was so bad," Aunt Edith said. "Adele, it must have been hard for you to live with the knowledge he was such a scoundrel, even for a day."

"It was," Aunt Adele said. "I saw the prop trunk and the rest is history. In retrospect, I'm not surprised you only disabled him, Edith." She sniffed. "You never were able to finish a job and really that's all I did."

"This is just peachy," Sue said. "The police suspect me and you two are guilty. Do they make jail cells big enough for three?"

"Oh, I wouldn't worry," Aunt Adele said. She disappeared upstairs and returned five minutes later clutching a sheet of paper. Her eyes glittered. "I've made a list," she said. "Now who shall we frame?"

Tourist Town

by Steve Shrott

*Steve Shrott's short stories have been published in numerous print magazines and e-zines. His work has appeared in ten anthologies—two from Sisters in Crime (*The Whole She-Bang, *and* Fishnets*). He recently published a mystery novel entitled* Audition For Death. *His comedy material has been used by well-known performers of stage and screen, and he has written a book on how to create humour,* Steve Shrott's Comedy Course. *Some of his jokes are in* The Smithsonian Institute.*

Roy owned the only drive-thru funeral business in Jasper County. It's located in our little town of Crenshaw. Population, 700. Two of them is pigs. The Mayor made 'em honorary citizens so's we'd be designated a tourist town, and get written about in all those glossy-type magazines. Course no one ever did.

Even with the quick-like funerals.

Old Roy was totally against the tourist thing. Said the town was perfect the way it was. We didn't need no drifters disturbin' things. That was Roy for ya. See, when a stranger stumbled into Crenshaw, Roy decided, on the spot, whether he liked 'em or not. And usually it was not.

Now don't let me give you the wrong idea 'bout Roy. He didn't care if you was black or white. Rich or poor. He hated everyone pretty well equally.

Course, I was on the other side of the fence on the tourist issue, seeing how I own the town souvenir shop—Sam's. I sell all kinds of knick-knacks, like a small plastic monkey that has Crenshaw written 'cross its butt. Unfortunately, everyone in town already owns one of them suckers.

Actually, Roy was a pretty nice guy in his younger days, but that's before his old lady kicked the bucket. Kinda strange about

85

that. Never sick a day in her life, then Roy makes her breakfast in bed, and boom she's gone. No one ever did figure out what happened to her. A good woman, Eunice was. A little hard on their daughter, Sally. Word is she kept her locked in the basement for a whole lotta years. But I reckon you have to be tough with kids sometimes.

Still, it didn't seem to hurt Sally. She grew up to be a bee-you-tea-ful twenty-three-year-old woman. Every man who looked into her deep blue eyes fell under her spell. And that was the problem— Sally seemed to fall in love with every man, too. And I'm guessin' that's why Roy was so bothered about drifters visitin' Crenshaw.

If anyone showed the slightest interest in Sally, Roy would get this weird look in his eyes, sort of like the mean look Betty Sue's one-eyed snake got when she didn't give him his food on time.

I remember the time Billy Swanson came up from North Dakota. Seemed like a good ol' boy. Tall, and clean as the dickens. Was mostly friendly to everybody. Even Roy. Course, Roy just looked at him, twisted his nose to one side, and muttered somethin' under his breath. He was even more fired up when he saw how keen Billy was on Sally, and Sally on him.

"What's she doing goin' after some stranger?" he hollered at me one day.

But Roy surprised me, and became Billy's best buddy, even took him out for drinks one night. That's when the story takes a strange turn. From what I heard, he got Billy all sauced up till he couldn't see an elephant if it was sittin' on his lap. Then he told Billy he had somethin' he wanted to show him at his shop. He called it a shop rather than a funeral parlour, 'cause he didn't want to give people the creepy-deepies.

Anyway, I'm not exactly sure what happened that night. But no one saw Billy no more, and Sally was heartbroken.

Well actually, I did run into Billy again. See, my souvenir shop was in a real bad slump back then, and Roy offered to let me work part-time at the funeral parlour. The smell was horrible, but for some reason it reminded me of Matilda, my last girlfriend. She worked in the smeltin' factory, the next county over.

One of my duties was to load the bodies into caskets. But I gotta admit, on my first day, I really messed up—put Miss Peabody, the town's short scrawny school teacher, into a "Wide and Long." What was I thinking? If that weren't bad enough, I tried to squash three-hundred-pound Festus Curby into a "Slim Jim." Wow, I really had a lot of learnin' to do in this business. I got so flustered I went into

86

the back room and sat down and moped for a while, chewing my craw. Just outta curiosity, I opened up a casket sittin' in the corner. But that turned out to be one heck of a bad idea.

When I saw Billy Swanson's face smilin' at me, like he was just sayin' "How dee doo," I jumped back, my heart beatin' faster than a fox chasin' a 'coon. Roy heard the commotion and raced over as much as he could with his limp. He saw me lookin' at the body and I think he was sizin' me up about what I was going to do about it.

Course there was no proof that Roy done anythin' to cause Billy's demise. Still, he hadn't told anyone Billy had died, or it would have been splashed 'cross the front page of the Crenshaw Daily. I had to know the truth. So I looked Roy right in his thick eyeglasses. "I never heard about this guy dyin', Roy. When did it happen?"

He gave me an angry stare. "Don't worry your head about things that don't concern ya. Just help me bury him."

That's when I figured Roy musta had somethin' to do with Billy's death. I gotta tell ya, my insides froze solid, but I somehow managed to dig.

I sorta forgot all about this for a while. You know how you like to forget about the bad things in your life like bills and buyin' insurance and stuff. But then about a week or two later, Judd Crowley comes to town looking for Billy.

I remember it as if it were yesterday. I was sittin' in The Tumblin' Weed Bar, with Roy. We was suckin' back Boilermakers, and Roy was tellin' jokes like he liked doin'. I remember laughin' my guts out when I heard the one about the crocodile, the farmer and the one-eyed snake.

Unfortunately for Roy, Betty Sue was at the next table a listenin' in. I guess when she heard the part about the croc eatin' the snake, it got her all riled up cause the next thing I know she's pourin' beer all over Roy's fancy new haircut.

Anyhow, Judd walked into the bar. Immediately, I could see that he was some kind of policeman, you know, with the badge and all. He came up to the two of us, took out his pad and asked if we knew anythin' about where Billy was at. Roy gave me that look again that said I better keep it buttoned. So I let him do all the talkin'.

"No sir, officer, I don't recall the lad. So many people come in and out of this town, it's real difficult to keep track."

The officer looked a mite disappointed and put away his pad. "He was my cousin, said he was coming here. Maybe he never made it."

Roy nodded. "I guess that be so."

Later, I saw the policeman talking to Sally at the town soda shop and I sensed trouble brewin'. After he left, I cornered Sally, and she told me she'd fallen in love with Judd. He was gonna meet her the next mornin' at Mandy's steak joint to propose.

My heart started pumpin' real fast like the time Doc told me I only had two months to live. Course Doc was just ribbin' me and we all had a good laugh about that. Even though right after I had to go to the hospital in Calhoun for res-pi-tory failure.

I wanted to tell Roy about Sally and Judd. After all, he was my employer and a fellow member of the Crenshaw Historical Society, but I was frightened as to what he might do. So I left it alone.

The next morning, I regretted my decision. Sally was sittin' in Mandy's, alone, in tears. The water just a floodin' down her cheeks like that broken septic tank of Wally Hudson's.

I headed back to the funeral parlour, but my heart wasn't in it. I saw Roy was workin' late and a strange idea climbed into my brain. I don't know what caused it—the drink, Sally's tears, or Billy sayin' "how dee doo" from the great beyond—but I picked up a shovel and banged Roy on the noggin. I figured he was dead, although truth be told, with Roy, it was difficult to tell.

I loaded him into one of the empty caskets. Then spent all night diggin'. About three in the mornin', the deed was done. I was all tuckered out, but I felt free.

The next day, Roy's death was all over town. Amazin' how fast news travels. The only one I told was Harley Jessop down at the Hardware Store. Course I couldn't give him the straight truth. Said how Roy had gotten all liquored up last night and accidental-like nailed himself into a "Wide and Long." Harley just nodded, and said, "Sounds like Roy, alright."

Course, I felt bad about lyin' and everythin', but I thought I had done the town a good turn, just like when Hattie McDonald took the oxygen tank off her daddy to re-sus-see-tate Wilber Pike's pet gopher. Good people.

I headed over to see Sally, sat down on her couch and tried to console her. Eventually, she seemed to feel a mite better and we got to talkin' about Roy, Judd and Billy. Then Sally surprised the dickens out of me by sayin' she was in love with yours truly. I told her it made me feel good to know because I had always secretly loved her.

She offered me a glass of Juniper Juice and I thought we was gonna live happily ever after. You know, like in the storybooks. Roy was dead and Sally had just confessed her love to me. But it's funny, you can know someone your whole life and still not really know 'em.

She said she was worried what she was gonna do, now that Roy was gone.

"What do you mean?" I asked.

"You know, with the bodies."

She went on to explain that she had this quirk. See, the thing about it was that once a man confessed his love to Sally, she lost interest. But she didn't know how to tell 'em, so's she wouldn't hurt their feelin's. That's when she gave them the Juniper Juice with the poison in it.

Then her daddy, being in the funeral business and all, would bury the bodies for her. She said up till now it had worked out pretty good. Roy was happy 'cause they got rid of all the tourists, and Sally was happy cause she didn't have to break up with nobody and cause all that hurt.

Course, afterwards, she felt lonely again, and cried till the cows come home. (Not Elmer Randy's cow, Sybil, of course. She ain't never come home.)

Anyways, when I heard all this, I stopped drinkin' the Juniper Juice, even though I was still a mite thirsty. I could understood how Sally felt, but it didn't make me like it much better. I'm guessin' that long stay in her mama's basement may have had somethin' to do with her thinkin' quirky-like.

Right now, my stomach is a gurglin' and I have a real bad headache. Even so, I do feel a mite sympathetic watchin' the tears a fallin' down Sally's face and her screechin', "Who's gonna bury the bodies now?"

Hammered

by Helen Nelson

Helen Nelson is a life-long reader and storyteller. Her first published stories appeared in The Whole She-Bang *and* Nefarious North. *She is past president of the Toronto Chapter of Sisters in Crime and co-chair of Bouchercon, the world mystery convention, to be held in Toronto in 2017. An IT consultant in her day job, Helen is looking forward to retiring to a life of crime (writing).*

Absolutely nothing seemed to compute and Jinx was not going to open her eyes until at least one thing did. Her head felt like the morning after six—no, make that ten—Jäger bombs. Voices droned. She wanted them to shut up.

Slowly, one voice came into focus, but it made no sense. None. "He didn't take the other bitch's word for it, he wants proof. We have to wake her up. We can't take a picture of her like that. Her old man isn't going to believe she's alive if she's totally passed out. We need her to talk."

A somewhat coherent thought came to Jinx. *Me? They want to wake me up? Okay, Jinx. Don't be opening those eyes just yet.*

"He says he'll pay up but we have to prove she's okay." Same voice.

Pay up? My old man? My father's... well I don't really know where he is at the moment. Jinx's father was something of a free spirit, a hippie really. *No money there,* she thought. *I don't have a boyfriend, or a husband. Other bitch? Do they mean Kate? Stop thinking; start concentrating on what they're saying.*

She heard another voice, "Look, Richards is stalling. We just have to tell him where to dump the cash and then let him know where to find his spoiled little girl."

Jinx decided to think of them as Frick and Frack. She had to keep these guys straight in her head. Frick—that was Mr. Impatient.

Mr. Sleep Disturber became Frack.

"Come on man—you didn't talk to him. I did. He sounds like a pretty cold dude. Basically told me we wouldn't see a penny till we showed him a picture of Kate alive and well. I believe him. So let's wake her up, prop her up against a tree and take her picture. Better yet, make a recording. I brought back a copy of today's *Globe* for her to hold up."

OMG, they think I'm Kate. Dead meat, that's me all right. Keep your eyes closed girl—give yourself a chance to figure a way out of this mess before they find out there is less than zero money to be had.

On Monday around noon, Jinx and her friend Kate Richards had decided to drive to Vancouver. Kate's new camper van. Kate's money. Jinx had nothing—no car, no money and at the moment, no job. So why not? She could leave Toronto behind for a couple of weeks or months if it came to that. By late that evening they were in a bar in Sault Ste. Marie, telling a couple of losers that Jinx was Kate and Kate was Jinx. Jinx was throwing around Kate's money and telling the losers that her dad was rolling in it. The losers—they would have been Frick and Frack. Well, they had said their names were... Bill and Bob? So she had seen them. And so had Kate.

But the hangover? Drugs—it has to be, Jinx thought. Kate and Jinx only drank Virgin Caesars. Jinx was sure of that. The plan had been to get a hotel room for their first night on the road and then head off to one of the parks along the north shore of Superior early the next day. *No Virgin Caesar ever made me feel like puking in the nearest shoe—and, oh boy, this is so much worse.*

Jinx forced herself to calm down, to think about what she knew. She made a mental list:

I am stuck here (Where is here? That is a huge question) with Frick and Frack, Bill and Bob, Dumb and Dumber...
They think I'm Kate.
The other bitch? That must be Kate so Mr. Richards must know they have me, not Kate.
Kate's dad doesn't appear to be giving the game away. He must be playing for time.
I know Kate will beg her dad not to call the cops, man I hope he doesn't listen.
I have the worst hangover ever. But I had zip to drink (total rip

92

off—all pain, no gain).

These guys are dumber than a sack of hammers. They don't even know they don't have any nails.

And whoa—I'm lying on a bed. And they don't even have me tied up. WTF?

I'm not hurt. I haven't been beaten up. Or raped. (Drugged though, majorly drugged.)

So what's to lose? They think I'm Kate, and if Kate's dad isn't going to give the game away, I can play along—I can be Kate. So, let's get this show on the road.

Jinx let out a tentative groan. And allowed herself to look at the world through eyes veiled by her lashes. Frick and Frack were there in a flash, hovering over her. Beyond them she could see a rough cabin. Probably an old fish camp. Everything was made of logs or rough wood. And everything wasn't much. A table. A couple of things that might be called chairs. Bunks on the far wall. A wood stove. Dirt floor. Some kind of gas lamp. Primitive would have been a compliment.

"Oh, God, am I hung over. Hey Jinx, you okay?" She still hadn't totally opened her eyes.

"Sorry, sweetie, Jinx isn't here. We left her in your camper back in the Sault with a note to take to your daddy—well, when she comes to." There was a chuckle in Frick's voice.

"Actually, she must have called it in. Because when I phoned him he already knew about it," Frack said.

"What?" Jinx took a dive over the side of the bed and made as if she were about to puke on their feet.

"Easy does it," said Frack and helped her back onto the bed. "I see you aren't feeling so well. But, see, we need your help. So you can get out of here and back to your daddy."

Jinx groaned again and look stupidly at them. It wasn't much of a stretch to play sick and stupid.

"We're going to write you a little speech for you to make to your daddy. And we're going to make a video while you read it," said Frick.

"Why?" she croaked.

"So he'll know you're alive and pay the ransom and then you can go home." That was Frack.

"Oh. Can we wait till my hangover is done?" Jinx played for the time she desperately needed to think this through. She felt like someone had beaten her up and puked on her.

Waiting was never in Frick and Frack's cards. Delayed gratification didn't seem to be their thing.

"Come on bitch—haul your ass out of that bed. Time to shine. You're going to be in the movies." That was Frick. And Jinx was on her feet with more than a little help from her impatient buddy. She really did almost toss those cookies and wondered again what drug they had given her.

Frick had a firm grip on her arm. In a substantial twist. He used that stranglehold to propel her outside. After a short walk on a path through the trees they arrived on a stunning pebble and sand beach. Beach, hills, trees, water as far as the eye could see. And nothing else. Really nothing else. No hydro poles, no road, no sign of anything resembling civilization—or a population of more than the three of them. She felt that to run away was to risk being eaten by a bear or at least to get seriously lost. *No wonder they didn't bother to tie me up. Are you ready to hear me curse?*

"Hey guys—can I go for a swim? It might help with my hangover."

Frick twisted her arm more and said, "Sure—if freezing is what you have in mind." He threw her to the ground. "Off with your shoes Katie—dip your toes in that pond."

"Don't call me Katie. I hate it." It was one of the things they had bonded over in high school. Kate refused to be Katie or Katherine or anything but Kate. Jinx refused to be Jess or Jessica or anything but Jinx.

She peeled off her shoes and socks, rolled up her pant legs and stood up. She hit the water running. Cold didn't even begin to cover the sensation. Jinx was surprised there wasn't ice floating there.

Late May, water that must barely have the ice off it. Probably near the Sault. No other land in sight. She was beginning to have a sense of where she might be. Not that she would be able to pinpoint the location on a map—it covered a lot of ground.

Frick and Frack laughed their heads off as they stood on the shore. "Warm enough for you, bitch?" asked Frick.

"Refreshing," said Jinx "Life's a beach. I'd take a proper dip, but modesty prevents me." In fact the shock of it had cleared her head a bit but she had no urge to swim in a place where icebergs must be so very close at hand.

"Here—go over this." Frack thrust a piece of paper into her hand.

It read: "Hi I'm fine. Don't call polis. Give what they ask. They will let go. Today is Tuesday May 21. Headline on globes is about

Ford and Gaker".

"Can I make a suggestion? How about I add, 'Hi Daddy?' And can I say something about how I'd like to go fishing with him when you let me go? It would just make it all more personal."

"Sure," said Frack as Frick said, "No way. No changes."

"But it's too cold and impersonal. He'll think you're hurting me." She decided not to add that the grammar and spelling were pitiful.

Frick glared at Frack and grumbled, "Okay, okay. Whatever. But nothing funny."

Apparently Frack was the movie maker. "Okay—over by those trees there; do your stuff." Frick pushed her over to a stand of what she thought was maple, although the trees were still leafless so she might have been wrong. But she doubted it as there were more than a few desiccated maple leaves on the ground.

"Okay, start... now," said Frack as he waved his arm like a fancy movie producer.

I'm going to pull out all the stops here, let's see if they catch me. Jinx inhaled and...

"Hi, Daddy, today is Tuesday, May 21st. The headline on today's Globe is about Rob Ford and Gawker. I'm fine, so please don't not call the police. Give them what they have asked for. They have promised to let me go when you pay. When I'm out of here we'll go fishing again—just like we did when I was ten—the same place. Okay?" Frack filmed and Jinx held up the copy of the Globe.

"Hey, bitch, that's different than what we wrote." Frick said.

"I just changed the order around a bit," Jinx said. "But really it isn't any different than what we agreed on."

"It's fine." Frack shut off the camera and headed off down a path through the bush while Frick strong-armed Jinx back toward the cabin.

This time, Frick tied Jinx's ankle to the bed frame. And Jinx added to her mental list of things she had learned:

They must have some vehicle down that path.

Frack is off to contact Mr. Richards with the video, or at least the sound part of it. When he comes back, I'll have an idea of how far I am from civilization. I hope.

We are away from even cell reception, or Frack wouldn't have to leave.

I'm by a really big, really cold lake. I think I know which one, but I'm not sure yet.

Dumb, these guys are dumb. Not only are there no nails, but

I'm not even sure about the sack.

Frick and Frack hadn't caught the double negative in my message. Would Kate and Mr. Richards?

Would Kate and Mr. Richards try to find my dad to figure out what the fishing stuff was about? Kate will know it is important. I hope.

Mr. Richards seems like a sweetheart. But I can't see him forking over a bundle for me despite my status as Kate's friend.

I've probably seen too much for them to let me live regardless of what Mr. Richards does. So I have to figure out how to get away.

When Kate came to in the camper she felt only marginally better than Jinx would a few hours later. She read the note and called her father right away. He told her to call the cops. Kate wept profusely and pointed out that the note said not to bring in the cops. "Dad, they said they'd kill her—and they think she is me." Her father backed down, for the time being. He also wanted to come to Sault Ste. Marie immediately, but Kate persuaded him to wait for the phone call that the losers had said to expect.

After the phone call, which came from Kate's cell phone, there was no putting him off. The cops were called. Kate had been subjected to every kind of blood test for drugs—but there were no results so far. The cops had the camper and were going over it for fingerprints and other possible evidence. They had the note. And they had questioned Kate at length. Kate's dad forwarded his calls to his cell phone and joined her in Sault Ste. Marie. Cops were standing by, ready to listen in and record the next call. To trace it if they could. Within hours, Jinx's Mom would be joining them and everyone—siblings, friends, Jinx's Mom—was trying to hunt down Jinx's dad.

They were finally in a hotel suite—along with several cops.

"Explain." Aaron Richards said. "How did this happen? And why do these jokers think she is you?"

Kate was blubbering. "We were in the bar. They asked our names. It's all my fault. I told them I was Jinx and before she could do anything I said her name was Kate. I told them her daddy had just bought her a fancy camper van. Well, you did for me. I passed her a couple hundred under the table and suggested she should buy rounds for everyone. We just had Virgin Caesars. That's all. But I told them who you were.

"We went to the can and laughed ourselves silly. They must have put something in our drinks. They just seemed so dumb and gullible. We didn't taste anything weird—the Caesars were so spicy. We were just having fun.

"I remember wondering why I felt so terrible. They helped us back to the camper. And then I woke up. I had both our purses but both cell phones were gone. They couldn't have even looked at the rest of the stuff in our purses or they would have known. And I had the note. You know the rest. Daddy, you have to do what you can. Please!"

By the time the phone rang, Kate was weeping inconsolably. Her father's glare as he answered his phone put a damper on that.

"Hello." Aaron Richards sounded gruff.

"Just listen, don't talk. Save your questions for later," said the voice on the other end.

They could hear Jinx. Brave, strong Jinx. "Hi Daddy, today is Tuesday, May 21st. The headline on today's Globe is about Rob Ford and Gawker. I'm fine, so please don't not call the police. Give them what they have asked for. They have promised to let me go when you pay. When I'm out of here we'll go fishing again—just like we did when I was ten—the same place. Okay?"

There was a pause.

"Right," said the voice. "Three million dollars should about do it in exchange for your daughter. We'll need the money tomorrow. Cash. Packed in plain duffle bags—no marks on the bags or the bills. We'll call you at noon. When we have the money and can see the bills aren't marked and can't be traced—that there is no GPS or other crap like that attached, we'll call again and tell you where you can find your girl."

"I can't do that—I can't get that kind of money in less than twenty-four hours." Aaron Richards was following police instructions to a T. "I need till Saturday. And when you call again, I'll need more proof that Kate is fine. I need a picture. No, I need to talk to her—not just hear a recording. And I want an exchange—I give you the money. You give me Kate.

"And give me a rough location—will we meet in Toronto? If that's what you want I'll have to go back. I've come to Sault Ste. Marie to help my daughter's friend. She is pretty shaken up by what you jerks have done to them."

"Richards, my heart bleeds bitter blue tears for you. The drop will be in the Sault on Thursday—big guy like you can pull the strings to make it happen. No pictures. No way to get them to you. We'll have a new recording. But you're going to have wait to talk to your girl till we know we are safe. Bye."

The connection broke.

"So, did either of you learn anything from that?" asked the cop.

Aaron Richards shook his head. "No, I don't think so. I don't know Jinx all that well though."

Kate started to speak tentatively. "Jinx is scared. She sounds brave and strong, but she would never use a double negative. Just never. She wants us to call the cops; she needs help. So Daddy, I guess you were right about that. And I don't know what that stuff about fishing was about. She went fishing and camping with her dad when she was ten. That is true. But she hated it. Just hated it. She likes to camp but she said she would never go fishing again, not if her life depended on it. She has to be telling us something. Maybe her Dad will know... If you can find him..." Kate trailed off.

"Maybe she just wants to make her Dad feel better if something happens to her," the cop suggested.

"No," said Kate. "Not a chance. She is saying something... I know it."

They had less than forty-eight hours to find Jinx.

"Hey, I'm hungry." Jinx complained.

"So, does this look like a restaurant to you?" asked Frick. "Bill will bring us all some food when he gets back from talking to your old man. Well, you'll get some if your old man is cooperative. Otherwise—no point feeding a corpse, is there?" Frick, such a barrel of laughs. He thought so anyway.

"Okay then how about something to drink—I have a hangover, you know."

"You stupid bitch, you don't have a hangover. Drugs is what got to you."

"Well then, I'd rather risk a hangover tomorrow than feel like this now. Come on something—wine, beer, scotch, whatever." An idea was forming in Jinx's head. She didn't so much want to drink as she hoped that Frick would drink too, get good and drunk, and just maybe pass out. *It might not work. But nothing ventured, nothing gained. In for a penny, in for a pound. I sound like my grandmother.*

Water. He gave her bottled water. A plastic bottle. *No weapon there.* But he did have a beer himself. *Can I get my hands on that glass bottle before Frack gets back? Much easier to deal with them one at a time if I have to get physical.*

Frack had been gone about two hours. Frick was getting restless, and Jinx was getting hungry. Dusk was setting in. She could see the sun setting through the trees. She added that to the collection of things she knew: *We're facing west across the big, cold lake.*

A few minutes later, she heard the crunch of steps approaching the cabin. Frack had returned. She knew that as soon as she ate, she would have to feign sleep to hear what they were up to. But she had to eat.

Frack brought burgers from a fast food joint. The kind you could only get in a bigger place like the Sault or Sudbury. They were cold. And limp. The cotton bun had absorbed the cheese and grease and ketchup. As unappetizing as they were, Jinx managed to choke down the burger and fries and the dead flat pop, conscious that they were calories and no more. She hoped that if she didn't get food poisoning, the sustenance meant she could fight if the opportunity arose.

She rolled over on her cot and tried to keep her breathing as shallow and regular as she could. It worked. Shortly Frack said, "I think she's asleep." She heard beer caps popping.

"He said he can't get the money till Saturday. I told him Thursday, like we agreed. He wants to talk to her just before he pays up. I said he could have another recording. He wants an exchange— I said no way. He's in the Sault, so I said we'd get the money from him there. He won't be pleased at a change of plans, but I think Batchawana Bay isn't that far from the Sault, so it should be okay. Good and open anyway, hard to hide cops."

"This bitch is a real handful, wants food, wants a drink, has to piss, swim, changes the message," said Frick. "I'm real glad we don't have to try and keep her after Thursday." He paused. "We can't give her back."

Jinx's heart sank. It was as she expected, but it also made the stakes for her crystal clear. She had to find an escape.

"Oh, man, she's not that bad. Maybe we can just phone and let them know where she is when we're safe," said Frack.

"Think about it, dude. She's seen us. Anyway we don't have to actually do anything—no one will ever find her here."

Their talk drifted off to how they were going to enjoy spending their three million dollars. How sweet the beaches were in Mexico. How cold the beaches were here. Every now and again Frack would moan a bit about how it was too bad Kate would have to die. But then hadn't she said it herself? "Life's a beach." And they both laughed. The beer caps popped. And popped. And popped.

It seemed to Jinx that they must have had six or eight beer each. Their speech began to slur and they pretty much stopped making any sense. Finally she heard snoring—and Frack asking his companion, "Hey you 'sleep?" And another beer cap popped. Then both of them were snoring.

Now she knew. *I have to be on Lake Superior. On the west shore, north of the Sault and north of Pancake Bay. Probably south of Lake Superior Provincial Park and if those were maple trees, south of Wawa for sure. The beach looks like some of the ones I camped on with Dad on that fishing trip. There are only a handful of places along there where we could be more than a few kilometres from Highway 17. It has to be a few though—there are no traffic sounds.*

Jinx knew she had to risk it. There might be a better chance later, but this was the chance she had now. She had to untie her leg, grab Frick and Frack's flashlights and either make it to the highway or die trying. Frick and Frack had been so dumb, so cocksure that she couldn't go anywhere. They hadn't even tied her hands.

She was at the door when she heard Frack's voice.

That's it, it's all over for me. Just shoot me now guys.

And then what Frack was actually saying penetrated her consciousness. "Go for it, kid. Take the path I took this afternoon. He'll be out till morning now. I gave him the last pill—the one I was supposed to put in your drink. I'm not a killer."

Jinx ran.

A month later, in Vancouver, Kate and Jinx rehashed it all. They had been back to the beach on Lake Superior. They had walked the beach and admired the rugged, lonely beauty. Nonetheless, the place gave Jinx the creeps, and awe-inspiring as it was, she hoped never to set sight on it again.

It had actually been about eight or nine kilometres to the highway. Jinx had come across her captors' truck a few hundred metres from the cabin. But no keys. She memorized the plate number and everything else about the vehicle. From the truck there was a bad road, a pair of ruts really, but it made a good walking trail with hills that left her gasping by the time she reached the top and her knees aching by the time she got to the bottom. Between the flashlights, the cloudless sky, and the fact that it was only a few days from a full moon, she had been able to see well enough. When she finally got to the highway a few hours later, the first truck barrelling down on her had stopped and taken her to the Sault. To the police station.

Unbelievably, Frick and Frack—the brothers Bob and Bill Johnson as it turned out—had tried to brazen it out and collect the ransom after Jinx's escape. It hadn't gone well for them. *No nails, no sack, and, well, in the end not even any hammers.*

Beyond the Locked Door

by P.M. Jones

P.M. Jones, always an avid reader, devours eloquent words and quirky tales with gluttonous velocity. In 2012, she shared her other secret passion—her love of writing. Her other, more well-known passions include creating spicy gastronomical feasts from around the globe to the rhythm of excellent music at a seaside retreat, while enjoying a glass of fine red wine in the company of good friends. From her experiences as a traveller, a woman of many different careers and the priceless gift of motherhood, P.M. Jones has much to offer as a writer. After honing her craft and experimenting with many different genres, writing mysteries seemed to be the right fit. Whether light and comical, historical, or ominous chillers, she loves to weave a multifaceted tale of intrigue. P.M. Jones lives outside Toronto and is busy writing and following one of her favourite sayings, "Live Life Like You Mean It!"

The exhibit's grand opening had caused quite a stir. A new 'Matadori' was being sold by auction, with an opening bid of one-hundred thousand. Until the gallery was forced to close for a week. But of course, murder trumps artwork...

Dane Wells began his investigation by request of the wife of the gallery owner. Her husband had been under police scrutiny since the starring artist was found dead in the workroom of the gallery the night before the grand opening. The doors had been locked, alarm set and the lights turned off. Things looked pretty bad for the only person who held the keys and the security code. Private Investigator Dane Wells knew he had his work cut out for him.

The gallery was only a year old, but highly successful. The owner had an eye for up-and-coming artists as if he possessed a mystical sense. Leo Greenwood had "discovered" three very different artists in a short period of time, using his connections to launch careers of relative unknowns into stratospheric heights. The life-size charcoal sketches by Davis Matadori were breaking records in the art world. The commissions off his pieces to the gallery were twenty percent. To Dane Wells's mind, Greenwood would have been a fool to kill the golden goose.

After pounding the pavement investigating the employees, the catering company, the security company and basically anyone who had access to the gallery, Dane Wells knew he had to go hat-in-hand to the police department.

Dane sat down in front of Detective Nivens's desk and cleared his throat.

"Hey, Teddy. Brought you a coffee so you don't have to drink the swill they brew around here," Dane said, sliding the brown paper cup across the desk.

"If this is a peace offering you'd better remember how I take it," Teddy Nivens said, locking eyes with him.

Dane's piercing blue gaze took in the woman across from him. Ex-co-worker, ex-fiancée, Detective Sergeant Teddy Nivens. Damn, she still looks good, Dane thought.

"Peace offering and bribery. Here's a chocolate chip muffin to sweeten the deal," Dane said, handing her a bag.

Teddy snorted a laugh as she folded back the plastic tab on the lid of the cup before pulling the muffin out of the bag. She took a long sip, bit into the muffin and sighed.

"Okay, you got it right. Coffee's good. Muffin's the clincher. What's the case and what kind of information do you want, Dane?"

"Just a little thing. Why do you like Greenwood for the Matadori homicide? And why was it called murder?"

"First, it's murder because the victim ingested poison from the lemon-ginger cream on his tea cake. Think he baked himself a toxic aconite snack?"

"Probably not. So where'd the killer dessert come from?" Dane asked with a hint of humour in his voice.

Teddy shot him a dry stare. "No idea. The catering company didn't supply it and there isn't anywhere locally you can buy it. Must have been homemade."

"Okay. So why is Greenwood on the radar?"

Teddy pulled a file out from under the heap on her desk. "The accessibility to the victim, plus the gallery owner will probably get ten times the amount for Matadori's work now that the artist is dead. Greenwood has six more sketches in his possession to be exhibited at the gallery next month. The commission alone creates motive."

Dane Wells pulled up to the gallery just before closing time. Leo Greenwood was closing the supply room door as he came in.

"How's things?" Dane asked, shaking his hand.

"Pretty good, for a suspected murderer," Greenwood said, with an ironic smile on his face. "Getting anywhere?" he asked Dane, as he loosened his tie, his brown eyes hopeful.

"No. But the cops don't have anything more either," Dane said.

"They don't have anything else on me because I didn't kill him," Greenwood stated matter-of-factly. He pushed a hand through his dark hair, sweeping it back from his forehead. "Matadori must have been in the stock room when I left. It's the only room I didn't check every night before leaving. I damned well do now though."

Dane Wells's next stop was the pricey Toronto townhouse where Davis Matadori had lived until a few days ago. He rang the bell as a precaution. It was a good rule of thumb before picking a lock.

Dane wiped the look of surprise off his face as a tiny elderly woman opened the door a crack, peering out cautiously before asking him what he wanted.

"Investigator Dane Wells, ma'am. I'm looking into the murder of Davis Matadori," he said, taking a small step forward to give the woman a sense that he wanted to be invited in. "May I ask you a few questions, Mrs...?"

"Dezaki," she filled in. "Come. Come in and sit. I'll bring tea."

Dane sat in the eclectically furnished living room, taking in the space.

Tray clanging with mismatched china, Mrs. Dezaki waddled in, setting the tray down on the coffee table. She poured the tea and shoved a cup into Dane's big hand.

"I clean the house. Cook a little bit now and then. But I'm old. I don't like standing so much anymore," Mrs. Dezaki volunteered.

"Is this all Davis Matadori's artwork?" Dane asked, looking at the artwork adorning the walls.

Mrs. Dezaki put her cup down on the table. "All Matadori," she said, sweeping her hand around the room. "Your questions?"

"Just a little background information, if you don't mind," Dane said, taking out his notebook. "How long did you know him?"

Mrs. Dezaki smiled. "Since he was born."

"Any siblings?"

"He had a sister."

"You mean she's dead?" Dane asked, wondering if there were family skeletons that could account for Davis Matadori's death.

"No, I said 'had' because he is. His sister lives in Haliburton."

Trying not to sound disappointed about the way he was interpreting Mrs. Dezaki's clipped responses, he asked for the sister's name.

"Isadora," she replied.

"Do you have a phone number for her?"

"Yes, but it won't do you any good," Mrs. Dezaki said with a strange, wistful looking little smile.

"They were estranged?"

"No, but they haven't spoken for years. And she won't speak to you, so don't bother going to the trouble."

Dane's blue eyes searched the care-worn face of Mrs. Dezaki, trying to figure out what she was getting at. Aside from volunteering her role as cook and cleaner for Davis Matadori, getting anything else out of her was like trying to get a rooster to lay an egg.

"I think I'll give it a try anyway," Dane said, standing to take his leave.

Mrs. Dezaki laughed a little.

"Something funny?"

"No. Not funny. There's nothing funny about Isadora. Just funny about you, trying to talk to her. Isadora hasn't said one word in twenty years. Since she was six. Isadora lives at the Millbrook Institute. She can't help you, Mr. Wells," Mrs. Dezaki said, before gently shutting the door.

Dane Wells pulled up Matadori's website to have another look. Ten years ago, at the age of twenty, Matadori had his first art show at a small gallery in the Distillery District. An instant success. The website highlighted Matadori's career in the art world, finally leading up to the big break he got last year when one of his hauntingly lifelike sketches was used as the cover art for a major best-seller.

Greenwood had signed him on just before the big wave of fame hit and highlighted him as his new star at Shadowbox Gallery. Since then, the steady increase in value of a Matadori had created a major buzz in the art world.

One small detail latched onto Dane's analytical brain which he'd missed before, and he knew just who to ask about it.

"Hello, Mr. Greenwood. It's Dane Wells calling."

"I think we're past the formality, buddy. After your investigation, you probably know more about me than I do. Just call me Leo."

Dane laughed his deep hearty chuckle. "Ok, will do."

106

"Are we in the clear yet?" Greenwood asked.

"Not even close, I'm afraid. But I do have a question about Matadori's exhibitions. Do you know why he chose to have his art shown only in the spring?"

"That's a good question. I wondered that myself. I wanted new pieces to add into my fall exhibit and asked Davis for his latest creations. 'Nothing until March', he said. When I asked him to give me a couple of small sketches or paintings, he balked. But I pushed him for something to keep him in the public eye. He gave me three unsigned paintings, which quite frankly, were close to terrible. Looked like a kid had painted them."

"Did you use them in the show?"

Greenwood laughed. "I put them in as 'artist unknown' because I'd pressured Davis into giving them to me. I took them down after the first night when the critics starting asking me why I was showcasing my five-year-old daughter's artwork."

"Did you tell Matadori about that?"

"I didn't have to. He was standing right there. He took off that night and I didn't hear from him for about three months."

"That must have had you worried."

"Not really. I'm used to artists' temperaments," Greenwood laughed. "Although when he still hadn't resurfaced by February I wanted to kill him. Figuratively speaking, of course."

Dane chuckled. "Of course. Did he ever explain his absence?"

"Not really. He just said he only 'creates' in the winter. I left good enough alone."

Time to pay another call on the odd little housekeeper at Davis Matadori's house, Dane thought.

This time Mrs. Dezaki wasn't there. A little B & E seemed opportune. A quick search of the ground floor showed little more than sparse decor and a plethora of Matadori's artwork, all signed with a big swirly D and 'matadori' in lower case. Seems like this guy was really into himself, Dane thought, taking it all in.

An inspection of the second floor proved to be a little more fruitful. One of the rooms had clearly been used as his studio. The floor had been covered in canvas drop-cloth and empty easels stood in disarray around the room. A cupboard holding artists' materials stood ajar on the far side of the room. Dane ambled over and took a look inside, finding dust covered palettes and dried out tubes of paint. The brushes looked either brand new or crusted with dry paint. There were no half-finished paintings or rough sketches laid out. A small box of charcoal pencils sat on a stool with a couple of pencils missing, the rest of the box pristine.

Guess this guy really did only get creative in the winter, Dane thought. He slid open a drawer of the wide cabinet on the far wall of the room, hoping to find some small clue. What he did find were many small paintings, crude and unsophisticated. Juvenile at best. It was as if Davis Matadori were two different people. In the winter brilliantly talented, and the rest of the time, staggeringly awful.

A loud crash at the end of the hallway startled Dane out of his ruminations. He shoved a door open while his brain played catch-up with his quick dash down the hall, his eyes widening in shock as he took in the room.

A wizened old man with a thin shock of wispy hair lay on the bed, his arm stretched out over the bedside table where he'd knocked a glass of water onto the floor, shattering it. The old man opened his eyes a crack, taking in the tall Norse-like figure standing in the doorway.

"Come to take me away, finally?" he whispered in a hoarse voice.

"No, sir," Dane said, stepping into the room.

"Why are you here? Come to take him away finally, then?" the man cackled.

"Who, sir?"

"The boy, of course. I warned him. I told him to stop, but why would such a brilliant young artist listen to a feeble old man like me?" the man snapped, a sneer upon his weathered face.

"Stop?" Dane asked, hoping the old fellow was coherent enough to give him some answers.

"Stop!" a shrill voice sounded out from the doorway. Dane turned, coming face to outraged face with Mrs. Dezaki. "You have no right! Get out, get out! Get out now," she raged, shooing him out the door.

"I heard a crash and thought I'd better help," Dane said, as he was shepherded down the stairs and out the front door.

"You go away! And stay away," the angry little woman huffed before slamming the door with a resounding bang.

Oh, *shit*... that did not go as planned, Dane thought, climbing into his car. Thoughts on how to figure out what Davis Matadori was up to before he died occupied his mind for the entire drive.

"So you've come back for more information, Dane?" Teddy said, as she opened the door of her condo suite.

"You caught me," Dane said, eyes twinkling at the one that got away.

"Well, what is it?"

"I was wondering what you've found out about Davis Matadori's underhanded or illegal activities?"

Teddy laughed. "What are you talking about? That man had no record, no shady dealings, and no skeletons in his closet."

"What about the old man who lives with him?"

Teddy brushed her chestnut hair off her face as she looked up at Dane with her hazel eyes. "You mean his father? He's not mentally competent enough to make any statement," she said, narrowing her eyes. "How do you know about him anyway? Please do not tell me you broke into that poor man's house to snoop on the victim."

Dane cleared his throat, but kept his eyes steady on hers. He knew from experience that Teddy could smell bullshit the way a hound finds a fox, and he really didn't want any of his appendages mounted and stuffed and sitting on Teddy's mantelpiece.

"I went over to talk to Mrs. Dezaki. I met the old man while I was there."

"Uh hunh," Teddy said, clearly not buying it fully. "And when Mrs. Dezaki invited you in for tea, what did you discuss?"

Ah, good, Dane thought. The truth about having tea with Mrs. Dezaki was his out. "Well, she made us green tea and we talked in the bizarrely furnished living room. I found out that Matadori has a sister in an institution and that he really loves his own artwork. His good stuff anyway. The winter work."

"Ya, I know about the sister and the house. What are you talking about, his good stuff? Winter work?"

"I had an opportunity to take a look around the studio and it looks like it hasn't been used in ages. The only 'artwork' in there was awful. Shoved into a drawer and forgotten. And when I talked to Leo Greenwood, he said Matadori would only show the pieces he created over the winter. And rightly so."

"That's interesting. Mrs. Dezaki wouldn't let us into the studio. You must have charmed her with your winning personality and sparkling smile." Teddy grinned. "And how did you come to meet the old man? She wouldn't let us talk to him either."

Dane drew in a breath and instantly knew he'd goofed. Teddy knew when Dane Wells was bracing himself for some serious shit shovelling. Instead of outright lying, Dane decided some skating around the question was called for, so he skipped right into the conversation with the old man, recalling it verbatim.

Teddy sat back in her chair, mulling over what Dane repeated to her, her eyes focused on the ceiling.

"So?" Dane said, interrupting her chain of thought.

"So, shut up for five seconds so I can think. Or I'll arrest you for breaking and entering."

Dane flinched, and she snorted a laugh.

"Transparency, thy name is Dane."

"You haven't been charged so far," Dane said to Greenwood as they sat in the Brewhouse, each of them nursing a draft the next night. Dane was apprising his client of his progress. Or non-progress as the case would be.

"Well, let's drink to that," Greenwood said, with a hint of humour. "I'm pretty sure I will be arrested by this time tomorrow, though," he continued, looking as if he felt slightly ill.

"What makes you say that?"

"I got notice from my lawyer today. All of Matadori's works in my possession are now legally mine. Apparently it's a clause in my standard contract. All consigned artwork belongs to the gallery in the event of the artist's death. I called the cops to tell them about it."

"What!?" Dane said, almost lifting himself off his bar stool. The entire population at their end of the bar looked over.

"Sorry," Dane said to Greenwood using his inside voice, looking around at the nosy bar-flies. "I mean what the hell did you tell the cops for? They would have found out eventually anyway, and it would have bought us some time until I found out who the hell really did off young Mr. Matadori."

Greenwood chuckled. "I'm not trying to hide anything and I want the cops to know that. Aren't you going to ask me about the artwork I now own? It's bound to be worth a pretty penny once this is all cleared up."

"Don't need to, mate. I know a straight shooter when I see one. And as your charming wife said when she asked me to take this case, she would never have a husband who murdered people for money. And Tasha Greenwood strikes me as a pretty straight shooter, too."

"Now, that I really will drink to," Leo Greenwood said, taking a big swig from his pint.

No stone unturned, Dane Wells thought, as he drove up the highway to the Millbrook Institute the next morning. You really know your investigation has gone to hell when you're going to interview a person who doesn't speak, he said to himself.

His radio station turned static as he drove out of range. The King's voice filled the space as the CD changer selected one of

110

Dane's driving discs. "A Little Less Conversation" came on first, causing Dane to crack up at the irony of it. The next one was "Suspicious Minds." He switched over to the Tragically Hip for the rest of the drive.

Millbrook was a beautiful place in the spring. Soft green rolling lawns, blossoming gardens and big old trees graced the grounds. Many of the residents were outside, walking along the paths or sitting with visitors on the sun-shaded wrap-around porch.

Dane approached the middle-aged woman behind the reception desk and asked to see Isadora Matadori.

"Are you family?" she asked, peering out from behind funky red framed eyeglasses.

"No. I just came to, uh, ask her a few questions," Dane replied, knowing how stupid that sounded.

The receptionist stared for a blink. "I'm sorry sir. But unless you're a family member on the visitor's list or have court ordered permission to speak with her, I'm afraid you're S.O.L.," she said, smiling sweetly.

Well that's just goddamned terrific Dane thought. A three-hour drive for nothing.

"Well thanks anyway, Mrs..."

"Perkins. Miss Perkins."

"Miss Perkins. By the way that's a lovely dress you're wearing, if you don't mind me saying so. That colour of blue really brings out your eyes, and with your red hair it really says something."

Miss Perkins laughed a little. "Well, thank you Mr..."

"Wells. Dane Wells," he said reaching across the desk to shake her hand.

"Just what is it that you want to see Isadora about, Mr. Wells?"

"It's Dane. And I really just wanted to meet her. I'm involved in the investigation of her brother's death and though probably fruitless, I thought I may as well pay a visit."

"Ohhh, right! He was murdered, wasn't he? I saw that on the news. I heard the police were close to making an arrest. Can you tell me who? Why was he killed?" she asked in a hushed, excited tone as she leaned closer.

"I really can't divulge the details in an ongoing investigation. The police department tends to frown on that. I was just hoping to get a better sense of who Davis Matadori was by meeting his sister and maybe talking with the people here who might have known him."

Miss Perkins jumped up from her seat. "I'll take you to meet her.

Don't tell! And I knew Isadora's brother, a little. I'd be happy to help a bright young officer like you."

"I'm a detective," Dane said, covering himself in case he was accused of impersonating the actual police.

"Well of course you are, Detective Wells. How silly of me," Miss Perkins said, taking him by the arm and leading him to the recreation room.

"It's just Dane, remember?"

Miss Perkins giggled.

Having met Isadora, a sweet, gentle young woman with large brown eyes, and a trusting smile, Dane was saddened by the fact that such a lovely young woman would never know a normal life. She lived in a little world of her own, humming and flitting around the room straightening books then staring dreamily out the window.

Miss Perkins sat beside Dane on the couch as she chattered on.

"It's really too bad we didn't get to see much of her brother. He only visited a couple of times a year. I suppose he was awfully busy. But he brought her gifts and she seemed to enjoy his visits. She's such a chipper little thing. Well, most of the time, anyway."

"We all have our good days and bad," Dane said, smiling at the way Isadora's profile looked with the sunlight streaming on it. So innocent and serene.

"Oh, no," Miss Perkins said. "Isadora doesn't have bad days. She..."

An overhead intercom paged, "Miss Perkins to the reception desk please."

"I'm sorry, I have to be going... Dane," Miss Perkins said with a little twitter in her voice, as she sashayed out of the room.

His jacket pocket vibrated, reminding Dane that he'd set his phone on silent. Tasha Greenwood. Texting him in shouty capitals. The police were there to arrest her husband.

Dane dialed the first number that came to mind.

"Detective Sergeant Nivens." Dane recognized Teddy's "official" I'm-on-a-case voice.

"Theodora. You know you have the wrong man. Why the hell are you arresting Leo Greenwood?" Dane barked into the phone.

"Just a moment please, detective. I can't hear you. I'll have to go somewhere quieter."

Dane listened to Teddy's marching footsteps and a door closing before she blasted him.

"Now you listen to me, Dane Wells. I'm doing my goddamned

job and I do not answer to you. I answer to my Chief and he is the only one allowed to call me Theodora, by the way, because he knows I won't shoot him. Christ, Dane, that's almost as bad as calling me Dora!"

Dane had to laugh. He used to call her that for fun. She was damned sexy when she was mad.

"My apologies," Dane said. "I was merely trying to save you from public embarrassment when this case blows up in your face. Leo's a damned nice guy, by the way, Dora."

"Davis?" a soft voice said from across the room.

Dane Wells's eyes bugged out, cartoon-style, he figured, when he heard that gentle voice.

"Holy shit, Teddy. I've got to go."

Dane raced up the hall to the receptionist desk. Miss Perkins looked up as he reined himself to a stop.

"She spoke. Isadora spoke."

Miss Perkins laughed. "She doesn't speak, Dane. She hasn't said a word since her brother brought her here ten years ago."

"Ten years? I was under the impression she'd been here for twenty? Since some accident?"

"There was an accident twenty years ago. Isadora, her brother and her father were in a terrible car crash. Her father was paralyzed, poor soul. Her brother lost the use of one of his hands. Isadora was in a youth facility before she came to us."

"Well, I'm telling you she just said 'Davis.'"

Dane had been right. Isadora had spoken. And continued to speak when addressed as "Dora". It seemed as if whoever addressed her was "Davis" to her. Only her brother had known the secret key to her mind.

And he'd kept it to himself, selfish bastard, Dane thought, as he drove away from Millbrook. What kind of a brother pays top dollar for a facility like that to care for a sister he supposedly loves, then doesn't share the fact that she can communicate? A brother who doesn't want her to talk.

Dane checked his rear-view, did a U-turn and headed back to Millbrook.

Isadora's bedroom was like nothing Dane had ever seen before. Paintings, drawings and sketches of every kind covered every bare surface of wall and ceiling. They were brilliant.

"Does she paint every day?" Dane asked Miss Perkins, who had kindly agreed to show him Isadora's room.

"Oh, gracious no. That's what I was starting to tell you earlier.

Isadora only paints when she's blue. That only ever happens in the winter. The doctors diagnosed her with SAD—you know, seasonal affective disorder. The rest of the time she's as happy as a lark."

"And you said her brother only came to visit her a couple times a year?" Dane asked, wheels turning. "By any chance would that be in the fall and the early spring?"

"Aren't you a clever detective!" Miss Perkins exclaimed. "How ever did you know that?"

"The gifts he brought were art supplies?"

"Why, yes..."

"He took the artworks she made for him when he came back in March, of course." Dane said. He had a hard time keeping the anger out of his voice.

"He did," Miss Perkins said, with a quiver in her voice, staring at his thunderous face.

Dane drew a breath and lightened his voice. "Miss Perkins, may I ask you who else visited Isadora?"

"Well, only one other person that I can recall. Her mother, of course."

Dane's head was reeling. Why had no one ever mentioned the mother? "Let me guess. She goes by the name Dezaki..."

Miss Perkins smiled. "She does. Do you know her?"

"I've met her. Perhaps you can fill me in, Miss Perkins."

"She was an artist too. Quite famous, from what I hear. She was a child prodigy. That's why she used her maiden name. She said it made her remember who she was. After the accident she had a terrible time of it. The extra medical bills just about wiped them out. Then Davis began making money on his artwork and paid for his sister to become a resident here. Mrs. Dezaki was so happy that her daughter was being well cared for. She loves her Isadora very much. Drives up here every week with little treats."

"Did anything happen recently, between her and Matadori, that you know of?"

"Funny you should mention that. On his last visit they had a terrible argument. It seemed as if they'd made up before he left though. He hugged his mother and kissed her on the head before he drove off. That was the day he died."

Dane knew he had to ask, and if it weren't for Leo Greenwood being hauled into jail for a crime he didn't commit, he wasn't sure he would've even bothered.

"The little treats Mrs. Dezaki brought. They were little green-tea cakes with lemon ginger cream, weren't they?"

114

"Dane, you really are a wonder! They were Dora and Davis's favorites. They had a little tea party every time the three of them were together."

Dane Wells went out to the grounds and walked around in stupefied silence. He dialed the phone, intent on verifying the facts before jumping to conclusions. A short conversation later, he was sure about who it was that really killed Davis Matadori. His next call was to Teddy.

Sirens blaring, three police cars careened to a stop in front of the building. The sobbing woman was escorted out to one of the cruisers. She looked back at Dane Wells through the rear window of the car as it pulled away, the sun glare reflecting off her red-framed eyeglasses hiding the look in her eyes.

Dane slid into the booth and looked into Teddy's warm hazel eyes.

"She confessed everything," Teddy said. "She did murder Davis Matadori. Turns out she's been responsible for quite a few 'mercy killings' over the years as well. This one was different though. She really seemed to love Isadora, and killed Davis because he was using her. How did you ever figure out it was Miss Perkins?"

"I called Mrs. Dezaki. I couldn't believe she'd murder her own son. She was a protector, not a killer. She did admit that she just found out that Davis was stealing Dora's artwork. Then I simply asked her if she'd given the tea cakes to Matadori to take home. Turns out she had, and Miss Perkins took them to the kitchen to pack them up for the trip."

"That doesn't make her a killer though."

"Then there was something Miss Perkins said when we were talking about the last visit. She referred to Isadora as 'Dora', as though she were used to calling her that. I figure she'd discovered Davis's secret to Isadora's mind and had created her own self-serving co-dependent relationship with her. I knew that was the workings of a sick mind."

"Dane Wells, you are one fine detective."

"Do you mean fine as in 'competent' or fine as in 'let's go home together?'" Dane asked, his blue eyes crinkling up at the corners.

"Come a little closer and I'll tell you," Teddy said, a mischievous little sparkle in her own eyes.

Revenge is a Treat

Linda Wiken

Linda Wiken is a former mystery bookstore owner who now writes the Ashton Corners Book Club Mysteries as Erika Chase. Her short stories have appeared in the Ladies' Killing Circle anthologies, and in magazines. She's been short-listed for an Arthur Ellis Award from Crime Writers of Canada for Best Short Story, and for an Agatha for Best First Novel.

"Looks like he didn't get any treats, ma'am."

"Well this sure as hell isn't a trick, either." Detective Constable Anne Mason noted the knife protruding from the front left pocket of the plaid lumberman's jacket. Must have gone right through the heart or damned close. "Run through it for me, please."

The patrol officer grunted, pulled his notebook from his pocket and read from it. "We got the call at 00:40, arrived on scene at 00:43. The owner of the house, Mrs. Gayle Shelton, found the body when she let her cat out. Says it's the man from two doors down, a John Deaver. Says the last trick-or-treater came at about 21:30. After that, she heard and saw nothing. Was watching TV. Her husband is a cop, Harvey Shelton, a constable with Division Twenty-One. I asked Dispatch to get in touch with him."

Mason sighed. "Someone's either very ghoulish or very clever. Well, you'd better get your partner and start the house-to-house questioning. Do you know Shelton?"

"I know he's been around for a while. Never worked with the guy, never even met him, but..."

"Stop hedging, Richardson. Just say what's on your mind."

"OK ma'am. I heard he'd made Sergeant but got knocked back down a couple of years back, just about the time of amalgamation, for some rough stuff."

Anne nodded. "And Richardson..."

"Yes, ma'am?"

"Please don't call me 'ma'am'. It's Mason or Detective. OK?"

He glanced at her face. "Uh, right, Detective."

"And would you find out what's keeping Ident? I want this cleaned up fast before we draw a crowd."

"At one a.m.?"

"As soon as you guys start knocking on doors and the neighbours see the lights, they'll drift over. You can be sure. I don't want kids seeing this mess and he's sure as hell visible. Is this your first homicide?"

"Yeah."

"Some Hallowe'en, isn't it?"

The constable nodded and left the porch. Anne took another slow scan of the scene. Jack-o-lantern shining in the living room window of the placid white clapboard bungalow. Front porch big enough to hold a single park bench. And two figures sprawled on it, partially illuminated by the shaded porch light. One a sexless pair of jeans and shirt stuffed with plastic bags, a noose just under its pumpkin head. The other, male, very real, but dead.

He looked to be in his mid-forties, dark hair, medium build and height, wearing dark corduroy pants, dirty sneakers, dark plaid jacket. And the knife.

Anne studied the white clapboard fifties-style bungalow, its front porch sliced by the yellow police line tape. The house fit right in this peaceful neighbourhood—crisp paint job, well-tended small front yard, wide porch which, this morning, was devoid of the dead body. The tape was definitely out of place, though.

Anne had spent the past few hours two doors down, at John Deaver's house, the same model but laid out in reverse, searching through his life for clues to his death. She'd come up with a dandy. She ordered her thoughts, took a deep breath and went to question her suspects.

The door was opened on the third knock. Gayle Shelton looked like she'd spent a night similar to Anne's, one with very little sleep. Her eyes were puffy and red. She wore a green terry housecoat tied with a red plaid belt, likely from a man's bathrobe. Stains, probably coffee, dotted the right cuff and front lapel.

"Do we need to do this now? Harvey is sleeping. He's on midnight patrol, you know."

"I need to talk to both of you, Mrs. Shelton and it can't wait. This is a murder investigation."

"I told you everything last night." She gestured to the kitchen and poured them both a coffee while Anne sat down at the square maple table.

"I know. This is upsetting, especially when you had the shock of finding your neighbour, but it needs to be done. You may remember something that slipped your mind last night. You must have been very distressed."

Gayle waved the notion, or maybe it was the questions, away. "All right. I'll help however I can."

"Good. Now, do you remember anything else from last night? Any unusual sounds, movement on the porch, voices?"

She wouldn't have heard the murder being committed. The body had been moved after death. Deaver had lost his life in a dark unlit space under an aging apple tree in his own back yard. A massive blood stain had seeped into the grass. Signs of four small wheels, possibly a child's wagon or something similar, approaching the site and leaving, with a heavy load. Rubber-soled shoes or boots. Probably the latter. Not clear enough for a good print, though.

The wagon—the assumption was—had been pulled across two back yards and wheeled to the side of the Shelton house. The body had then been lifted out and carried to its final location. That's how it played out until proven otherwise.

"I can't help you. There was nothing," Gayle said. She blew on her coffee and sipped, then sat staring at it. Or at nothing.

"Mrs. Shelton, Gayle, how well did you know John Deaver?"

"What? Oh, yes. Well, we'd met often enough out on the street. At the corner store. Things like that. We'd talk. He was a nice man. A kind man, it seemed."

Anne glanced at the closed kitchen door. She hadn't heard any noises in the hall. "I'm going to have to ask you—was there anything more? Were you lovers? You see, I went through Mr. Deaver's things this morning."

Tears formed at the corner of Gayle's eyes. Her hands clutched the mug. She chewed her top lip and nodded.

"Your husband didn't know?"

She shook her head, pulled a tissue out of her pocket and wiped at her eyes. "No, he didn't. You won't tell him, will you?"

"I'm afraid we'll have to. Everyone's a suspect at the moment and the affair gives your husband a motive."

"But he was on duty."

Not, 'but he wouldn't do that,' Anne noted.

"Yes, he was on duty, but alone in a patrol car." And he didn't make contact with dispatch for forty-five minutes around the critical time. Not suspicious in itself—at that time of night if there are no calls, it's just a matter of cruising around, eyes open. No reason to call in if nothing's happening.

"Did he talk to anyone?"

"No."

"Well, what's the problem? Don't you think he'd cover himself, call in to give himself an alibi, if he were planning to murder someone?"

"Possibly." But why go on record with something that could be traced rather than just staying quiet? Following normal routine. If he'd received a call, he could then come up with an excuse as to why he didn't answer—going to the can being the most likely.

"How long had you and Mr. Deaver been involved?"

"It was two years ago last month when it started."

"How did you meet?"

"At the corner store. He said he'd noticed me in the yard." She smiled at the memory.

"Did you argue much?"

"No, not really. Just the odd misunderstanding. Nothing important."

Anne looked at her a few moments before continuing. "What sorts of things did you misunderstand?"

Gayle looked startled. "Well, ummh, once I couldn't get out as planned because Harvey booked off sick. John didn't like that. But he got over it quickly," she added.

"Had he mentioned having problems with anyone, being worried about something recently?"

Gayle shook her head.

"What was his job? Where did he work?"

"He was a computer consultant of some sort. I never really understood what he did. Anyway, he worked out of his home."

That explained the well-organized office Anne had seen.

"Did he have any family?"

"Only a brother in Charlottetown, I think. They didn't keep in touch much."

"Can you think of any reason for him to be killed?"

"No." She started to cry.

Anne gave her a couple of minutes to compose herself then said, "I have to question your husband now. You'd better wake him up. And Gayle," she added as the other stood up, "I have to talk to him

120

alone."

Anne summed Shelton up the minute he staggered through the door. The way he planted his overweight body right up close. His eyes, still drooping with sleep, but sending out a challenge. A burned-out cop just waiting to get his years in. Not caring about the job. Not taking any guff from the public. Not to be under-estimated.

"Have a seat, Constable. I have some questions to ask." She'd stood up before he came in and remained standing.

Anne waited until he'd dropped into a chair before continuing. "How well did you know John Deaver?"

"I didn't."

"But you were neighbours. Didn't you talk, nod, wave to each other?"

"Nope." Shelton pushed out of the chair, grabbed a paper towel from the counter and blew his nose.

Anne gritted her teeth. "When did you find out about Deaver and your wife?"

Shelton spun around and stared at Anne, his mouth hanging open. "What do you fucking mean?"

"Their affair. Come on now, Shelton. You're a cop. You must have caught on."

His hands gripped the edges of the counter behind him, the knuckles turning white. "You're a fucking liar."

"No. You are. I don't believe you didn't know. In fact, I think you knew and planned this whole thing. You had the perfect alibi, didn't you? We wouldn't suspect one of our own. But you're wrong. You're at the top of my list."

He didn't answer. She knew she wouldn't get anything else out of him at this point. But later...

Someone was watching. The white lace curtain fell back into place, but not before Anne caught a glimpse of movement at the top right window across the street from the Sheltons'. Maybe that person had been watching last night, regardless of the assurances from all neighbours that no one saw nor heard a thing.

Anne's fifth knock on the door was answered by a white-haired well-fed woman with a heavily-lined face, standing at eye level with Anne, height about 5'7". She wore a long-sleeved striped beige polyester blouse, tails hanging out over brown slacks, and an annoyed look.

"Yes?"

"Excuse me for interrupting, ma'am but I'm Detective Constable Mason with the Regional Police. I'd like to ask you a few more questions about what happened last night across the street."

The door opened to admit her. "Come and sit in the living room, Detective. I can't help you though."

"You never know, Mrs.???"

"The name is Bertha Collins. I'm a widow. My Lewis died last year. A heart attack. One year ago, yesterday."

"I'm sorry. It's probably not a good day for you, but I won't take long. I just need to know if you remember seeing or hearing anything after midnight."

The woman shook her head. "No, I didn't. Like I told the officer last night, I go to bed early and sleep like a log. I didn't know anything had happened until he rang my doorbell. And then it took a few rings to get me up. Sleeping's not my problem."

"Did you know your neighbour, Mr. Deaver, the deceased?"

"No. I don't mix much with the neighbours these days."

"What about Mrs. Shelton, across from you, do you know her?"

"We nod. That's about it. I don't keep track."

Which, I'd bet, means you do, Anne thought. "So, you wouldn't know if they were acquainted?"

Mrs. Collins snorted. "No, I don't. Is that part of what happened?"

"I'm just asking questions at this point, Mrs. Collins. No conclusions as yet."

"Well, come to think of it, I may have seen them talking together the odd time. Yes, I'm sure of it. Several times, in fact. Late at night, too."

"Uh-huh." Anne jotted a few notes down. "And do you live alone here?"

"Why do you ask?"

"In case there's someone else I should speak with. The photograph of the young boy, on the mantel—is he a relative?"

"My son. Herbie." She pushed herself out of the chair and ran her hand along the edge of the picture frame. "He died, too. When he was five. A neighbour left the cover off his pool. Herb fell in and drowned."

"I'm so sorry. That's very tragic."

"Yes, yes it was. But he's still here with me. I can feel him. They're both here with me."

122

"Uh-huh. Well, thank you, Mrs. Collins. I appreciate your time. I'll just show myself out."

She left the woman holding a photograph in each hand.

Anne had gone back to Deaver's house and was sorting through the drawer of knives, a photo of the murder weapon on the counter. What if the murderer had been someone Deaver had known? They'd been in the house, arguing, Deaver had gone out back, the murderer had grabbed a knife and followed. A long shot, sure, but it would narrow the field of suspects. Possibly to the dozen or so names written in the brown address book found in the desk.

The front door burst open and slammed against the wall. Damn, she should have locked it. Anne touched her gun in its shoulder harness and shoved open the door to the hall.

"Shelton, what are you doing here?"

"You know fucking well what I'm doing here, Detective. My wife was having an affair with the prick, as you pointed out. I just wanted to see where it happened."

"What, the murder or the sex? Shelton, get out of here."

He remained in his spot, staring at her.

"I mean it, get the hell out of here. This a crime scene and you're a suspect. I'll haul your ass downtown if you don't leave. Now."

"You're going to have a fucking time proving it. I already told you, I didn't know about them."

"You sure about that? You sure you didn't know long before this? Maybe you found out and were just biding your time. Waiting for the right moment to kill the guy who was screwing your wife." Her words hit home.

Shelton clenched his right hand and drove it into the wall. Plaster crumbled. He look surprised.

"I didn't. I swear to God, I didn't know a thing. I didn't kill the bastard. But I'll tell you this, if I'd done it, I would've pulverized the prick. I would've taken it out of his hide, one fist at a time."

Anne believed him. Shelton acted on impulse. He would have found out, sought the guy out and dealt out the blows. She was glad she didn't have to partner with him.

Still, she'd do some more checking before he was totally off the hook. Given enough time, even a short fuse could burn long enough to plot a cold-blooded murder.

Every street has its self-appointed overseer. Someone who sees all that happens, knows why and who the players are in each event. Someone who likes to talk, eliciting information and then distributing it when necessary.

Anne found that someone living next door to Mrs. Collins. A seventy-year-old widow by the name of Marion Claybourn. She came by her role naturally, having lived in the house since it was built, forty-seven years earlier. The Collinses had moved in the following summer. They were the first two houses in the then-new subdivision. By the next fall, the street had houses on each lot and only three were vacant.

Marion Claybourn could recite the names of the majority of occupants in each house over the ensuing years. She had gotten to know them, their occupations, family members and where they'd eventually moved to. It was her life.

"John Deaver had been married, when he was in his twenties that was, and only for five years. They moved in right after the honeymoon, you know. Just like my Fred and I did." Marion offered another home-made chocolate chip cookie. Anne swore off dessert for the next two days as she bit into her third cookie. Mid-life gravity was winning the battle.

"Mr. Deaver didn't want children. She did and that's what eventually broke them up, you know. I heard she'd remarried and has four young ones, bless her. He stayed in the house and never remarried, although he had someone living with him for a couple of years. She couldn't put up with his compulsive neatness, you know. Moved out and to Toronto. That would be about ten years ago. He's been on his own since. Not alone every night, of course. But nothing permanent."

Anne waited until Marion had sipped some tea before asking, "How about lately? Did he have many visitors? Anyone in particular that you knew of?"

Marion didn't seem embarrassed at the question but rather delighted at being able to share her knowledge. "I don't like talking out of turn but since it is a murder investigation, you should know about Mr. Deaver and Mrs. Shelton. They've been seeing each other on the sly for a couple of years, you know."

"Was there anyone else?"

"Oh, yes. He's had several women visiting him overnight, you know, for many years."

"At the same time he was seeing Mrs. Shelton?"

"Oh my, yes."

Another angle to follow up. "Well, it sounds like Mrs. Shelton and Mr. Deaver weren't overly careful about their liaison."

Marion laughed, a musical sound. "Of course they were. They didn't want Mr. Shelton to know. Especially after the last time."

"What last time?"

"Well, before Mr. Deaver. Mrs. Shelton had herself another man and one day Mr. Shelton came home early in the afternoon and caught them. He gave the man quite a beating. Never saw him around again. So this time, they'd get together when the Mister was working nights mainly. I'd see him drive by the odd time in his police car, slow down in front of his house, then drive off. Still does that on occasion."

"You don't think he knew about this affair?"

Marion shook her head. "I doubt many others knew about it. I'd see her sneaking over there, through the back yards. Sometimes he'd go to her place. But always at night. Late like, you know. You can ask Bertha Collins, too, if you don't believe me."

"But Mrs. Collins said she didn't know anything about the neighbours. She keeps to herself."

"Only since her Lewis died. A real sad thing, that. Kids playing tricks again. Every Hallowe'en there's something. Dumped a load of leaves at the end of their driveway. Next morning, Lewis Collins shovelled them out of the way and took a heart attack. Died right on the spot." Marion drew in her breath and let it out slowly.

"Since then, Bertha hasn't talked to many people. Only me. Of course, she hasn't really had too much to do with neighbours ever since her son drowned. That would be forty years ago. That was so sad. She blamed the Stewarts, of course. They lived next door on the other side. Wanted to sue them but it was ruled an accident. She hated them fiercely. They moved very shortly after the whole thing."

"She's had a very sad life," Anne murmured. "But she told you about seeing Mr. Deaver and Mrs. Shelton go to each other's houses?"

"Well, yes. We'd spoke of it. Here, have another cookie, child. You could stand to have a bit more meat on you."

Oh, sure, Anne thought. "No, thank you, Mrs. Claybourn. Getting back to Mr. Deaver, did he have any trouble with any of the neighbours?"

"No. He got along well with us all. Everyone liked him. Such a practical joker. A kid at heart. Maybe that's why he didn't want any, do you think? Wanted the attention himself. But, you know, he never visited with us. Didn't have any of us over. You know, there

125

was a time when we used to have spur-of-the-moment parties, in the back yards. Several families getting together. Then the kids grew up and people moved away and that doesn't happen anymore." She sighed and fell silent.

"I have a few more questions to ask, Mrs. Shelton. It won't take long," Anne explained.

Gayle Shelton was down on her knees, scrubbing the front porch. "I couldn't stand the thought that there might be some of his blood or something."

She dropped the brush in the pail and stood up. The paint-stained light blue shirt she wore had holes at each shoulder, obviously her husband's old uniform with the patches cut out. Green paint stained the left pocket where his name tag would have been pinned and bleach spots formed an overall tie-dyed effect.

Her blonde hair, badly in need of a washing, was held back in a mini pony tail, loose ends all about. Her face needed much more than a soap and water scrub to erase the pain of the past twenty-four hours.

Anne was suddenly conscious of her own appearance. Short auburn hair in its usual fly-away mode, lipstick long since nibbled away, green rayon blouse wilted in the surprise heat of a late summer after-thought, and beige pants in need of a pressing. Not the most authoritative-looking cop on the block.

"How would you describe your relationship with Mr. Deaver?"

Gayle looked startled. "I'm not sure what you mean. We weren't really in love, at least I wasn't. We had a lot of fun. He was certainly exciting in bed. But nothing more."

"So you weren't upset that he was seeing other women?" Anne watched closely for a reaction.

Gayle's eyes widened. "No. No, I wasn't."

"You did know about them?"

"Of course I did." She reached into the pail and pulled out the scrub brush. "Yes, I did. Like I said, we weren't in love or anything."

"Did you talk to anyone late last night, after the kids stopped coming by?"

"No. Nobody. Why? You don't think I killed him?"

"We have to look at everybody involved, Mrs. Shelton."

"Well, I didn't." She dropped onto her knees and attacked the porch again. "I couldn't."

Anne turned towards Deaver's house. It wouldn't be hard to see

126

visitors arriving. She looked back at Gayle working, trying to imagine her hefting the 180-pound corpse up the stairs and into the chair. Rage could unlock that strength. But what would have been the trigger?

"Just a couple of questions." Anne squatted at Gayle's level. "Had you seen or talked to John Deaver yesterday?"

Gayle shook her head.

"Gayle," Anne reached out and stopped the moving of her arm. Gayle looked over at her. "Did you two have an argument?"

Tears welled in Gayle's eyes. "No. I thought he was out of town."

Anne sat in her unmarked car, parked in front of the police building, jotting down notes before going inside. It all added up to the killer being someone in the neighbourhood, someone who knew about the affair. If Gayle Shelton had done it, or Harvey, why leave the body on her own front porch? Or was it meant to look too obvious so therefore a set-up? Is that how they'd operate? She shoved the notebook in her purse and went to her next stop, the Human Resources office.

The only incident worth noting on Constable Harvey Shelton's sheet was the one that had led to his demotion. A few notations about warnings, but nothing major. Obviously the former lover hadn't pressed charges. Not surprising. So, what if Shelton, learning from past behaviour, had decided to play it cool this time and take out the competition permanently? A warning to his wife not to try it again. Kill two birds with one stone, as it were. Being a cop, he'd think he'd know how to get away with it, too.

Anne checked her watch. Eight p.m. If she waited around another hour she could probably catch Shelton before parade. But he'd be hyped up, ready for the streets. She wanted him when he was tired and worn out. She'd call it a day and be back at eight a.m., as he was coming off shift. Corner him. Question him.

"So, Shelton, it would have been easy for you to slip back to your neighbourhood while on duty, park the cruiser a block or so away, go to Deaver's house, knife him, then dump him on your own front doorstep." Anne leaned against the wall, staring down at him, seated at the small table.

"Why would I do that? It would look pretty obvious, don't you think? Leaving him on my own fucking porch?"

127

"Obvious only if we knew the reason. A warning to your wife. The desire to hurt her. Finding her lover's body must have been quite a shock. Do you think she felt as badly as you felt after learning about them?"

"How should I fucking know? Ask her." He sat ramrod straight in the wooden chair. Body rigid, even after a ten hour shift. His eyes gave away just how tired he felt.

"I'm asking you, Shelton. Because, as you know, the spouse is usually the number one suspect."

"Yah, but it's not my wife who bought it. And if that's so, how come I'm still on active duty?"

"We're not through here, yet. You do admit to motive and opportunity."

"Yah, yah, detective. I read the manual. But for fuck's sake, I didn't do it. I didn't know about them so I didn't do it. What part of that don't you understand?"

Anne tried not to grind her teeth. She hated that line. But what irritated her more was knowing she wouldn't get a confession. The jerk hadn't done it.

"So, Shelton, start thinking like the great cop you think you are. Who would you finger as the killer? What's happened on your street?"

Shelton's shoulders sagged, pushing him lower in his chair. He ran his right hand through his thinning hair. "Beats me. I never much liked the guy, seemed too phony with his 'How're you doing?' and 'Great weather, isn't it?' I'm sure he's the one who tied all the handles of my garbage cans together, too. Pouring rain out and I couldn't move the fucking things. Heard him laughing on his front porch. Guess he's not laughing now."

Shelton smiled.

Noon. The murderer was probably eating lunch, not expecting another visit from the police. In fact, she very likely thought she'd gotten away with it. Who would suspect a little old lady of stabbing an adult male, pulling him in a wagon across two yards, and hauling him up a set of stairs?

Anne hadn't. Not at first. Not until the pranks.

"Mrs. Collins, I need to speak with you again."

"Oh, all right. I'm eating though. What do you want?"

"I want you to tell me all about how you murdered John Deaver."

128

Bertha's eyes narrowed then she broke out into a wide grin. It didn't reach her eyes. "How'd you figure it out? I thought I had it all planned. But it doesn't matter. I guess I knew you'd find out sooner or later."

Anne let out the breath she'd been holding. "You don't have to tell me now. We'll go down to the station and wait for your lawyer."

"It doesn't matter. I did it and I'm proud of it. Me and my Herbie, we got back at the neighbours who'd taken my family away from me. It was Herbie's wagon, you see. I'd kept it all these years along with most of his things. Locked away in his bedroom. It seemed fitting he'd help revenge his father's death."

Anne touched her elbow and steered her to the couch. "Why did you do it? Was it because of the leaves?"

"Yes, that was the final straw. That John Deaver piled those leaves there. As a joke. He always did something stupid on Hallowe'en. Lewis used to get so mad at him and his practical jokes. Never paid attention to us any other time. Never offered to help Lewis shovel the snow off the driveway. Young man like that. He killed my Lewis and he had to pay for it." She stared out the window. Back rigid. No tears. And continued.

"I grew up on a farm. Helped with all the chores. I may be old but I'm still strong. He didn't know how strong I was. I could slit the throats of chickens. I hefted bales of hay. I knew what I needed to do. And I knew when I should do it."

Anne spoke softly into her portable radio. She heard the cruiser pull up outside. The two officers, one male, one female would enter momentarily.

"Tell me, Mrs. Collins, why did you leave his body on the Sheltons' porch?"

She shrugged. "It seemed fitting. That Mrs. Shelton never even sent a card at Lewis's passing. That same night, those two were back at it. I saw them. Didn't seem right. Anyway, what are they going to do to an old woman? I don't have many years left. Don't have any family. What can they do to punish me?"

"But, you knew it was murder."

"No, dear. An eye for an eye. Like it says in the Good Book. Not murder. Revenge."

No Honour Among Thieves

by Lesley Mang

A former English teacher and editor, Lesley has published book-length non-fiction. Her first published fiction appeared in The Whole She-Bang.

I was leery about taking the job.

I knew the guy's reputation.

If I was unsuccessful, not only would I not get paid, he might try something nasty. Everybody knew the guy flew off the handle for almost nothing. But I was short of cash, so I agreed to it. There are fewer jobs for freelance break and enter artists these days. Most of the operations are run in one way or another by gangs.

I actually knew the guy slightly. His name was Douglas Crawford. He'd been a year ahead of me in high school. His parents pulled him out of school in the middle of the year when he was sixteen and sent him to a boot camp in the States. I don't know how long he was there or if he ever returned to school. I left in the middle of Grade 12.

Anyway, I met Douglas by chance in a bar not far from where I lived. We semi-recognized one another. He was pushing forty, a little pudgy, a little gray, but fashionably dressed. I wasn't much younger, although I wasn't fat. We were about the same medium height. After a few beers, we talked around what we worked at. I told Douglas I was a service provider, not specifying the service, but he knew what I did. Among other things, I knew he imported illegal weapons. I also heard he romanced rich older women.

He started off nice. "Thing is, Robbie," he said, "You could maybe help me out. There's this house in Rosedale that needs some attention. I'd make it worth your while—how about half the jewellery? The old lady has a ton." I wondered why he wanted to do

131

a B & E when he probably could have asked for anything he wanted.

"No, no, she's not one of my ladies," he smirked. "Just someone who lived near us when I was a teen. I used to see her going out in the most fantastic glitter. Anyway what do you say, pal?" He gripped my wrist. "This is a very good deal. I give you the source, you give me your expertise. That's fair."

He didn't note that the risk was all mine. He was also going to wait in a car outside while I did the job.

I did some preliminary work casing the place, noting the type of security and what I would have to do to disable it. Then Douglas picked me up on a cold spring night around eleven and we headed over to Rosedale.

We didn't talk much en route. I thought about how I ended up doing B & Es for a living.

My dad had left and my mother was struggling to support us with her job waiting tables at a greasy spoon in the east end of the city. I had a job, myself, briefly at a coffee chain, but the pay was so low, it hardly made a difference. My options were limited. I could deal drugs or find some other way to make money. I considered the drugs, but decided I liked living more. Young drug dealers, unless they are super tough, have a very short shelf life.

An acquaintance of mine, Billy B., introduced me to the art of break and enter. He was pretty good at outwitting security systems and showed me what he knew. He wasn't so smart about some of the people he worked for. The last job he did was for a large company that wanted to claim insurance for inventory losses. He stole the required items. Then, when he went to be paid, the guy who set up the deal shot him, said he was scared when he found an intruder.

I decided to stay away from commercial deals as much as I could. I've done a few, but only for small businesses. Mostly, I've worked for individuals who want to make insurance claims. Occasionally, I've broken into places that smell of money. Almost always, if I haven't found the safe, I've found an art object that made the effort worthwhile.

We parked on a dark, tree-lined street. The leaves weren't out but I could see the swollen buds bouncing in the breeze.

The easiest place to break in was at the back of the house. I took out the motion sensors without anyone noticing and one of the back doors had a lock that could be picked. I was ready to take off if there was an alarm, but the house was silent when I pushed open the door.

That door led to basement stairs and to another door for a storage room in the main part of the house. I was about to ease myself out of the storage room when a light went on in the kitchen next to it. I pulled the door so that it was only open a crack. A middle-aged woman dressed in scrubs stood with her back to me. She was filling a kettle with water. Douglas had told me the old lady lived alone. This clearly wasn't her.

I always wear gloves and carry certain equipment with me regardless of the job, so this was not too big a problem. I had a hard rubber club and some lengths of light rope. I slipped out of the storage room and whacked her on the head. The kettle clattered into the sink as she fell. I tied her hands and feet with the rope and knotted a tea towel over her mouth. Then I turned out the kitchen light.

Douglas had told me the old lady kept her jewellery in a safe in her bedroom. This was going to be tricky. The old lady wasn't well, if there was a nurse present. That meant she was most likely lying in bed in her bedroom. I hoped she was asleep. I had no appetite for harming an old woman.

I hurried up the curved oak staircase. Then I glided along the hall from door to door, pushing each one open a crack. The rooms were empty. None of them held a stick of furniture. At the end of the hall, I could see a night light glowing through the half-closed door. I slid into the room and stood for a moment orienting myself.

There was a large four-poster bed with its head against one wall. In the bed lay a small figure propped up on pillows. It was hard to tell if she was awake. I noticed an IV drip and an oxygen tank.

Douglas thought the safe was behind a large painting that hung on the opposite wall. I made my way to the painting. It was of a huge bouquet half spilling out of its vase. I was just about to take it down when the woman in the bed spoke in a breathy whisper, "Douglas," she said, "I'm so glad you've come. I'm not very well. I need to speak with you, my son. It's been far too long. Come closer."

My eyes widened. Could she be...? Then I turned to face her, thinking quickly what to do. I thought I better humour her, because I didn't know what call system she had access to. I walked to the end of the bed, where my face was in shadow.

"I don't see very well, anymore," she continued. "Come sit beside me. I want to hold your hand."

I pulled up a chair on the side of the bed opposite the night light. Then I pulled off one of my gloves and took her papery hand in mine.

"I've so longed for this day," she said after a few minutes. "It's been twenty years. I never forgave your father. Can you forgive me for not making him see how wrong he was?"

I muttered something under my breath.

Then she said, "It's all gone, Douglas, all of the money. Clark sold the stocks and all of my jewellery to pay the bills. You remember Clark. He's our lawyer. You can check the safe if you want. He's even sold that painting over it. The house will be next. Go on, check it."

I got to my feet, walked over to the painting and lifted it off the wall.

"The combination is in the night table top drawer," she said. "Your father changed it just before he died. He was worried you might come back and rob us. I told him you would never do that."

I retrieved the combination from the drawer and opened the safe. It was empty. I closed it and rehung the picture. Then I went and sat down beside her. I took her hand and whispered, "It's OK."

"I knew you would come," it was becoming difficult for her to talk. "I saved something for you. It's under my pillow. Clark doesn't know." She pushed my hand toward the edge of her pillow.

I felt under the pile of pillows. There was a hard round object that I drew out and held up to the light falling from the lamp. In my hand was the largest sapphire I had ever seen.

"Mother gave it to me when I got married. She said I should keep it just in case..." she trailed off and her breathing became more laboured. "Clark would be so angry." Then she muttered, "Mary."

I thought, *Mary's the nurse.* I slipped the sapphire into my pocket, and pulled on my glove. Then I kissed her forehead and murmured, "I'll find Mary."

In the kitchen, Mary was just beginning to regain consciousness. I pulled my hoodie over my head and rolled up my turtle neck to cover my face. I untied her hands and feet and said, "She needs you right now. Go to Mrs. Crawford." Then I bolted out through the storage room and the back door.

Large cast iron planters stood on the outdoor patio. It was too early for spring plants, but they were ready. I ran over and tipped one up. There was a hollow in the base that would hold the sapphire. I tucked it in and put the planter down.

When I got back to the car, I shouted at Douglas. "You didn't tell me this was your mother's house."

He shrugged, "What difference does it make? She has a lot of jewellery that she's too old to wear."

"Couldn't you just have asked her?" I demanded.

"Asking never worked with them."

"Anyway, she's dying. She was confused and thought you had come to see her. She was very happy about it. I don't think she has much time left. If you want to see her, you should do it now." I knew that was a risky suggestion, because if he did go, his mother was sure to mention the sapphire.

"I have nothing to say to her. She was always under my father's thumb. Too scared to do anything for me. So where's the jewellery?"

I told him what his mother had said.

"That's ridiculous," he roared. "They were dripping in money."

As we sat in the car, we heard the wail of an ambulance and saw one pull up in front of the house. In a few minutes the paramedics were carrying Mrs. Crawford out on a stretcher. Mary, the nurse, followed and climbed into the ambulance.

When they were gone, Douglas said, "Come on. We're really going to check out the place."

I followed him around to the back door, which was still open.

Douglas first went through all of the rooms on the ground floor. The only room with furniture was a small dining room next to the kitchen. Two large formal rooms were empty, as was the room that had clearly been the library. Even the shelves were bare. The sun room looking out on the patio and planters was unfurnished.

"I can't believe this," Douglas muttered as we climbed the stairs. He checked each of the rooms I had looked in.

When he saw the painting in his mother's room he smiled. "At least she kept that. It's worth something." He lifted it off the wall and put it on the bed. I told him she said it had been sold. "So what," he replied. I gave him the combination for the safe. He was enraged when he saw its black emptiness. "They've left me nothing."

"What about the house?" I said. "It's worth a pile."

"Yeah, maybe," he said. "I know it was mortgaged several times to pay for some of Dad's business schemes. All I've got is that paint-ing. I'm pretty sure it's worth a bundle. So when I dispose of it, I'll give you a cut. OK Robbie?"

I always demand immediate payment for a job. "I think you can find the funds now, Douglas," I said. "I can give you an invoice, if that helps."

"Pick up the painting, Robbie," Douglas said. I turned to do so and everything went black.

I woke up with a ferocious headache, just as gray dawn light was filtering into the room. Douglas must have whacked me on the head

135

with the butt of his gun. I lay listening for human sounds. A car went by on the street, but the house was dead quiet. I got to my knees, then hanging on to the bed stood up. The painting was gone. I staggered down the hall to the bathroom, sat for a few minutes, and told myself to get out of there. I was lucky Mary was so worried about Mrs. Crawford that she hadn't called the police right away.

I made my way down the oak staircase hanging on to the rail, then slowly found my way out the back door.

I retrieved the sapphire and slipped it into my jeans pocket, walked to Bloor, and hailed a cab.

I had no provenance for the sapphire, but my Internet research told me it was likely worth a lot. The gemologist I took it to confirmed this, but cautioned me that it was worth less without the papers. I sold it on the black market for about a quarter of its value.

Then I used the money to go to school. I learned how to be an electrician and I moved away from the city.

Now, I'm never without well-paid employment.

There are scam artists among electricians, too. People only care if the lights come on. They can't see what's behind them and they don't care. Shoddy, dangerous work usually reveals itself several years after the fact. I take a lot of pleasure in cleaning up those messes. I know whatever work I do is safe and will last a lifetime.

I bless whatever spirit made me take Crawford's job. And I bless the spirit that confused Mrs. Crawford. I even bless the mean spirit that stopped Douglas from speaking to his dying mother.

I'm glad I don't have to do B & Es any longer.

There is no honour among thieves.

Women's Work

by Melodie Campbell

Billed as Canada's "Queen of Comedy" by the Toronto Sun *(Jan. 5, 2014), Melodie Campbell achieved a personal best when* Library Digest *compared her to Janet Evanovich.*

Winner of nine awards, including the 2014 Derringer (US) and the 2014 Arthur Ellis (Canada) for The Goddaughter's Revenge *(Orca Books), Melodie has over 200 publications, including one hundred comedy credits, forty short stories and seven novels.*

Melodie got her start writing stand-up. In 1999, she opened the Canadian Humour Conference. She has a commerce degree from Queen's University, but it didn't take well.

Melodie has been a bank manager, college instructor, marketing director, comedy writer and possibly the worst runway model ever. These days, she is the Executive Director of Crime Writers of Canada.

Constable Tiffany Ellis stood over the body of an old woman, which lay crumpled at the bottom of the basement steps. She shivered, even though the air was hot and muggy. It was July. The dead body had been there a few days, making it not too pleasant for the constable and her boss.

"Took a tumble from the stairs, no doubt," said Kevin, the senior officer.

"I don't know about that," Tiff said, trying to hold her breath. All her life, she had wanted to be a cop, even though some said she was pretty enough to model. Even though her whole family and much of the force said it wasn't women's work.

Determined to beat the stereotype, she tried hard not to appear squeamish.

"Look at the evidence! Rickety old stairs and rickety old woman. Bad combo."

Tiff shifted her eyes to her boss. He was a tall, heavy guy, formerly fit and tough, but now running to fat. She knew he was looking forward to retirement in a few months, and that he sure wasn't looking for any trouble in the meantime.

"Let's wait to hear what the coroner says." Her instincts were good. And she could see better than her boss, who relied on glasses for both distance and close up.

The coroner was a whip-thin middle-aged man named Glen who wasted no time.

"Hit on the back of the head with something flat like a frying pan. No doubt about it—it's murder. Body was flung down the stairs after being hit."

"Son of a bitch," muttered Kevin. "All I need. Okay, team. Go do your stuff."

Several hours later, they met back at the station. As Toronto stations go, this one was old and shabby. Just like the neighbourhood.

"No sign of burglary, but there are two obvious suspects, Sir." Tiff flipped open a notebook. "A son and a daughter. The son is thirty-nine and lives above a store two blocks from the house. The daughter is thirty-six, teaches Grade One, and lives alone in a small apartment in Scarborough."

"So. Money a motive?"

"It's always a motive," Tiff grinned. "Guess what? Apparently, the old lady had over two million dollars tucked away in a high interest savings account."

"Holy shit!" Kevin said. "Two mil—that's a motive. How did she all get that?"

"Apparently, she inherited a bundle from a relative a few years ago and just socked it away."

"Do the kids need money?"

"The son runs a second-hand bookstore on the Danforth that appears to be going broke. You know what it's like these days. Bookstores closing all over the place. The daughter seems to like casinos a lot."

"Good enough for me. What was the old bird like?"

"Tight with her money, the neighbours say. Didn't spend a cent on the house, as you could tell when we were there, and never gave to charity at the door. There's one other thing you ought to see."

Tiff put a package on the Sergeant's desk. "We found this sheet in the back of the linen closet." It was in a plastic evidence bag.

Kevin leaned forward and peered at the sheet. "Blood stains. Good work, Tiff. It looks as if someone tried to wash them out."

"Didn't get it all out, obviously." Tiff looked hard at her boss, and waited.

"So you're thinking someone wrapped the woman in the sheet to drag her to the stairs?"

"Either that, or used the sheet to mop up the blood upstairs. But why they would keep the sheet, I can't imagine." This was the part that puzzled Tiffany.

Kevin shrugged. "Not so easy to get rid of a sheet in July. Can't burn it in the fireplace—too hot out. Can't throw it in the garbage— we'd check that. And besides," Kevin paused. "If the lady was as frugal as you say, her kids probably picked up that trait and wouldn't throw out a perfectly good sheet."

"Good point," she agreed. It was hard to break habits, she knew, even when you were under stress. *Particularly when you were under stress.*

"So..." Kevin leaned back in his chair. "Which of 'em did it? Got any ideas?"

She frowned. "If these are the only two suspects, I know for sure who did it."

Kevin snorted. "What—are you a witch?"

Tiffany perked up. She smiled enigmatically. "No. But I'm a woman."

Kevin peered over his reading glasses. "Explain."

One week later, a small group of law enforcement colleagues celebrated over pints at the local pub.

"Solid case, boss. Congratulations!"

They all clinked glasses.

Kevin grinned. "We got the evidence—finally. But Tiff here put us in the right direction." He punched her shoulder lightly with a fist.

Four heads turned to Tiffany.

"So?" said Glen, the coroner. "Give!"

Tiffany's brown eyes looked over her beer mug. It was tough being the only female in a pack of male cops. Always being tested— and yes, they were testing her now. Good thing she was on her game. "It was the sheet," she said.

Now she had everyone's attention. Most looked puzzled, but she saw Kevin smile, and she grinned back at him.

"I knew it had to be the son because of the sheet," she continued. "But then, there's proving it. Everyone helped with that."

"Sheet? What did the sheet have to do with it?" blurted the coroner.

The young constable collected her thoughts. "The fact that there were bloodstains on the sheet even after it was washed. Every woman knows the way you get blood out of fabric is to rinse it thoroughly in cold water."

She paused for effect. This was her big moment. "The sheet was obviously washed in hot water, and the stains remained. The daughter wouldn't have made that mistake. No woman would."

Glen sat with his mouth open. "You're kidding, right?"

Tiffany glared at him. "Who does the laundry in *your* house?"

Glen's face went red.

"Thought so," Tiffany said, with grim satisfaction.

"Everyone knows laundry is women's work." Kevin rocked back in his chair. He winked at Tiff. "And so is policing."

There Goes The Neighbourhood

by Elizabeth Hosang

Elizabeth is a Computer Engineer who wants to be a writer when she grows up. Her interests include poisons, art fraud and convincing her mini schnauzer that squirrels in the yard do not constitute an emergency. A fan of a well-told story in any genre, she especially enjoys mystery, urban fantasy and science fiction. Her first short story was published in The Whole She-Bang, *an anthology produced by the Toronto chapter of Sisters in Crime. Not content with being a one-hit-wonder, she continues to hone her craft, enjoying the freedom to use adjectives, adverbs and pronouns, unlike when writing code, but still needs to practise not writing run-on sentences. Her short stories can be found via her Goodreads page.*

The day the moving van pulled up in front of Agatha Dearing's old house, Edwina had a bad feeling. She watched as the men dragged her new neighbour's furniture across the lawn, holding her breath as they came close to the edge of the flower bed. When they finished, with no major damage, Edwina sighed in relief. She made herself wait half an hour before venturing over with a basket of muffins and her best "welcome to the neighbourhood" smile.

The man who answered the door was a little taller than Edwina, with white hair, black-rimmed glasses that made his eyes look small, and a rounded gut. "Can I help you?" he asked, his voice a pleasant tenor. She wondered if he sang.

"I'm Edwina Pritchard from next door. I wanted to welcome you to the neighbourhood."

"Uh, thanks. Jeff Warkentine." He took the basket from her hesitantly.

"Is your family with you?"

"No, it's just me. I retired last month after forty years working in oil and gas. Thought I'd move back home. I grew up three blocks from here."

"In that case, welcome home." Edwina's smile broadened. A single man. How interesting. "I just had to see who bought Agatha's place. The poor dear was getting on in years. I helped her out as best I could, especially with the garden. Such a lovely big yard, being on a corner lot as it is. It was so nice to be able to coordinate the colour scheme across both our yards."

"Oh." His smile faded. "So you live in the house with all the gnomes?"

Edwina felt her own smile fade a little, but she soldiered on. "Yes. I do so love my little family. They give the yard a sense of whimsy, don't you think? Agatha wasn't fond of them, but she did like flowers. It was nice for her to be able to sit at her window and look out over all the colours. Of course I know how much trouble they can be. The roses in particular have to be fertilized, and the clematis needs to be trimmed back in the fall. If you aren't sure about how to do it, I'd be happy to help."

"Right. Well, thanks for the muffins. I'm afraid I've got a lot of unpacking to do."

"Of course." Edwina recoiled a bit as the door shut firmly in her face. Well, maybe he was too busy to discuss flowers today. In a week or two she'd approach him again. She just hoped he didn't make any major changes. It had taken forever to get the azaleas to come in properly.

A week later Edwina pulled into her driveway, humming to herself. She parked the car and walked around to get the bags of groceries out of her trunk. As she closed the lid she glanced up at the house next door. With a gasp she dropped the bags, and sharp pain radiated through her chest. She sagged against the car, her legs unable to hold her up. The garden, Agatha's garden, the one she had tended with loving care, was gone. Only black dirt remained, gaping holes and torn leaves bearing witness to the violation that had been wrought upon the landscape. Jagged trails of soil led from the barren flower bed across the grass to the driveway, where small tire tracks indicated that a wheel barrow had been used to cart the broken green bodies away. Here and there stray petals punctuated the black, the colour stark like drops of blood.

Edwina leaned against the trunk of the car, shock leaving her weak and trembling. She panted a few more times, trying to catch her breath. After resting a moment she bent to pick up her groceries, which had scattered across the concrete. She was on her hands and knees picking them up when Mr. Warkentine walked around the corner from his back yard. The knees of his khaki pants and his work-roughened hands were stained black and green. On seeing him Edwina stood up, trying to summon as much dignity as she could before confronting him. To her surprise he walked towards her.

"Hi. Groceries getting away from you?" he asked.

She felt her cheeks flush with embarrassment and rage. "You destroyed the garden!" Her voice shook.

He shrugged. "A garden needs a lot of work. Grass looks just as good. They're coming to lay the sod in a week."

"Just as good?" She wanted to scratch his eyes out. "I told you I'd be happy to help..."

"Thanks, but no thanks." There was a definite finality to his tone. He brushed dirt off his hands before speaking again. "It's my yard and I like things simple."

Edwina spluttered, but words failed her.

"Edwina, is it? Look, I know you like flowers. But all those gnomes and cartoon animals? They're kind of an eyesore."

"Eyesore?"

"Yeah. They're hokey. This isn't Disneyland, this is a residential neighbourhood. The way your house and yard look can affect everyone else's property values. It was great for me when I bought my place, but houses are an investment. I don't want to lose money on this deal." He crossed his arms, staring directly at her. "I'm asking you to think about your neighbours. It's time to stop playing with dolls."

Black spots appeared on the edges of Edwina's vision. She glared at the man, shell-shocked, as he turned around and walked away. He was gone by the time she could speak again. She turned to look at her own garden, but for once the whimsical landscape failed to calm her. She kept her back to the neighbouring yard, but as she went about gathering up her groceries all she could think about were the gaping holes next door where once there had been beauty and colour.

"I'm sorry, Ms. Pritchard, but there is nothing we can do." The head of the neighbourhood association smiled sympathetically, but the condescension in his voice was clear. "By your own admission,

Mr. Warkentine didn't damage anything."

"But he did! He ruined a very carefully cultivated work of art."

"Which you can easily re-establish. You said so yourself, he didn't deface or destroy any of the statues."

"But he removed them from my yard!"

"And moved them to your backyard. It may be mischief, but it isn't vandalism. Now if you don't mind, we need to discuss the annual neighbourhood yard sale."

Edwina looked around at the others in the school gym for support, but no one met her eye. On the far side of the room Jeff Warkentine sat, arms crossed, with a hint of a sneer on his face. She fought the urge to rush over to slap him. She took a deep breath, hoping she could keep her voice even.

"Do you have any idea how many hours I've spent on that yard? Every figurine has a name and a place. They were carefully arranged to present an aesthetically pleasing tableau..."

"And you can put them back again. Look, Ms. Pritchard, if you didn't actually see him do it..."

"Who else could it be?" The words exploded from her as she whirled around to face the association chairman again. "I never had any problems with my yard until he moved in. Anyone who could destroy such a beautiful garden..."

"I thought you said the flowers weren't disturbed."

"Not my garden, his." She thrust an accusing finger in her neighbour's direction, but her eyes were locked on the chairman. "The first thing he did when he moved in was rip out Agatha's beautiful flowers."

At this Warkentine finally spoke up. "It's my house, and I'll do what I want with it."

She turned to glare at him. "You have no respect for aesthetics, for harmony, for beauty..."

"If you want to talk aesthetics, let's talk about those stupid statues."

Edwina clenched her fists, digging her nails into her palms in an effort to control her rage. "They're not stupid. They're darling."

"They're tacky and stupid. Why do you think they call you the crazy gnome lady?"

Edwina gaped at him. "What?" She looked around the room again. This time people were clearly avoiding her eyes, staring at their feet, their cell phones or their watches.

"I, I..." Edwina stammered, finally looking back at the meeting chair.

"Look, Ms. Pritchard, if you and Mr. Warkentine need some form of mediation to get along, maybe someone can help you after the meeting. But this is a neighbourhood association meeting, and we have an agenda we need to get through."

Edwina felt the heat rising in her cheeks. She had never been so humiliated. She grabbed her purse and walked out of the school gym as quickly as she could. As the door closed behind her she heard the rumble of a male voice, followed by voices laughing. Tears of frustration finally spilled over as she fled to her car.

Two weeks later Edwina sat staring grimly out her living room window, waiting. In the days following the disastrous meeting someone had started moving her statues around, arranging them in obscene poses. She'd put motion-triggered nanny-cams in her yard hoping to catch Warkentine in the act the next time. The cameras were mounted in the eyes of little ceramic frogs. The frogs hadn't really fit in with the family of deer on the left side of the garden, nor the mushroom cluster on the right, but she told herself that it was a small sacrifice to make to preserve the garden. Along with the cameras she had installed flood lights. The lights and cameras were triggered by motion sensors, meant to catch her neighbour in the act. Instead she'd caught a group of teenagers giggling, drinking and trying to impress each other by messing about in her garden. She'd tracked them down and spoken to their parents, but the look in their eyes made it clear her pleas were pointless. She really was the crazy gnome lady.

After that the overt acts of mischief had stopped, but it had taken her several days to catch on to the next crime. Every morning she would stand in front of her living room window and survey her garden. Instead of a sense of peace, the view now gave her a sense of claustrophobia, an uneasy feeling that her darlings were menacing her. The feed from the nanny-cams, which should have been triggered by motion, showed her nothing but the odd cat wandering through the garden.

Realizing that the vandal must have recognized what the frogs were for, she'd installed new cameras inside her home at the top of her front window, overlooking the garden. The next morning she'd been rewarded. The camera playback showed a black-clad shape that had to be Warkentine. The figure had come up on the garden from the side of her house. Very slowly he lowered a cloth over the frogs. Some Internet searching later showed her that the speed and the fabric may have foiled the motion detectors. He'd then moved each of the remaining figurines closer to the house by one inch, rearranging the mulch at their bases so that the movement wasn't obvious.

The grim satisfaction of knowing she was right hadn't lasted long. It wasn't enough that he had violated his own yard. Now he was trying to turn her little oasis against her. Well, if he wanted to play dirty she could play dirty. She'd made her own little nighttime visit to his yard, exacting a little revenge that would take time to become obvious. In the meantime she had forced herself to endure the effects of the continued nocturnal visits of her neighbour so as to not let him know she was on to him. She sat in her chintz arm-chair now, looking out over her territory and sipping tea, waiting. Her darlings were closer still to her window, and she could almost feel their anguish at this violation. Just a little while longer, she told herself, and she could restore harmony.

It had been four days since she took action, and as she gazed out the window she saw the fallout come storming up her walk. Her doorbell sounded then, an angry staccato instead of its normal dulcet tones. She rose and made her way to the front door. Warkentine was standing there, his face red, his fists clenched.

"You poisoned my sod!"

"I don't know what you're talking about."

"All my sod is dead. I know you did it."

Edwina crossed her arms. "I know nothing about it. Sod is a very tricky thing. You have to water it constantly if you don't want it to die."

"Bull. This is you getting revenge for me moving your stupid gnomes." He took one step into her entrance, looming over her. "What was it, weed killer?"

Edwina stood her ground. "Chemicals sometimes end up in new grass. You really have to be careful who you deal with."

"This isn't over." He spun on his heel and stormed down her front steps. Edwina firmly closed the door and walked back to her armchair, reaching it as her knees finally gave out. It hurt her to be vicious, but it was too late now. The battle was joined.

A flash of light woke Edwina from her restless sleep on the couch. She had been waiting for this, the next offensive. The motion sensors were now attached to floodlights with a one minute timer delay, meant to catch the culprit in the act. She surged up, staring out into the night. The lights showed Warkentine crouched in the garden, night-vision goggles strapped to his head, a paintbrush in one hand, a terracotta bunny in the other. As she stared he dropped the rabbit and fumbled to rip off the goggles. With an angry glance at her window, Warkentine grabbed a can from the ground beside him and fled back towards his own house.

The next morning Edwina sat in her armchair, the terracotta bunny cradled in her arm, stroking its head like it was alive. "There, there, Miss Bella." She gazed lovingly into the large blue painted eyes. "Mommy's not going to let the bad man do anything else to you and your sisters. It will be all right." She murmured soothing words to the rabbit as she looked out over her garden.

The doorbell rang steadily, as if it was being held down continuously. Warkentine glanced through the window, surprised to see Edwina on his doorstep. He'd been expecting her to call the police after she caught him outside her house, but since the liquid he'd coated the figurine with was clear he hadn't been worried. When he opened the door she was looking down, cradling something in her bare arms, stroking it lovingly. With some alarm he recognized it as the rabbit he'd painted the night before. "Can I help you?" he asked.

She raised her eyes to him, her head still bent over the figurine. "Miss Bella has something she'd like to say to you."

Homicide detective Erica Ridgeway walked up the path, past a neatly trimmed green lawn with patches of dead sod next to the house. She stepped into the hallway. A trail of blood led into the living room, where the homeowner's body lay stretched out on the floor, his head a bloody pulp. Fragments of terracotta littered the wound and the floor around him. Crime scene technicians looked up at the detective. She took in the scene from the hall, then gestured for them to continue with their work before heading to the next room. A uniformed officer greeted her as she entered the kitchen.

"Nasty business," she commented. "Who is he?"

"Jeff Warkentine. Apparently he and the lady next door had a running feud over their yards."

"And she went crazy and attacked him?"

The officer nodded. "With one of her garden statues. But it may not be entirely her fault." He pointed to an open door that led to the basement. "Apparently he's a retired chemist. We found a small lab in the basement where he was cooking something up. The lab techs think he was making PCP."

"He set up a drug lab in his own house?"

"Probably not to sell. He had a can of horse liniment as well. It contains," the officer checked his notebook, "dimethyl sulfoxide. DMSO. It's used to make drugs absorb through the skin. He had a can with some strange liquid in it, and a paintbrush."

Ridgeway frowned. "What's that got to do with the neighbour?"

"She was sitting on the front step of this house when we got here. She was petting the head of a clay rabbit, talking to it like it was alive. She sure looked high. She wouldn't let us take the rabbit from her, but there's blood on her hands and chunks of what looks like its body in his living room. She's been hauled off for psychiatric evaluation."

"Why would the victim drug the woman with PCP?"

"Make her look crazy, I guess. According to some of the other neighbours they had a big fight at the last association meeting."

The detective considered this. "So he drugged her, and as a result she went crazy and killed him."

Ridgeway nodded. "I guess so. And it looked like such a nice neighbourhood."

Poetic Justice

by Susan Daly

Susan Daly has two claims to fame in the world of crime fiction. She shares her birth date with Kinsey Milhone, though, unlike Kinsey, she's moved beyond the 1980s. And, in 2007, she was thrilled—and chilled—to make a guest appearance in Meg Gardiner's thriller, The Dirty Secrets Club, *as a victim who suffers a particularly horrible death. Susan has been writing for more years than is mathematically possible, considering her age. But she started young, aged nine, with a mystery novel for a school assignment, with illustrations by the author. Now she's left her day job behind her in the soul-searing world of corporate finance, to focus on murder and mayhem, with side trips into romance, where she is published under another name. She no longer illustrates her own stories.*

Deputy mayor Louie Pimento arrived in his office at City Hall with yet another great idea for saving taxpayers' money. He could see the news stories already.

The Toronto Comet: *Louie Pimento's brilliant plans will save millions in taxpayers' dollars by implementing efficiencies in the library system.* Yeah, he couldn't actually say "close libraries" because the artsy fartsy intellectual types would get in a snit.

The Toronto Mirror, of course, would twist it all around. *Pimento has declared war on books. War on children, war on reading, war on immigrants.*

"Add 'hardworking' in front of taxpayers," he said to the Efficient Babcock an hour later, as she took notes.

"We've used 'hardworking taxpayers' fourteen times in the last three weeks, in speeches and press releases." Was she trying to tell him off?

"They *are* hardworking." Or at least, they liked that he thought

149

they were. Or they *thought* he thought they were. He frowned. Did that make sense?

"Fine." She didn't sound like it was fine.

"It's important to find cost-effective measures," he went on. "Yeah, I like that..." He let his tongue roll over the words again. "Cost-effective measures."

"Six times in the past two weeks."

"Geez, Babcock, what are you? Some kind of computer?"

Babcock's gaze floated over him.

"Economies." Pimento dipped into his mental stock of buzzwords. "Money-saving economies. Tax-saving, cost-cutting, downsizing, right-sizing... Oh hell, *you* come up with something."

"Very well." She waited for him to go on.

"The elected members of council have a duty to the taxpayers..."

"Not taxpayers again."

"Okay, voters."

"Too blatant."

"Families, then. Hardworking families." You couldn't go wrong with *families*. Stephen Harper used it all the time.

"Too exclusionary. And families tend to use libraries."

"Citizens, then. Residents. People." Damn, what happened to the good old days when you could talk about *The Working Man*?

Maybe there was an app for this.

The Efficient Babcock snapped her notebook shut. "I'll consult a thesaurus."

"Yeah. Whatever."

Catherine Winters caught sight of the picture and caption in The Toronto Mirror.

"More libraries than doughnut shops in TO," says deputy mayor.

"Well, isn't *that* interesting..." She settled back with her paper and her mug of Indian spiced chai, inhaling the aroma before drinking. "Whoever thought Louie Pimento would be proud of how intellectual Toronto is."

But after reading the accompanying story—*Louie Pimento Declares War on Libraries*—she slammed down the hand-crafted mug, splashing Nestor the Cat, who gathered up his dignity and took himself off to clean up.

"Wage war on libraries, will he?" The familiar fire of righteousness ignited in her soul. Anyone who'd been on the front lines in last

150

year's War Against Superfluous Apostrophes (or as The Toronto Comet insisted on calling it, Winter's Obsession with Apostrophe's) would recognize the signs. And run for cover.

That man. Again.

Three months ago, when the elected mayor had been laid low with a mysterious lower body injury, the deputy mayor had made it more than clear he was ready to step up to the plate and stickhandle the job until next year's election. When, it was clear, he'd run for mayor.

City council had let him, unwilling to hold a by-election for a term of less than a year.

Since then, he'd become a kidney stone in the systems of all unions, teachers, artists, cyclists, environmentalists, street people and social workers.

And now he was setting his sights on everyone with a library card.

She took a deep, energizing breath. Not for nothing had she been named for the patron saint of libraries.

"He wants war, he'll get war."

Nestor shivered on his perch on the back of the chair and leaped up higher, to the top of the bookcase.

"Catherine Winters is on your private line, sir."

"What's she want?" The name sounded vaguely familiar. The woman from the Save Our Airport Committee maybe.

"About libraries."

"Everyone's got their shorts in a twist about libraries. Hell, you'd think I'd proposed a surtax on Double-Doubles the way they're carrying on."

"I think you'd better take the call, sir."

"No way. I'm already getting it from all sides. Teachers, librarians, people who read. Even bookstore owners, if you can figure that one out. Why should I talk to this woman?"

The Efficient Babcock rewarded him with a long cold look of disapproval.

"It's *Catherine Winters*." As if she were explaining who the Queen was. "Internationally renowned poet? Nobel prize winner?"

"Oh." It was ringing a faint bell. "Yeah, of course. *Catherine Winter*. Sure."

Babcock wouldn't leave until he took the call.

"Louie Pimento here. What can I do you for you, Mrs. Winter?"

He pulled up Ninja Bupkis on his tablet, making sure the sound was off. "Or is it Miss?"

"It's Ms. of course. But you can call me *Doctor* Winters, since I have several honorary degrees and three or four real ones."

Well, lah-di-dah.

"Heh heh. I'll know who to call if I need my appendix out, then."

"I'd be happy to oblige. Actually, Mr. Pimento, I'm just calling to set you straight on something I read in this morning's Mirror."

"Uh-huh..." Yes! Two Bupkis Broads down. 4,500 points.

"There *aren't* more library branches in Toronto than doughnut shops."

"Is that a fact?" Zap! Another Bupkis Beanie bit the dust.

"Indeed. There are, in fact, ninety-nine library branches in Toronto. And, not including kiosks at gas stations, there are 2,456 doughnut shops."

Aw, geez. He shut down the game. This was going to require focus.

"*Mzzz* Winter, it may surprise you to hear I was merely using poetic justice." Was that right? What had Babcock said?

"Poetic justice?"

"I mean poetic licence. You know what that is, right? You being a poet and all." Or should he have said "poetess"?

"I've heard of it, yes. So are you saying you exercised poetic licence to demonstrate how Toronto is criminally over-served in libraries, or just underserved in doughnut shops?"

"Uh, yeah."

"Which?"

"Both." He glanced at his watch. All this talk about doughnuts was making him hungry. "Uh, look, Mzzz Winter, it's been really nice chatting with you, but I have a meeting with, uh, the Premier in a few minutes, so if you'll excuse me..."

"The Premier's in Sudbury today."

"The Premier of Quebec. So listen, if you want to defend free books for people who don't want to buy them, why don't you write a letter to The Toronto Mirror. Hey, you could even make it rhyme. Heh heh heh. Thank you for calling."

He disconnected.

"Babcock!"

The Efficient Babcock appeared.

"Send Rufus out for doughnuts, will you?"

"Assorted? Including banana cream?"

The deputy mayor leaned his chair back and felt his tension start to ease away.

"Yeah. And some with those little coloured thingummies on them."

Catherine Winters was not a complete stranger to being hung up on. Especially by egocentric, right-wing, has-been jocks.

"Poetic licence indeed." She was surprised he'd even heard of it. Or of her, for that matter. And *Poetic Justice*? The title of her first volume of poetry, 1974. Was that just a coincidence?

Be that as it may, this man was dangerous. He had a lot of hard-core budget-obsessed councillors on his side, only too ready to see universal access to knowledge and ideas as a dangerous, subversive tool of a Socialist society.

Which, of course, it was.

She reached again for her phone. Fortunately, she had the twitterverse on her side.

"Any more questions?" deputy mayor Pimento looked around at the reporters and various gate-crashers, assessing the distance to the escape door near the rear. Geez, he hated these public scrums. And today it was more crowded than usual. He'd allow one last question, and then...

"Deputy mayor Pimento." Damn, his worst nemesis, Nicky Nickerson from The Mirror. "I understand you're planning to wage war on books and reading."

A murmur of unhappy reaction stirred through the room.

"No, now that is a complete and total..." Shit, what was that word Babcock had told him to use instead of "lie"?

"...*misstatement*. This council is *not* waging war on books. We *love* books. But this council's mandate is to find efficiencies, and save the har— the taxpayers' money. And we can do that, while still delivering the same services—*better services*—if we Streamline the Process." He'd come up with that phrase all on his own.

"Streamline the process?" Nickerson repeated. "What the hell does that mean? Close branches, cut hours, buy fewer books? Close down the Reference Library?"

The restless hum grew stronger.

"Not necessarily any of those. Our committee will look into any and all possibilities."

"Why not just privatize the whole system?" came another voice, a man's. "Kick out the union and buy all the books from American publishers' clearances?"

Not a bad idea. He'd mention it to the committee.

The grumble of discontent became more threatening. Now would be a good time to end this. He tried edging towards the exit, but more questions were being thrown from the floor. Pimento almost felt he had to physically duck.

"What about the people who need the libraries for Internet access?"

"What about spaces for literacy classes?"

"What about immigrants who need to learn about opportunities...?"

And so on. The crowd seemed to have swelled into hundreds. How could that have happened?

"Wait!"

A single voice rose above the clamour. Silence fell. Everyone turned to look at the speaker. A pint-sized woman in blue jeans and a sweater. Heck, she had to be at least sixty, but the whole crowd seemed to part for her, looking to her, waiting for her to speak.

"Mr. Pimento..." The woman stepped forward, her sharp, commanding voice filling the room. "You claim Toronto has more libraries than doughnut shops."

The rabble rumbled, like some kind of angry chorus.

"Yeah, I did. I was using a hyperbowl to make my point."

"Really. And you further implied that was not a good thing."

"Ma'am, I don't know who you are..."

A horrified gasp went through the crowd, and he realized from some nearby murmurings she must be that interfering poetess.

He raised his voice to enact some quick damage control. "I don't know who you are... in the habit of dealing with in the poetry world, Mzzz Winter, but let me assure you that we at City Council take our mandate very seriously, and the hardworking taxpayers of Toronto have elected me to curb the reckless spending that's been going on too long in past years..."

"What has that to do with closing down library branches? Depriving students and immigrants and taxpayers and voters—your own people—of access to information and knowledge and fine literature and worlds of adventure and romance and ideas."

Yeah, whatever.

"Any more questions?" he said, deploying his favourite avoidance tactic.

Several hundred angry questions were fired at him, involving

154

words like short-sighted and mean-spirited and ignorance.

He smiled. "Okay then, if there's no more questions..." He made it to the back door and slipped out, to find Babcock looking pissed.

"I told you, it's pronounced *hyperboly*."

Catherine Winters poured coffee for her friend Lexington Brody, just returned from a six-week tour for his latest book. She added a generous shot of Inis Mór single malt to both mugs.

"I don't trust him," she muttered.

"He can't act alone."

"I don't trust City Council."

"They're not all idiots." Brody's faith in the political wing of humanity was touching but hardly warranted.

"Mostly I don't trust his hand-picked Axe the Libraries Gang." It was actually called the Libraries Efficiencies Committee.

"What about your million blog followers? I thought you were going to have them inundate him and all the councillors with phone calls and emails."

"They've done that. Even real letters. Library supporters all over the city have an ongoing campaign in all the media, showing libraries as the good guys and Louie Pimento as the troglodyte he is. Hundreds of people from all walks of life have testified how libraries helped them make good."

"Well then...?"

"Pimento is one solid brick wall. He keeps hammering home how expensive 'the current system' is and how he can save money and still deliver. And some people, especially the rich and ignorant, want to believe him."

"Well, making knowledge universally available *is* expensive."

"Ignorance is even more expensive."

Brody nodded and gazed into his coffee.

"Worse," Catherine went on, "he claims he's actually pro-library. That his streamlining the delivery will make libraries better, for less."

"Maybe he's never actually read a book."

That was evident. His claim, "I never used the library when I was a kid, and look at me today" was highly popular with Planet Pimento. And more so with those opposed to him.

"Maybe if someone actually gave him a book...?" Brody went on.

Catherine shook her head. "He wouldn't know what to do with it. He'd hand it to his nearest assistant to read for him, or give it away as a present."

"What if lots of people gave him books? Maybe one of them might catch his fancy."

Catherine gave a derisive sniff. "Right, I can just see it. Louie Pimento's office flooded with books. Or... wait a minute." The wheels in her head clicked into gear.

"What?"

She shrugged. "It might be worth a try."

The Toronto Mirror: *Give-Louie-Pimento-a-Book Campaign.*

Toronto poet and Nobel Laureate Catherine Winters is spearheading a plan to promote reading in the deputy mayor's office. For the past five days, books of all kinds have been arriving at City Hall from people who want to introduce Louie Pimento to the joys of reading.

Pimento's executive assistant, Myra Babcock, reports he's received more than 300 books, with more coming in each day.

When asked if he's planning to read any of them, the deputy mayor, who has been known to say that books and reading can be dangerous, stated, "I'm a busy man. I've got a city to run. And more taxpayer dollars to save."

"What's Rufus doing in my office with all that stuff?"

"He's assembling a bookcase. The committee thought it would be good PR for you to be seen keeping all the books you've been sent. To show you have an intellectual side."

"Watch it, Babcock. And who authorized spending public money on a bookcase?"

"It was a gift from an admirer. It arrived from Ikea this morning."

Yeah, he had a good idea who the admirer was. He entered his office, stepping over the boards and books all around the floor.

"Make it snappy, Rufus. I have work to do."

"Almost done, sir. I just have to position the shelves, attach the anchors, arrange the books. Do you want them alphabetical or...?"

"Never mind getting fancy. That thing's not staying. As soon as the new library budget is approved, that shit is all out of here."

They were blocking his wall of hockey memorabilia.

"You're not going to like this," Brody said, as Catherine joined him backstage after her reading at the Authors' Festival.

"What?" Her reader's high evaporated.

He handed her his phone, misery oozing from every pore in his face.

Catherine hit Play. There was Louie Pimento at his desk and behind him a wall of books, arranged by colour.

"I'd like to thank all the generous people of this great city who sent me these books. Don't they look great in my office? I'm very happy to have some good reading material to while away the idle minutes I have between council meetings and budget meetings and meeting with my constituents.

"And you know what else I got this morning, presented to me personally by the Chair of the Library Board? My own library card." He held it up for the camera. "Look at that. A passport to the world of reading. And guess what, folks? I found out today there's actually a library branch right here in City Hall, on the main floor."

"It's been there for decades," Catherine muttered.

"So I went downstairs to the library to see what all the excitement's about. And look at what I found."

He held up the book on his desk so the camera could get a good look at it.

"Oh shit," Catherine said.

"That's right. *Fifty Shades of Grey*, available at the library. And there are two hundred and three copies of it. Not only that..." he picked up another object. "...thirty-five copies of the audiobook, and..." another item "...the Large Print edition. Twenty-seven copies. On top of that, it's available as an eBook for downloading." He indicated a stack of books to his left. "And they have it in French, Italian, Spanish, German, Filipino, and even..."

He held up one more book. *Gŭrei ŭi 50-kaji kŭrimja.* "That's right. We have dirty books in Korean at the Toronto Library." He smirked. "I'm not sure what to make of that."

He put the last book down and folded his hands in front of him, staring earnestly into the camera, as though about to make a pitch for laxatives.

"So there you have it, taxpayers. The Toronto Public Library—or should I say Toronto *Pubic* Library, heh heh heh—makes pornography freely available to the children of this fair city. Using *your* tax dollars.

"I've said it before, books can be dangerous. And here's a prime example.

157

"Now, I've been accused of exaggerating when I said there were more library branches in the city than doughnut shops, and maybe I was. But believe me when I tell you this: there are more libraries in City Hall than doughnut shops." He paused and picked up a doughnut from behind the books and took a huge bite.

He continued with a full mouth and a gloating grin. "And I say that's a damn shame."

"I'm going to kill him," Catherine murmured. "I'm totally going to kill that man. I'm going to send him six dozen doughnuts sprinkled with arsenic."

"The doughnuts alone might do the trick. Though I don't know how he can eat so many and still stay fit."

"I want him dead."

"Uh, Catherine..."

"I don't care if he chokes on a doughnut hole or gets mangled under the wheels of a streetcar, or if they find his body in a car parked in a bike lane with a bike-lock-shaped dent in his skull. Just as long as he's no longer a menace to the people of Toronto."

"Go easy." Brody sneaked a look around. "Anyone with a phone could be recording this conversation, and the next thing you know it will be all over the net."

"Hah!" She grabbed her phone. "I can get a hundred witnesses, a thousand, to give me an alibi. I can even get them to do the deed. I can..."

"Stop it!" Brody grabbed her phone. "Calm down. Killing him is not the answer."

Catherine took a few deep breaths and allowed Brody to see she was calming down. "Okay. Okay. You're right. It wouldn't do any good to kill him now."

"That's better."

I should have killed him when he first ran for council. I'd be out of prison now.

"*Fifty Shades of Grey!*" Louie Pimento was laughing so hard he felt tears coming to his eyes. "Geez, those pinko intellectuals are wetting their pants!"

"Yes, sir." Babcock stood patiently by.

"That was brilliant finding out that book was in the library. How did you know?"

She shrugged and eyed the stack of *Fifty Shades* editions on Pimento's desk. "Shall I take them all back to the library now?"

158

"Yeah, sure." He managed to control his amusement at last. "They've served their purpose. Get them all out of here."

Babcock wrangled the books into her arms, and headed out of the office, kicking the door shut behind her.

Pimento got up and went over to the bookcase. Geez, he hadn't felt so tickled in years. Feedback had been flooding in, in all variety of media, ever since the video had hit the Internet this morning and gone viral.

It was better than he'd hoped. Furious backlash from the lefty bookworms about freedom to read and all that crap. Hundreds of messages of support from Planet Pimento all saying, essentially, keep up the good work.

Best of all, outraged emails and phone calls from the tight-assed crowd who were shocked, *shocked* to learn about the filth being spread by the library system, all pledging their support to Pimento for whatever he could do to Make It Right.

He tugged a book free from the tightly packed shelf. The English language print edition of *Fifty Shades*.

Maybe there was something in this reading business after all.

Now then, where was he?

"Have you seen the report from the Axe the Libraries Committee?" Brody asked, joining Catherine at their table at the Elsie Street Ukrainian Tea Room.

"Of *course* I have." Online reaction and emails and phone calls had been pouring in for the past twenty-two minutes. An ever-rolling stream, like the morning Margaret Thatcher died.

Except this was bad news.

"Every member of my twitterverse has taken it upon themselves to tell me about it. Even those living in Kuala Lumpur. Along with the entire membership of Planet Pimento."

She pulled out her flask and added a generous slug to her cup of Icelandic Kelp tea. "It's just a recommendation." But Brody's voice was steeped in dejection. "Council won't vote on it for weeks."

"Right. Time enough for that doughnut-devouring, erotica-bashing jerk to whip up more council members over to his side. Did you know after the *Fifty Shades* diatribe, three councillors changed their position on libraries?"

"Aw, they were swithering anyway."

"And there are more smarmy, pseudo-religious namby-pamby switherers ready to join them if their holier-than-thou constituents

159

find more things to complain about in the library."

Catherine stood up and made to leave.

"Sorry, Brody, I've got to run. Believe it or not, I have an appointment with the deputy mayor. He invited me to drop by his office."

"You're not going, are you?" His horrified tone suggested she planned to attend a public stoning.

Catherine unscrewed her flask and knocked back the remaining Inis Mór.

"I think meeting him on his home ground is an opportunity too good to miss."

"Doughnut?" Louie Pimento indicated the box on his desk.

"No thank you." Catherine glanced with revulsion at the sugar and crumbs and two remaining doughnuts. "I'm wondering why you invited me here. Unless it's to tell me you've seen the light about the value of libraries."

He grinned. "Not a chance. By the way, have you heard about the proposal the Libraries Efficiencies Committee came up with?"

"No. Why don't you tell me about it?"

"Privatization. That's the way to go." He pulled the penultimate doughnut from the box and took a bite.

"You mean, hand the libraries over to a private company to run. A company who will naturally expect to make a profit. Perhaps you could explain to me the logic behind that approach to saving money."

His smile was wreathed in superiority and a dollop of red jam. "Economies of scale. We've had a proposal from a firm whose humungous book-buying clout brings them huge discounts."

"An American firm, no doubt." Catherine didn't even try to explain everything wrong with that, starting with the massive drop in local and Canadian books, to the impact on the publishers' bottom lines if they had to sell their paper stock at rock bottom prices.

"Don't worry, Mzzz Winter. We would still make a point of keeping *your* books on the shelves. You are, after all, a Canadian icon."

"That's right, I am." Also a National Treasure and the Voice of the People.

"There would be other cost-cutting measures. The unions would be out, of course."

"Of course. So that would cut down on the big bucks library

workers are pulling in."

"Exactly. More volunteers, unpaid internships, less librarians. We don't need to pay over-educated women just to stand there all day stamping books and telling people to shush."

"Yes. I'm sure any high school drop-out could handle that." Catherine mentally ticked off five more aspects of his vision that were completely out to lunch and deducted a demerit for the grammatical mistake.

"You're catching on, Catherine." He crammed the last of the doughnut into his mouth.

"It'll never pass, Mr. Pimento. I believe there are still enough city councillors with IQs over eighty to make sure that plan is relegated to the trash heap of bad ideas."

"Haven't you heard?" He brushed the powdered sugar off his suit jacket. "It's not cool to throw things out any more. We recycle everything."

Saint Catherine, give me strength...

"Well, Mr. Pimento, much as I'd like to stay here all day chatting with you, I have to go and write some more poems. What exactly did you ask me here for?"

"Right." He picked up a book from the desk. "Look what some kind citizen sent me."

The sight of her own first book of poetry in his hand gave her a jolt a nausea. Worse, she saw it was a first edition.

"Ah, I see. My poetry. And are you enjoying it?"

"Some of it's not bad. I've been taking it to council meetings, and reading a poem or two during the breaks."

Or when someone you disapprove of is speaking.

"Though I admit bits of it are pretty heavy going for me. I guess I'm not highbrow enough."

"Perhaps not." Would this man ever get to the point?

Pimento flipped open the book and found a passage. "Yeah. For example, this poem here. 'Small Remainders.'" He cleared his throat and declaimed, "Across the lucent nadir of delight..." He looked up at her, sincere puzzlement on his face. "What does that mean?"

Catherine held back a sigh.

"Taken in isolation from the rest of the poem, it has no meaning in itself..."

"Yeah, I thought so." He snapped the book shut and handed it to her. "Anyway, I wonder if you'd autograph it for me? I'd like to keep it as a special souvenir."

161

"I'd be delighted," she lied, opening the slim volume to the title page. "And shall I inscribe it to you personally?"

Pimento's grin got wider. "Oh, yeah. That'd be great."

Of course it would. An association inscription, from her to him, would make the rare volume even more valuable.

For Louie Pimento, as a momento of stirring political times. Catharine Winter.

She added the date and handed it back to him. No doubt he'd try to hawk it on eBay the day after the council's vote on the library budget.

The three spelling mistakes would render the inscription deeply suspect.

"Thanks." He put it on the desk without even glancing at the inscription.

Now or never.

Catherine turned her attention to the bookshelves. "What a lot of books. I'm glad to see you've got them here on display."

He nodded. "My assistant tells me there's at least seven hundred. I'm not sure where to begin."

She scanned the upper shelf, looking for a likely accessory before the fact.

"Oh. I see you have *A Mayor for All Times*." Mayor Bobcat Ryan's autobiography. A man after Pimento's own heart, who'd spearheaded the destruction of many of Toronto's heritage buildings and neighbourhoods during his tenure.

"Can you reach it down? I'm not nearly tall enough."

"Sure." He reached up to the book she'd indicated and tugged at it.

"Careful." Catherine stepped aside and placed her hand on the end of the bookcase. "I think it's a bit unsteady..."

"No problem..."

Oops. Oh dear.

Louie Pimento's right hand, just visible at the edge of the mountain of fallen volumes, twitched once or twice and then stilled.

Before the sound of running footsteps in the hall reached the office doorway, Catherine picked up the first edition from the desk.

"You were right, Louie. Books *can* be dangerous."

Poetic Justice. Indeed.

Testimony

by Madona Skaff

Jennifer Green wasn't sure if the churning in her stomach was due to excitement or terror.

Barely two months out of Aylmer Police College, and she was about to testify at a coroner's inquest. Her hands trembled on her lap despite the clenched fists. She glanced at Jake Cavalier, her partner and mentor, who immediately gave her a wink of encouragement. She barely managed a weak smile.

"OPP Constable, Third Class, Green," the court clerk called.

Her smile vanished as she put a hand to her mouth suppressing a gag. She looked back at her partner.

He placed a fatherly hand on her arm, whispering, "Relax. It's not like you're shy or anything."

With a grateful nod, she took strength from him and somehow regained her composure. Her mind raced as she was sworn in. What was he going to ask? What if they were the wrong questions? What if...?

The questions started before she felt ready. The lawyer was a friendly looking man wearing a nondescript dark suit. He had a round, plump face with a gentle smile that put her at ease.

"Tell us what you saw on Saturday, October 17th."

Her hands shook as she opened her notebook. Trembling, dry fingers clumsily flipped through the pages. Damn! Why hadn't she found the page before coming to the stand?

"That would be last month." The words were out before she could stop them. What a stupid thing to say. Everyone knew that. She cleared her throat. "At 8:25 a.m. my partner and I were patrolling West Carleton Township on Highway 17. We watched a small aircraft circling overhead, then suddenly it nose-dived towards the ground. Soon after it disappeared from sight, we saw smoke coming from the direction of Carp Airport. We called it in on the radio on the way to the crash site."

"And what did you find when you arrived at the crash site?" the lawyer asked.

She referred to her notes again, more to settle her nerves than to refresh the too-vivid memory. She would never, could never, forget the scene they'd found. "The Cessna one-seventy-two had crashed approximately ten kilometres east of the Carp Airport. I stopped the car on the road by a fence. It had crashed in the middle of a field, thirty metres on the other side of the fence, luckily far from any buildings. Plane wreckage was everywhere." She didn't say how they'd both sat in the car for several seconds, paralyzed with horror.

She continued. "The wings had broken off and lay smoldering on either side of the main body of the plane, which had plowed into the ground nose first. We looked in the cockpit, in the event there might be survivors. Body parts were everywhere..." Chin trembling, she clamped her mouth shut to regain control. Remembering to breathe, she continued. "We weren't sure how many occupants there were. Later we found out Andrew Ellis had been alone."

Jennifer shut her eyes. She hadn't realized testifying would be this difficult. She didn't say that she'd reached the plane before her partner. Looked in, then fell to her knees vomiting. In a foggy cold sweat, she'd sat on the ground gulping crisp fall air into burning lungs. She'd seen death before. But this...

She opened her eyes and blushed when she realized the lawyer was patiently waiting for her to continue. She sat up straight, squaring her shoulders. Cleared her throat. "We returned to the car to wait for the investigation teams to arrive." Jennifer paused to think and the lawyer jumped in with more questions, mostly about how the area had been secured and evidence protected. Finally, the ordeal ended and she was dismissed.

She held onto the railing for support and stood. A few deep breaths and she returned to her seat where Jake greeted her with a 'you did good' pat on the shoulder that she barely felt but acknowledged with a nod. She didn't dare look at him, afraid she'd lose what control she had. In a fog, she watched as the next witness was sworn in.

The air traffic controller sat down. He read from the transcript of the last radio transmissions from the ill-fated pilot. She wondered if her voice had kept cracking the way his did.

"Ottawa Traffic Control, this is Cessna one-seventy-two Kilo-Sierra-Tango."

"Kilo-Sierra-Tango, this is Ottawa."

"Ottawa, Kilo-Sierra-Tango. I'd like to take a quick tour over the city. Passing over the Parliament buildings, then west along the Ottawa River."

"Kilo-Sierra-Tango, Ottawa. Cleared for 1500. Altimeter, 29.9."

"Ottawa, Kilo-Sierra Tango. Descending to 1500 feet. Thank you."

The Air Traffic Controller stopped reading, looked up at the lawyer and said, "I didn't hear anything else from Kilo-Sierra-Tango until he was ready to leave the area." He looked down and finished reading.

"Ottawa, this is Kilo-Sierra-Tango. I'm leaving the control zone now. Thanks for the view."

"Kilo-Sierra-Tango. You're welcome."

The Controller cleared his throat and said, "That was the last I heard from Mr. Ellis."

"Did you notice anything about Mr. Ellis's tone of voice?" the lawyer asked. "Was his speech clear?"

"Yes, sir, he sounded very lucid."

Jennifer watched as the Controller shakily returned to his seat.

Next on the stand was an expert from the Transportation Safety Board of Canada who presented evidence that the plane had been in perfect mechanical condition when it had hit the ground, nose first at full power.

The pathologist was the next to take the stand.

"There was evidence of clonidine in his system. After checking with his family doctor, we discovered that he suffered from high blood pressure and had a prescription for the drug. The drug in his system was in high enough concentrations to cause drowsiness and quite probably unconsciousness."

Jennifer listened to one witness after another testify. The last was Ellis's family doctor, who confirmed the medical condition. "The clonidine controlled his blood pressure and made it possible for him to hide the condition from the Ministry of Transport doctor during his annual medical certification. If I'd only known that he was flying..." His voice cracked.

"Could the medication cause him to pass out?" the lawyer asked.

"In order to control his blood pressure, the dosage was fairly high. It is possible to accidentally take an overdose. If Mr. Ellis forgot that he'd taken a pill that morning and took another, it would be enough to disorient him and quite possibly cause him to pass out."

The coroner's jury left to make their decision.

Jennifer turned down Jake's invitation to grab a coffee, choosing to wait in the courtroom. She knew it wouldn't take the jury long to decide the cause of the crash. She'd seen the expression on their faces when the blood pressure condition was mentioned. A condition he'd purposely hidden. It was obvious that Ellis had passed out, falling forward on the controls. The plane had hit the ground at full throttle, partially burying itself into the ground. No wonder there hadn't been much left of Andrew Ellis.

Her first courtroom experience was over, but so much more wouldn't be. The image of the plane crash would never leave her nightmares.

She waited in the empty courtroom.

And remembered.

She'd knelt on the ground about six feet from the wreck, sweating despite the near-zero temperatures. She undid her thick jacket as she reached for some snow to put on the back of her neck. The light-headedness passed. At the moment she didn't care where Jake was, as long as he wasn't making a fuss over her.

She glanced at the plane again. There should be only one body.

Ellis had told her last night that he'd be flying alone the next day. He'd promised to look for her OPP squad car and circle overhead.

She'd met Andrew Ellis at a bookstore in the theatre section three weeks ago. They'd started talking about their favourite actors from days gone by, like Lillian Gish and Chaplin, then finished their conversation over a cup of café-au-lait at a coffee bar. She'd seen him frequently after that. He was so different from the men she usually dated. Not just that he was twenty years older, but he was always interesting to talk to, and knew so much about so many things. And he was always so very thoughtful.

The night before the crash, he'd invited her over to his place for the first time, bribing her with one of his famous dishes, duck à l'orange. He'd left her alone in the family room while he finished preparing dinner. With a cozy fire in the background, she looked around the room at his choice of interior decorating, wanting to get a better idea of the man she was falling in love with.

On the bottom shelf of one bookcase were several photo albums.

Cross-legged on the floor, she picked one at random, hoping he wouldn't mind her prying. Photos from a recent camping trip. She replaced it and looked at a few others. He definitely loved camping and fishing. Becoming bored, she quickly flipped through one more book. About to close it, a photo sent a stabbing pain in her chest. She truly wanted to believe that she was wrong.

There was no mistake.

A photo of her dad outside their family cottage and the business man, Johnson! After a day of fishing, they had proudly showed off their prizes; her father a ten centimetre minnow, Johnson a forty centimetre trout.

The photo had been taken one week before her father's death. She'd been ten. She'd gone to meet him at one of his construction sites, only to find his body, bent and broken, on the pavement. She'd felt a numbness overtake her as her young mind tried to imagine him simply asleep. But the odd angles of his arms and legs turned that fantasy into a nightmare. She would spend the rest of her life, seeing his eyes, looking up at the half-finished apartment building. He'd decided to step out into mid-air, rather than step into a court-room to face embezzlement charges and loss of his reputation.

Her father had been the victim of a smooth talking con artist named Johnson who'd taken millions from him and seven other investors. Only her father had been charged. The prosecution had insisted that he'd been working with Johnson to set up the others. The entire case hinged on the simple fact that her father had introduced Johnson to the rest of the partners.

As the girders had given the building shape, Johnson had emptied the bank account and vanished.

For sixteen years, without a trace.

Until now.

She gaped at the picture. It was old. That definitely was her dad. That other man was definitely Johnson. But was it Andrew Ellis?

She fought to breathe through heavy lungs.

Just then, Ellis came up behind her, catching her off guard. She tried to hide her feelings of hate and confusion, managed a toothless smile and accepted the offered red wine glass. When he noticed the album on her lap he laughed.

"From my wilder days," he said. "Hey, I remember when that photo was taken," tapping the one with her dad. "That guy was such a schmuck. But just like that fish he caught, he'd always be a little fish in a big pond. Always trying to play with the big boys."

"Where is he now?" Jennifer prodded.

"No idea. Never kept in touch."

"So," Jennifer swallowed hard and forced her voice to sound light. "That's not really you with the huge moustache."

"Yeah, but don't hold it against me. Like I said, from my wilder days." Then added, over his shoulder as he returned to the kitchen, "Dinner's almost ready."

Just like sixteen years ago, a numbness came over her. She tore out the photo and shoved it into the back pocket of her jeans.

The next morning, she sat on the ground by the plane wreck. She'd fantasized about his death for so long she was shocked that her plan had, in fact, worked.

She inhaled deeply then got to her feet, wondering where her partner was.

"Jake?" she called out as she looked on the other side of the plane. He was sitting on the ground, head bowed. She started for him and stopped. What was she thinking? She couldn't lose her chance.

She returned to the cockpit and forced sour bile down her throat. Where was it? She'd been careful about fingerprints. Still, she wanted it out! After several seconds of searching, she saw it. The small thermos. Jammed under the back seat cushion.

She took one last glance at Jake. He wasn't looking up. She inhaled sharply. Slipped on a disposable glove. Reached in. She deftly removed the thermos as blood streamed in to cover its place. Quickly she pulled out a large baggie from her pocket and slipped the bloody thermos in. Took off the glove and shoved it into the bag as well and zipped it shut. She tucked the thermos under her jacket. Last night she'd managed to sneak some of Ellis's pills from the bathroom and slip them into the small, two-cup thermos he took on flights. She'd remembered wondering if he'd rinse it out before pouring the coffee in.

Backing away from the plane, she knew he hadn't.

Trembling slightly, she went to Jake's side. He looked up at her, his face pale and sweaty. With a lopsided smile, he nodded at the evidence of his breakfast nearby and said, "I won't tell if you don't."

"Your secret's safe with me," Jennifer answered, as she patted the tiny bulge under her heavy jacket.

Special Delivery

by Linda Cahill

Linda Cahill writes moody crime stories about ordinary people who step across the line. Born in Montreal, Linda has a B.A. from Loyola College and studied Journalism at Carleton University before reporting for The Gazette *in Montreal and working as TV news assignment editor for both CBC and CTV News. Her first published fiction appeared in a UK anthology,* Oxford Prose. *More recently she contributed two stories to* Nefarious North, *an international anthology of short fiction, and is working on a novel about Michael Duluth, a Montreal police detective in hiding from his own criminal past. Linda is a member of the Toronto chapter of Sisters in Crime and is on the chapter executive. She is also a member of Sisters in Crime International and an Associate Member of Crime Writers of Canada.*

"She howls when the moon is full and asks for blood to drink. Now, hand me those inserts," Ricky had said when he instructed me on how to sort and deliver papers for his route. Ricky and his sister Giselle, my best friend, were going on a school trip and I wanted to earn some money.

She, the witch of Cranholme Street, was known to tear off her clothes while walking to the store. She yelled at kids playing in the road. When they threw stones at her, spitting and squinting, she foamed at the mouth, pulling at her dress and letting her boobs hang out.

Or so Ricky told me.

One thing I knew for sure, the witch lived in a creepy old cottage behind a weeping willow and some high bushes. I knew because the cottage was only a half block from our house. Kids crossed the street to avoid her. Once on my way to school, I saw her talking to herself

169

in her garden twisting bits of grass in her fingers, dirty hair hanging over her face. When she saw me she shrieked as if someone had stabbed her and I took off.

The cottage had been there my whole life, all ten years of it, before the other houses grew up around it. Ricky said someone had put a hex on the witch while she was young.

"Drinking blood? Come on!"

"The blood of a young child, to give her back her youth. She stabs them in the throat and drinks their blood. Like this!" Ricky had growled and clamped his teeth on his arm making sucking noises. He laughed as he did it so I knew he was kidding.

Still, our parents were always telling us about people or things to fear. Lately it was some story about a young couple who were trying to entice boys and girls into their car after school.

"I heard it from John's mom at St. Anne's," my mother said. St. Anne's Church is the only Catholic Church in Sterling, the town we lived in along the St. Lawrence River. It had services in French and English. "She heard it from Emile's dad—it happened to his sister's son."

"Emile doesn't go to our school." My mother gave me the look.

"OK, I'll be careful."

My mother wasn't keen on kids running around in the dark to deliver papers. I had persuaded her on other occasions that there were three of us, Gisele, Ricky and me. Nothing to fear. This time I left out the fact I was going alone.

I woke at 5:00 a.m. to a heavy snowfall. I dressed quietly so I wouldn't wake anyone and hurried out to pick up my papers in the lobby of the Tivoli Court apartments, Ricky's drop-off point.

The company agent looked suspicious. "Where's Ricky?" he demanded.

"Sick," I lied as I tugged at my tuque. "I'm helping him."

"Hmph. Can you carry that bag?" He pointed to the canvas hold-all I brought announcing "The Journal" in big blue letters.

"Course I can," I said, avoiding his eyes.

"Don't forget the inserts. Make sure you deliver every paper— and hurry!" He yanked the door open mumbling about Ricky needing to clear this with him and was gone, leaving a cold air blast and a line of snow drift in his wake.

I was excited. I had never done the route by myself. But I had a printed list of apartment buildings with subscriber numbers and the addresses of homes on my street and the next street. I also had notes from Ricky. "Back door, Mrs. Simmons doesn't want papers on her porch," or "Tivoli Court, Miss Allen wants hers on the mat not in the mailbox," or "Elegante Suites, leave Mr. Burke's paper with the Super." Nothing I couldn't handle.

But the papers were heavy and the wire cutter anything but sharp. Try as I might I didn't have the strength for the quick twist of the wrist Ricky used. I struggled for ten minutes to open the package of papers. Ricky started his route at the Tivoli Court but he was supposed to be gone before some tenant objected to a kid taking up space with papers and bag at the foot of the stairs.

Finally I put my knee on the papers to hold them down and tried turning and lifting the wire cutter at the same time.

Brilliant.

The papers flopped noisily to the floor. As I huddled over my task I was glad no tenant got up early for work and decided to start his day by chasing me out. My fingers would freeze if I had to do this outside. And the witch's home was nearby and Ricky and Gisele weren't with me...

Quickly I inserted flyers into each paper and loaded the stuffed papers into my bag. Lucky thing it was Tuesday. Tuesday was a skinny paper, maybe forty pages, and only thirty-two subscribers on my route.

The first four papers went to Tivoli Court. Easy. Grabbing the four copies, I risked leaving the precious bag of papers by the door away from the snow melt where the company agent had been, and raced to the fourth floor. Ricky always started at the top.

I left Miss Allen's paper square on her mat, as requested, then dropped two on the third floor on my way down and one on the second.

Banging down the stairs in my big boots, I glanced at my watch. Almost 6:00 a.m.

Pulling my tuque down over my ears so nothing showed but my eyes, I buttoned my coat up to my chin and pulled on my thick mitts. Then I pulled the bag onto my shoulder and almost fell over under its weight. Ricky was three years older and made it look easy. I was beginning to see why he liked Gisele and me to help him.

Gasping, I pulled open the doors and stepped into the cold. It had seemed warmer when I ran over from my house this morning. Frost and snowflakes glittered in the yellow light from the lamp posts.

The Tivoli Court sat on the corner of our street, Cranholme, and the main road, Chemin de Salaberry. From here Ricky turned east to deliver papers to the other apartment buildings then retraced his steps to the street we lived on, which intersected Salaberry at the top. As I moved out onto Salaberry, I saw a short, pudgy figure in the swirling snow. He was half way down Cranholme, smoking.

His head was bent but I could see a heavy coat and the tip of his cigarette as he stood outside one of the houses on my route. Usually there was no one about when we crept along the street and into the apartment buildings to deliver papers. Ricky did the apartment buildings first so I trudged in the other direction, east toward the sun. But there was no sun yet just a little lightening of the sky against the swaths of snow drifting down from the heavens.

My next stop was the Elegante Suites, with its shiny new grey brick and polished aluminum doors and railings.

I left three papers at the Elegante Suites and four more at Castleview Manor. Bag a little lighter, I went back along Salaberry. A few cars were whipping by for the early shift at the aircraft plant at the end of Salaberry. The plant employed most of the men and a few of the women in town. Like the couple driving slowly by me right now in an older Chevy.

"Hey kid, you want a lift?" the woman called out from the driver's side. "Yeah, we're going your way," the guy who was with her said in a dead voice. He tapped the ash off his cigarette. They scared me. Heart hammering, I took off in my heavy boots and snow pants. Rounding the corner back to our street, I ducked into the first of the four-family duplexes that lined Cranholme. The car disappeared toward the plant.

Whew. I could hear my mother's warning voice: "It's too dark for kids to be out alone," but I shut it down. I was safe on my own street.

The rest of Ricky's clients lived on Cranholme, a medium-size street, with two bends in it that tracked the stream that wandered through the empty fields behind our houses and off to the river.

As I climbed the stairs to the second floor of one of the four-family duplexes I heard a car crawl by, stop, then continue. One of the neighbours carpooled every day to the phone company where he worked. It must be his pickup, I told myself. With the papers a third done I grabbed my bag and moved on to the cottages and other duplexes that made up our neighbourhood.

"Need a ride?" The guy stepped out from a grove of snowy evergreens not twenty feet from Gisele and Ricky's duplex. I jumped. "No thanks," I squeaked. "I'm finished." It was the same guy I had seen in the car on Salaberry, the guy I had seen earlier on the street.

172

He was following me! And this time he was close enough to smell. He stank of tobacco. I pushed by him into the foyer of the duplex, dropped a paper and watched from a hallway window. The man looked around, then moved off toward the sidewalk, where he lit another cigarette. I could see his smoky breath hanging in the air.

Trapped in the duplex foyer, I unwrapped a bubblegum and tried to focus on how I would spend my share of Ricky's weekly collection. I wanted a pen knife.

As I waited and watched, a spooky tall figure emerged from the swirling snow on Cranholme and went up to the first man. It was beginning to get a little lighter out now but all I could see of this figure was blackness. He seemed to bring the darkness with him.

As they talked, he towered over the cigarette man. Hand on the door knob, I listened hard but they had turned their backs to the wind and to me and I couldn't make out what they were saying.

I waited a few minutes until they moved away, took a deep breath, and picked up my bag. These papers had to be delivered or Ricky would be in trouble. The good thing was my papers were more than half done and the bag felt a lot lighter. The bad thing was I had to pass the witch's house to finish my round and I was already scared enough.

I tried thinking about that knife but Ricky's stories about slashed throats mingled with my parents' warnings to shake my confidence.

The next six papers were simple, upstairs or downstairs in duplexes.

The road curves there and the two men were nowhere in sight so I began to feel better. There were some instructions to follow for these next deliveries if Ricky and I were to get a good tip.

Mrs. Karnecky, a widow in a semi-detached house, expected the paper to be brought to the back and carefully placed between the screen and the back door. This meant walking down a long driveway with Duke, an unfriendly German Shepherd, barking up a storm in the back yard next door.

The dog people didn't take a paper but they did collect junk on their front and back lawns, irritating their neighbours.

As I edged down the driveway, I saw the dog was guarding a broken old toilet complete with wooden seat. I breathed a sigh of relief when I reached the street again.

The next two papers were upstairs and downstairs in another small duplex like my own home. Unfortunately the outside door was stiff and I wrestled with it for some time before getting it open and placing the papers quietly in front of each door. Only a few papers left, including my own family's.

By now I was near the witch's cottage. She didn't take a paper so I stayed on the other side of the street to deliver the last papers. People said they heard terrible screams from the house especially on Hallowe'en when kids rang her doorbell or threw rocks at the windows, and I wasn't taking chances. Anyway, our parents told us to leave the witch alone.

"She's just a poor old thing," my Mother once said to me. "No family except that son of hers..."

"What about him?"

"Lives with..." she stopped. "Sucks her dry. Everybody says so."

"What?!"

"Takes her money—never you mind, curiosity killed the cat!"

The wind had picked up and the snow was dusting the tops of my boots and heading for my ankles. Home safe, almost, I couldn't resist looking over my shoulder toward the witch's cottage.

What I saw froze me to the snow-crusted sidewalk.

The tall, spooky man I had seen earlier stood with his back to me before the witch's rusty gate, his clothes dark against the snow. Facing him was the short, heavy guy who smelled of cigarettes.

"Go away," cigarette man shouted, but he wasn't talking to me.

Then the dark figure spoke: "Let me pass!"

I knew that powerful voice from Sunday sermons. It was Father Ephraim, from St. Anne's, in his long black robe and black hat. No wonder he blended with the darkness.

Rooted to the spot, I watched the two men. Father Ephraim held something in front of him covered by a heavy embroidered cloth. It must be the gold cup of consecrated communion wafers. The man with the cigarette backed off and turned away. Then Father Ephraim fixed his fierce eyes on me.

"Boy!" he called out.

"Yes, Father."

"Come here."

Dragging my feet, I walked toward the cottage and followed him through the gate. I had never dared come in here myself, just watched bigger kids throwing rocks or garbage at the witch's windows. There was a low chain link fence looped to small pillars sticking up that marked the path. The chain was white but old and dirty like the wood trim around the single broken window pane in the front of the cottage and the door I now faced.

"Move it," said the priest. "I have seen you at St. Anne with your family, non?"

"Oui, mon Père," I said with the few French words I had.

"Good, I need a witness."

I stepped into a tiny porch smelling of rubber boots, pulled mine off, and went slowly down a narrow hallway, my canvas sack with its last paper flopping from my shoulder. The priest paused at the door of a small blue-painted bedroom.

"What is the matter?"

I looked at my socks.

"They say a witch lives here. And it smells..."

A smell that reminded me of my uncle, a retired fireman who smoked cigars, came from the doorway.

"How old are you, boy?"

"Ten, I'm not..."

"And you serve Mass and know your Latin?"

"That's my brother Michael."

"You know the responses?"

"Yes but..."

"Boy, there are no witches here."

I followed him into the room. The cigar smell was coming from dead butts that filled an ashtray beside the bed. There were other smells too, chest rubs, musty clothes, an old body and an awful incense. They all came from a tiny figure in the bed, the scary woman of our fears, thin and dried out like a small pile of dead leaves. She was still as the grave.

On the night table there was a picture of the witch when she was young. She was smiling into the camera with her hand on the shoulder of the short man outside. Was he her son? Beside the photo was a glass, a teaspoon and a bottle of chocolate milk.

"Is she...?"

The priest shook his head. He sniffed the bottle.

"Put this in your bag." He shoved the bottle at me along with the spoon and the glass.

"And take off your tuque. We have prayers to say."

I fumbled with my tuque. Then I made sure the bottle was capped so it wouldn't spill and placed it and the spoon inside my bag.

I took out the last paper, the one for our home, and stuffed it into the largest pocket of my parka. Meanwhile the priest removed his coat and took the woman's tiny, claw-like hand.

"Eleanor, daughter of God, awake!" he boomed. The woman's eyes opened wide.

He began to pray in Latin. I knew it must be prayers for the dying. At the end of each prayer I knew to answer "Amen." I felt a presence behind me and looked back to see her son, a cigarette stashed behind his ear.

While he prayed, the priest had traced the sign of the cross on the woman's forehead and the palms of her hands. The woman's cheeks began to pink up and she raised herself a bit on her pillows.

Switching to English, the priest began the Lord's Prayer, and the old woman began to pray with us. At first we could hardly hear the words. By the end her voice got stronger. "Lead us NOT into temptation but deliver us from EVIL. Amen."

"Ten Hail Marys," Father Ephraim said, pulling out a large black rosary. We all joined in; even cigarette man mumbled along. After the second Hail Mary, Father Ephraim stepped back and pulled me along to let cigarette man get closer to his mother's bed.

Then he put his finger to his lips. As the man mumbled, his mother fell back against her pillow, gray and silent.

"Hail full of grace..." the man said and completing the prayer, he started over.

"Hail full of grace..." again he started over.

"Hail full of grace..."

Suddenly Father Ephraim shouted "Get out!" and shoved the man aside, blocking him from his mother.

"Depart! Vae te! Vae te! Woe to you!" He raised the crucifix from his rosary and pushed it right in the man's face.

Cigarette man ran from the house without saying a word.

The priest motioned me to resume the prayer.

I took a breath to recover and started. "Hail Mary, full of Grace, the Lord is with Thee..." At the sound of our voices the woman on the bed also began to pray again. When we finished the prayers the woman spoke in a strong, normal voice.

"Thank you, Father," she said, "And you, little one, I have seen you before, right? Thank you, too." I blushed as she smiled.

"I've called the visiting nurse," Father Ephraim said. "And the police. Don't eat or drink anything until the police check it." Then he bent to whisper something in her ear. She nodded. In the distance I heard a thin, wavering siren. Father Ephraim straightened up, took a communion wafer from the gold vessel and gave her communion. Then he gave it to me. Carefully gathering the communion cup, his rosary and the long coat he had left on a chair, he turned to me.

"I have another call to make. Don't leave. When the police come you give them this."

He dug into his coat pocket, pulled out a note and handed it to me. I caught the words "poison," "kidnap" and "children."

"Also the bottle, spoon and glass in your bag."

"What...?"

"Give them to the police."

He pulled me into the corridor.

"That man is living with a fortune-teller and has gambling debts," the priest whispered. "Big debts."

I knew he was talking about cigarette man.

"He will do anything to pay them, even kill his own mother to get his hands on her property."

I didn't know what to say. I looked again at the note he had given me for the cops. "How did you...?"

"I found her at the church door in the middle of the night. She was incoherent, talking about blood and thirst and her son. I took her inside and heard her story. Then I had someone bring her home and told her I would visit today."

I was still confused. "She put curses on people."

Father Ephraim shook his head. "The other way around. The son and his girlfriend put curses on her. But she didn't die, just went about screaming and crying and threatening to tell on them. So they decided to help her along."

Handing me the communion cup under its embroidered cloth, he slowly pulled on his long coat and then carefully took back the sacrament from my hands.

"He's been poisoning her," he said. "The evidence is in your bag. And be careful. The police suspect him and his girlfriend of trying to kidnap children also... but you don't need to hear about that."

"Father?"

"Yes."

"Why did you stop him from saying the Hail Mary?"

"Because he couldn't say the holy names. People engaged in the occult, in a certain kind of evil, they can't say the holy names," he said. "He never said 'Hail Mary,' just 'Hail.' And he couldn't say 'Jesus.' That's how I knew for sure." He paused and looked hard at me.

"After you speak to the police, go straight home. Straight home! The streets are no place for children at this hour. Especially little girls."

177

Try It Before You Die

by Elaine Ruth Mitchell

Elaine Ruth Mitchell's stories and articles have been published in journals and anthologies. She has been teaching journaling to women's groups for many years and has self-published Silver Fox: A Dating Guide for Women over 50. *Elaine is presently working on a one-woman play.*

"You're wanted at the station for questioning," said Daniel.

"Will you have to use handcuffs, Staff Sergeant Segal?" My tone was unbecoming for a woman my age, but I remembered when Daniel and I took turns owning the keys to the handcuffs.

"This isn't a joke, Emma," he snapped. "There's only one reason I would call you. Only one reason. Murder."

"What in the world do I have to do with a murder?" I asked, gulping a hit of caffeine.

"Doug Harcourt. The Conservative Member of Parliament from North Toronto. Quite a close connection of yours, in a manner of speaking." His voice was rough, the way it had been in tenderness. "Your name is in his smart phone. A drink date yesterday at four at Renny's. Just before he was poisoned."

"Oh! *That* guy!" I slammed down my coffee, spraying foamed organic skim milk on the pine table. "He cancelled. That was *Doug?* How did he find out my name?"

"You didn't know who you were meeting?"

"It was a blind date," I said. "No, I didn't know I was meeting the ex-husband of my ex-husband's lover."

"Who set you up?"

"A really blind date," I confessed. "I only know him under his site name—SilverStallion9. On AnyTimeLove.com."

Daniel laughed. Not a nice laugh.

I had dumped Daniel three years ago, even though I loved him.

179

Daniel, the guy who once solved big problems for me, including the one about how to make the earth move. "Do you want me to come down now?"

I shook my auburn (with only a few threads of silver) curls. "It's a truth universally acknowledged that a single woman of sixty, in possession of her marbles and some money, must be in want of a man."

"That is so last century," said my daughter Alex, as she fondled her accessory mutt, Sprinkle, who was wearing a new dog collar, pink leather with studs. Alex wore a matching collar.

"Two centuries ago," I said, ever the English teacher.

"Look at you. Still trying to find love with a man. As if."

"Three men, actually." I couldn't control a smile.

I sipped my skinny latte and looked around at the other tables on the patio. A typical crowd at the Yorkville Starmuggs—a young couple with a baby and French stroller, a designer-clothed middle-aged couple with shopping bags from Hazelton Lanes, an intense young man with an *Americano* and a computer. Across the street was the fanciest leather store in Toronto (which I've never entered). I am not a leather person: I dream of burgundy velvet bomber jackets and blue satin jeans.

"So who are the three men?" asked Alex.

"Jake, Daniel and a third man."

"Daniel? The cop? Sergeant Segal?"

"Staff Sergeant now."

"He's made a move? After three years?"

"You could put it that way."

"And what's with Jake? I thought he was history. He should be history."

"Not in my mind," I said. "He wrote me."

"You should clean out your mind. Don't answer Jake. Don't even think of it."

"Maybe he's changed."

"Thirty years of non-monogamy isn't a tiny thing," said Alex. "It's a lifestyle."

"Jake is older now. Well, a year older. Maybe he's realized how unsatisfying that way of life is. He's sixty-three." I licked the non-fat foam from the inside of the paper cup. Yeah, thinking of Jake.

"They never change, the screw-arounds. How come he wrote to you anyway?"

"I put an ad in the paper," I said.

"You're kidding. What did it say?"

I pulled my daybook out of my shoulder bag and handed her the clipped ad:

BEAUTIFUL AND ADVENTUROUS WOMAN, A SEXY SIXTY, SEEKING WONDERFUL MAN WITH WHOM TO WRITE A LOVE STORY.

"A bit cheesy. Where did you put it?"

"In the Saturday Globe. A week ago. In the National Personals section. It's anonymous—people reply to a box number."

"Who's the third man?" she asked.

"One of the responses to the ad. Sam. He sent a short note, but less is more. The thing is, Daniel doesn't realize he still likes me, and Jake didn't know he was writing to *me*."

"Are you really looking for a partner?" Alex asked.

"I'm searching for my soulmate."

"If you use that kind of language you'll get some weedy guy who tells you about his 'power animal' instead of being one."

"Don't you believe in the concept of soulmates?" I asked.

"As much as I believe in edible oil products," grinned Alex, as she took a last sip of her caramel soya macchiato.

"I've done enough solo inner journeys—I'm ready to journey with someone else."

Alex picked up her knapsack and pulled out a fat black spiral notebook. "That's a good one," she said.

"What are you writing?" I asked.

She looked uncomfortable. "Some notes for a comedy routine."

"I don't want to be immortalized again. That big lie about my paying eighty dollars for a feather to clear my aura."

"Do you ever hear that Drunk With Power chick's mother complaining?"

"Telling the world that I fed you nothing but chocolate when you were growing up."

She counted on her fingers. "Cappuccino yogurts, usually you threw in some candied chocolates—I would twirl them around until the dye came off—little containers of chocolate milk, chocolate bars, chocolate-covered raisins, Nuttola sandwiches, granola bars with chocolate chips—everybody wanted to trade me for my lunches at school. Especially since most of the parents wouldn't let their kids eat sugar."

"You're exaggerating."

"Of course. But there's a lot I could say about you that I don't. I'm very, very kind. Can I see the letters?"

"I don't know," I told her. "Some of them are sad, even pathetic."

"That can be comedic."

"Not if you're straight and have some compassion."

"I'm queer and like men better than most straight women. Why don't we go back to your house now?"

"I can't. I have an appointment in half an hour."

"Can I come over to your place after your appointment?"

"Why do you want to read those letters so badly?" I asked.

"I'm desperate for some material. I have a stand up gig at Under the Rainbow tonight," she said. "What kind of appointment do you have on a Saturday?"

"I'm involved in another murder."

Staff Sergeant Daniel Segal kept me waiting on a moulded orange plastic chair. When he finally came out of his office, I noted his large brown hooded eyes, Pacino nose, etched lips, flat belly (an unusual asset in the guys of the age that I date), and an air of authority and competence. It had not escaped my notice, nor my mother's, that he looked remarkably like my father in his fifties.

"Hello, Emma," he said. "Sorry to keep you waiting. Sergeant Chong is going to interview you—I'm afraid I have to run."

Maybe that's why I ran first. I always felt as if you were about to run.

"Hello, Daniel. I hoped I would see you again. Not, of course, under these circumstances."

He gave me a tight little smile.

"Didn't anyone at Renny's notice who was with him?" I asked. "Aren't you questioning the staff?

"Nothing conclusive so far. They remember a woman, medium height, red hair." He insulted me with a slow gaze. "A torn red rose was left beside Doug's single malt whisky. And a card, signed Soul-Mate 13."

"The Lady Internet Killer?" I asked. "You actually think I could be a serial killer?" The media had been splashing details of the two net-dating-connected murders over the past six months. Both men were killed in upscale bars. Both left diary entries for a late afternoon drink with a woman described as SoulMate 13. And a torn red rose was left beside each victim's drink.

182

"Does Segal really think you had anything to do with the murder?" asked Alex as she sat on my bed, tearing a teddy bear card from a baby blue envelope. "Listen to this one! *I may never be a wealthy man financially, but I wouldn't trade my life experience with anyone. I find it thrilling to be the existentialist I am.*"

I had dumped the small pile of letters, all addressed to Box 7743, on my chocolate brown duvet. "You have to kiss a lot of frogs to find a good letter," I said. "Here's a nice one but it didn't excite me: *I'm divorced now after a ten year marriage. My ex had a major mid-life change of direction and we had to split up.*"

"His wife discovered pussy," said Alex. "You should try it instead of hoping for love with a guy like this: *I believe in honour, fair play and ice cream. I used to pull into the Ice Cream Queen on a Friday night on the Queensway and order a three litre tub, with a swirl on top, scattered with nuts. I would sit out on the hood of a limousine and eat the darn thing.* Style matters. Where are the gelato-eating men?"

"Segal is counting me in as a possible murderer. I had a drink date with the victim, but I didn't go, and it turns out he's Doug Harcourt, Heather's ex."

"No reason for you to hate the dead guy. The contrary, I'd think."

"I only met him once, when I was still married to your father. I certainly didn't know SilverStallion9 was Heather's ex."

"Silver Stallion!" she hooted. "You're Internet dating too?" She tossed a few letters into the air and we watched them tumble down on the duvet and us. "But it's awful that you're a suspect. How was he killed?"

"Cyanide in his very good whisky. I'm sorry that he died but I never would have dated him."

"Or iced him. Any more letters for me?" asked Alex.

"I guess you could use this one in your act. A guy from North Bay."

Divorced for a decade, I'm ready to rock
Can cook and can garden, can clean up my sock
No paunch to display from too many beers
I'm in very good shape for a man of my years.

"There is definitely such a thing as being too straight," said Alex. "Just in case the crowd at Under the Rainbow tonight has any residual jealousy about the hetero lifestyle, this stuff will be so reassuring."

I poured myself a glass of muscadet and called my mother. "At what age do we stop talking about men?" I leaned back on my green velvet secondhand chaise lounge and sipped.

"I don't know. I'm only eighty-four. You're interested again in that Daniel?"

"Daniel contacted me and I think there's still feeling there." I took the phone to the fridge and poured myself a second glass. "Last night I woke up worrying that I'll never be with anyone again."

"You'll have a man if he meets your conditions. So many conditions. Available, attractive, strong but sensitive, funny, loyal, attentive, madly in love but able to give you all the space you want. His politics lean to the left, and he has to have children who love him because he's been such a good father."

"Ow! Am I that bad?"

"You're that good," said my mother. "You'll never settle. But maybe you could let go of one or two items on the list."

"Daniel contacted me for official reasons. He thinks I'm the cyberspace killer."

"What? He's crazy, but here you are a suspect again. The Goddess knows, I worry about you. It's going to work out, but being a suspect will hardly add to your statistically low chances of finding a new husband."

"I don't think Daniel really believes I did it. And I'm not looking for a new husband."

"Was he nice to you?"

"Cold."

"Maybe you should remember that he always blew more cold than hot," said my mother, who had changed her name from Patricia to Sophia when she became a Wiccan. "So were any of the letters to your ad interesting?"

"One told me about his difficulties in rising to..."

"T.M.I.! I don't like thinking about that. Besides, there are herbs."

"Listen to this from a former principal: *I silently nicknamed my former wife 'iceberg', although I later learned she had many lovers, so perhaps she wasn't always so cold; I am ready for a relationship again, in fact I've got a tiger in my tank, so better watch out... hahaha...* There were many other depressing letters. But there were two interesting responses. One from Jake."

184

"*Oy gevalt*," said my mom, who had picked up Yiddish words in her marriage to my dad along with various STDs. "Haven't you learned anything?"

"I don't think you ever get over the people you love," I said. "Those rituals you gave me for letting go haven't worked. I've visualized cutting cords from my second chakra to theirs, I've broken sticks in the woods, I've chanted stuff like 'the love that was hot now is cold.' There was one other good letter. A guy named Sam. He teaches Canadian history at New College. I'll email him in a week, after I lose a few pounds."

"My dear," said my mother, not for the first time, "it's wonderful to have a husband, especially as you grow older."

"Why a husband? Why not a wife?"

"Yuuuchh," replied my mother, who prided herself on being a free-thinking witch. "I can't understand those women. I can't help it—I like men."

I looked forward to repeating the conversation, complete with her exact coy intonation, to Alex. Let her use *my* mother as material.

Gary, Alex's Internet genius friend, told me that it was almost impossible to enter the "safe site" of AnyTimeLove.

"Then how did Doug find out my name?" I asked.

"Maybe he knew someone who worked there," he said. "Or he hired a hacker. You could do that if you want a list of who he's been in contact with. But the police will be able to subpoena that info."

Even if I could access the list, how could I know the real names behind the site names? Security was tight for non-hackers. I assumed it was also tough to crack for poor dead Doug. "What if I registered as a man, a man with a similar profile to Doug's? Maybe the serial killer will get in touch with me."

"Doesn't time matter?" asked Gary. "Aren't you like, kind of a suspect? Breaking into the site isn't an option for you—you'll have to use lateral thinking. There must be other ways of looking at the problem."

"I think we're having a communication gap," I said.

"I don't think so," said my mother. "It's got to be the wife. She's living with your no-good ex-husband, and she wanted Doug out of the way without having to worry about splitting assets."

"She's rich, mom."

"I heard from Tilly's cleaning lady, who also cleans for Heather, that there's trouble in their two million dollar condo. Your *farshtinkene* ex wants Heather to marry him and she's stalling on getting a divorce."

"I can't stand Heather, but why does it always have to be the wife or husband? Why not the crazy stalker? Did you ever want to kill dad?"

"Many times, but for anger, not for money. Your father had a few little friends—I know why you keep getting involved with philandering *putzes*. Anyhow, look into Heather."

"Stop looking at my hair," said Alex, "It's enough that I agree to have lunch with you in a place called *The Edible Complex*."

"When you dye your hair orange, you're screaming for hair attention," I said. "Can you think of any reason that Heather would have for killing her husband? He was still technically her husband. I found out that much."

"She's a bitch. Maybe she's just doing what bitch-protoplasms do, cause havoc, bully, kill." Alex examined her purple fingernails. "If you dyed your hair orange it might help you think outside your bourgeois box."

"I'm definitely of the sandwich generation—my mother keeps nagging me to get rid of the gray and find a husband and you keep nagging me to find a woman. Give it up. I'm not going to dye my hair and I'm not going to sleep with a woman. I'm happy with men."

"That's the funniest thing you've ever said," grinned Alex, taking out her notebook.

"Doug Harcourt was a Member of Parliament," said my mother. "I think the wife of a dead MP gets an amazing pension for the rest of her life."

"I've learned that Doug Harcourt has a sister in Oakville," I said. "Maybe she'll talk to me about him. I'm scared to phone Jake. I was so completely crazy about him. I couldn't bear to be in the same room with him without touching him."

"Forget him. He's too old to change."

"Maybe not. Maybe I left too soon and Jake would have changed for me. He said he would. And maybe I left Daniel too soon. I pushed a good man away."

"He disappeared every time you got close," said my mother.

"There were yo-yo strings sticking out from the back of your head when you were with him. Yes, call Doug's sister. She'd probably be happy to talk to you, the woman who got dumped by the woman who dumped her brother for your ex-husband."

"Think about this instead of the ridiculous idea that I'm a murderer." I glared at the cutest staff-sergeant in the world. "Doug Harcourt's sister told me that Doug wanted a divorce and Heather was hedging. She would get Doug's six figure MP annual pension for the rest of her life as long as she was still his wife when he died. Is that motive enough for you?"

"I'll look into it."

"The red flower was put there to make you think it was The Lady Internet Killer. I bet you Heather poisoned him. Guess she won't be living in luxury with my ex anymore."

"You hate her," said Daniel. 'That was a mean thing to say."

"Actually, I hate you right now," I said.

"I don't want you to freak out," said Sam, "But the other night was absolutely marvelous. I kept kissing my fingertips after you left."

I felt warmed in a new way, different than with Jake in our first go-round, or with Daniel or Cam, even when things were good. "It was great," I said, "but I don't want to lead you on. I'm too confused right now."

"Flexibility in one's planned life can be a good thing."

"I'm not sure I want a relationship with anyone. I'm always looking for an excuse to cut and run."

"You melted for me last night," said Sam. "Chemistry matters. I almost had to lick you off the couch."

"So you're going to take a chance on love?" said Jake.

"A big chance, with you. But you were the one who gave me confidence as a woman, and helped me with the reclamation of my sexuality."

"There's a mouthful. And speaking of that, you taste wonderful."

I flushed. "Because of you, I'm not inhibited anymore."

He leaned over and stroked my hair. "Only a little."

"It's amazing to me that I didn't know what the big deal about

187

sex was until I was in my fifties."

"You managed the learning curve very nicely." He stroked one of my breasts with one warm hand and two appraising eyes.

"And you took me on trips without a map."

"Metaphorically as well?" Oh, yes, Jake knew how to give a sexy stare.

"And hikes up mountains."

"You bagged your first peak with me," he grinned. "And you gave me support when I needed it."

"You too," I said. "You supported me in everything. You're the only man who wanted me to be myself—one hundred per cent myself. Everyone else wanted me to be less powerful than I am even though no one actually said that. Except my ex-husband. He was quite specific. He wanted me to reduce my personality by about eighty per cent."

"I like you exactly the way you are. Well, maybe a little more committed."

"I'm trying. My mom gave me a ceremony for letting go of my blocks. I've been lighting candles and muttering incantations."

"And I'm not just saying I intend to change." Jake's voice snaked into my ear. "I've joined a twelve-step program for sex addicts. You'll never have to worry about me again."

We kissed. I loved kissing him.

"So what happened to Heather?" Jake asked.

"They got her. Found a red wig in the condo, and a cyber trail to her site address. She confessed she found evidence that Doug was on a site while they were still married, and figured he wouldn't change his pseudonym, being Doug. She cruised adult sites until she found SilverStallion9, got in touch with him from a library computer using a false name and email address, met him at Renny's and told him some story, I guess. Anyhow, she poisoned his drink when he went to the washroom."

"So the red rose was a red herring," said Jake.

Jake's wit wasn't quite as fine as his kiss.

"Don't go off with him," said Alex.

"Whose life is it, Allie?"

"Just saying."

"She's right, Emma," shouted my mother above the whirring blender. "Jake's a good man to go to bed with, not to make your bed with."

188

"You rock, grandma! What are you making?"

My mother smiled. "Thanks, sweetie. I'm preparing a special potion with herbs I've wildcrafted to bring each of you a good husband. It won't fail. Trust me, I'm good." She poured the olive-green mush into two pottery goblets, singing, "Love and marriage, love and marriage, go together like...."

Alex and I locked anxious eyes. We both knew Sophia was good. Very good. Her business, *A Spell in the City*, was thriving, and she was famous in Toronto for the power of her manifestations.

Jake and I took off in a camper and traveled throughout Canada, the States, and Mexico without a single map. There was no map to heaven either, but we found it in the bed that took up most of the RV. Jake was a sex god, of course—all that capacity for fun, all that need to relate to a woman, all that unremitting experience.

But Alex is right. I should really give a woman a chance before I die. Sam doesn't believe it will work out with Jake. She'd take a chance with me anytime I wanted. And, since I always tell the truth, I'll be able to say to Jake that he's the only man in my bed.

Exercise Blues

by Carol Newhouse

Assembling the ski machine took an hour, because Wally Hendrig was not mechanically inclined. Now, the question of placement remained. The apartment was large, three-bedrooms-and-a-den large, but he nixed the den immediately. Exerting oneself in front of a fireplace? Too hot.

The casements in the living room offered a panoramic view. Wally imagined working out while observing the street below. He moved his glass-topped coffee table against the leather couch, then carried the machine across the room to place it squarely in front of the windows. He began to exercise slowly, simultaneously watching pedestrians strolling along the sidewalk. By diverting himself from the task at hand, he imagined skiing ten or even twenty minutes longer. But then he realized if he could look down, people could look up. The thought of them gazing skyward to see a fat man with flailing arms showcased behind glass repulsed him.

Wally walked down the hall to the kitchen, opened the fridge and poured himself a glass of water. Finding a home for the machine shouldn't be this difficult. Perhaps the manual included some suggestions. He sat at the kitchen table, pushed aside a stack of leaflets and started flipping pages. There were several images of smiling people using the skier in beige rooms. Invariably the machine sat in front of tub chairs or couches. He knew that after use it could be moved offside, but a metal skeleton at the side of the room would be an eyesore. Wait, maybe not. The machine would be a reminder to engage in regular physical activity.

Wally returned to the living room but this time stayed well back from the windows as he situated it to straddle the doorway. Then he climbed aboard and started again. Exercising was slow going at first but soon his arms and legs were extending fully. He couldn't see passersby and they couldn't see him.

Twenty strides in, he built enough of a rhythm to continue on cruise-control. Then he glanced beyond the doorway. From his vantage point he spied his new digital wall clock. The quest for fitness would have to be cut short. It was time to leave for work.

The staff sergeant logged the call at 14:00 hours. Wally Hendrig burned rubber, arriving at the Cyr University Athletic Centre in fifteen minutes. He joined the coroner, police photographer and evidence technicians outside the strength and conditioning area, which had been secured by the University security guard. After a brief conference, Wally and the medical examiner walked over to a person splayed on the floor beside a treadmill. The police photographer began snapping pictures. The evidence technicians waited. Groups of students huddled, speaking in hushed tones. Wally could see the victim was an extremely tall, muscled man, attired in gym shorts and a t-shirt with the word "Bowes" emblazoned across the chest. A defibrillator lay beside him.

"Shame," the medical examiner said, shaking his head. "Always worse when they're young. If it's straightforward, you'll have the autopsy results within twenty-four hours."

"Meanwhile, I'll see what I can unearth from the living," Wally said.

The young man standing beside the defibrillator self-identified as Alan Derose. He was early twenties, with bulging muscles. His t-shirt had "Clout" stamped across it.

"I'm here every day," he said. "So is Bob. I can't believe he's dead." Derose began wringing his hands. "I had no idea he had a problem. How could it happen? There was no sign. I mean I'm on my treadmill; he's on his, like always."

"You fellas talk?" Wally asked.

"While we're working out? No. No one says much," Derose said. "But I looked over and he's doing just like he does every day. Next thing I hear a thump. He's collapsed. Even before I get off my tread-mill I see his hand, quivering. My throat turned to sand; I could hardly swallow. Turned him over to start CPR and see his face, all pasty and gray. He'd aged one hundred years in ten seconds." Derose squeezed his eyes shut then covered his face with his hands.

"It's all right, son," Wally said. "Take your time."

Alan Derose took a slug from his water bottle before continuing. "Not more than three minutes. Wow, it seemed longer. Mike brought over the defibrillator and we tried bringing him back with the juice. Someone must've called 911."

"You did all you could," Wally said, in what he hoped was a comforting tone. "How long had you known the deceased?"

"I'm first-year," Derose said, "so we met just this semester."

"Did you consider him a friend?"

"We didn't hang out together. I just saw him here, exchanged observations about the machines, stuff like that, never more than a few words. I had no idea he had anything wrong with his heart, if that's what you mean."

"Any significance to the words on the t-shirts?" Wally asked.

"Oh that." Derose flexed his chest with pride. "New this year: Bowes and Clout are each sponsoring a team of University students for the state body building championships in the spring. Aside from the usual bragging rights, both companies offered scholarship assistance to anyone who qualified, so this wasn't just a try-out for t-shirts. It was tough going but I made Clout, which is a good thing because other things being equal, I really need the money."

"Did Mr. Greer need the money?"

"I wouldn't know."

"Any animosity from students who tried out but didn't make the teams?" Wally asked.

"Not towards me," Derose said.

The staff attendants, called "blue shirts" by the students, confirmed Greer completed his morning regime from 7:00 to 8:00 a.m. and his 1:45 p.m. workout on the cardio machines, something he did four times a week. They hadn't seen him speak to anyone.

The gym had free weights and strength circuit machines, two weightlifting platforms with bars and plates, bikes, medicine balls, stability balls, treadmills, stair-steppers and suspension trainers. Professional tools for the professional fitness buff, Wally thought.

"There had been complaints," one blue shirt said, "But they weren't health-related."

"Complaints?" Wally asked. "By Greer or about Greer?"

"Both." Two of the blue shirts grimaced. "Greer objected to the women-only hours in the conditioning centre," they said in unison. "Claimed he needed to work out at those times," said one. "Complained the centre was closed statutory holidays," said another. "Even started a petition to extend facility hours," they said, again in unison.

"Many names on that petition?"

"Are you kidding? Out of a membership of nearly seven

hundred, maybe thirty."

"So everyone agrees he complained regularly," Wally confirmed.

"Yes," they said.

"And who complained about him?"

"Think of it as a squabbling family," a blue shirt said. "I do. Some of the women found him intimidating. One gal said he loomed over her, though he had quite a physical presence, so it may have been unintentional. Several guys complained he left the rowers sweaty. Alan Derose, he's standing over there, said Greer used towels and discarded them on the floor."

"Did Greer ever talk about aches, pains?" Wally asked.

"Never. But you might want to check the residence don. He's the one who'd know about that kind of thing."

Arnold Gardiner had been a residence don for two years. "Most are senior undergraduates like me," he told Wally. "I love this job. I get room, board and a small stipend on the proviso I keep my grade point average above 2.3 and stay accessible to the residents evenings and weekends. Since I'm always studying or helping students, attending classes or at the gym, hanging around is no problem. I enjoy being the 'go-to' person."

"I'm here about Robert Greer," Wally said.

"Bob? Sure. Everyone calls me Arnie, by the way. One of his roommates told me what happened in the gym. I can't believe he's gone. My hands are shaking. Is it true he had a heart attack? Totally unbelievable, I mean heart attacks are for old men, not guys like us."

"I understand," Wally said. "You weren't aware of any health problems?"

"You're kidding, right? Bob is, I mean was, an icon of fitness, always working out. He even has some equipment in his room. I can't remember him complaining about a headache though, and trust me, if he'd had one, I'd have heard."

"Complained a lot, did he?"

"More than some. Besides, if he'd had some sort of heart condition, I'd know. Residents with chronic conditions have to register. That's University rules and they're strictly enforced. One of my first-years is diabetic, for example, so I made it a point to learn about the disease. But Bob was no sickie. He ate well, worked out all the time. If he had any health problems he never let on, to me or to the University."

"Can I check his room?"

"Sure."

Arnie got the key from his desk drawer, unlocked the door to Greer's room, then stepped aside. It was small and modestly furnished with a bed, a desk and a short cabinet. A poster of a body builder broke the monotony of beige wall. A rack of dumbbells sat underneath the window and a ski machine was stowed in the corner of the room. It looked the same as the machine he'd purchased except that padded hand grips had been added, presumably to make longer work-outs more comfortable. He opened the drawers in the short cabinet and the desk. Nothing. There were no bottles of pills or syrups in the shared bathroom either.

The case seemed open and shut. Funny how that worked, Wally thought. Here he was, having another go on his ski machine. Overweight, yes, but no history of heart disease. Should he worry about dropping from sudden cardiac death? It didn't seem likely, but Bob Greer must have felt the same way.

Still, people's lack of concern about Greer niggled at him. Everyone had been shocked and surprised, but no one had cried or said he'd be missed.

Wally's chest began to heave and perspiration beaded on his forehead. Even his hands were sweaty. He considered stopping after fifteen minutes. Overexerting on the first day could only lead to sore muscles. His ringing telephone ended the debate. He stopping skiing and in one motion wiped his hand on his pants then stepped off the machine to answer the phone.

"The autopsy results surprised me," the medical examiner said. "No signs of any disease. In fact, I'd say he's the healthiest fellow I've autopsied in years. His heart stopped, but none of the common findings that could have caused sudden cardiac death were present. Then I noticed burns inside his fingers, his palms and on each thigh."

"Burns?" Wally frowned. "I didn't see blisters, not even reddened skin."

"You wouldn't. Internal burns that weren't visible on the skin surface told me to test for hydrofluoric acid. Easily absorbed through the skin but, depending on the concentration of the acid, the burns may not appear on the skin surface until the next day. If he'd lived, his fingers would have become visibly grey and blistered, but since he didn't, burning is only evident on deeper tissue. Hydrofluoric acid poisoning caused his heart to stop."

"Burns on his hands," Wally said. "Give me a minute. Think maybe he picked something up or handled something coated with hydrofluoric acid?"

"Possibly, but the burned patches on his thighs need to be explained too."

"Right," Wally said. "You know this guy was fanatical about working out." Then he looked down at the sweat stains on his track pants.

The room had been stripped. All that remained was a sheet-less bed, empty side table and nude desk.

"It's only been a day," Wally said.

"They move quickly," Arnie said.

Wally jumped. He hadn't heard the residence don, who now stood behind him.

"I heard there's a waiting list. I'll likely be introducing myself to a new resident tomorrow."

"Where'd you store his personal effects?"

"I didn't, but the front desk would know. Unionized maintenance men do all the heavy lifting. Not that I couldn't." Arnie flexed a bicep and smiled.

"Everyone around here pump iron?"

"Not everyone. But most of us."

"I guess that contest with the t-shirts increased the intensity, right?"

"Bowes and Clout? A bit. But bodybuilding is always intense and competition-based, so the contest had more impact on the newbies."

"No hard feelings among the fellas passed over?"

"You gotta understand the community. We're bros. We're about spotting and teamwork and comparing notes. It's working together until you hit the stage."

"Well somebody didn't think they were Bob Greer's bro."

"I wouldn't know about that," Arnie said.

The front desk advised Hendrig that Robert Greer's brother would be picking up his personal effects in a few hours.

"I'm curious," Wally said to the head administrator, Ms. Farley, as they walked to the storage area. "The gymnasium seems very well-equipped, so I'm wondering why Mr. Greer would have extra equipment in his room. Do you have any idea?"

The administrator hesitated a moment before answering. "How should I describe the deceased? I suppose you could say he was unique."

"Is that another way of saying difficult?"

"I suppose so," Ms. Farley said.

"I remember the blue shirts in the gym mentioned he complained a lot. They also told me about a petition," Wally said.

"Oh." Ms. Farley smiled. "I'd forgotten about that petition. Administration found it more amusing than irritating. But yes, I think everyone would agree Mr. Greer enjoyed complaining."

"Did any person in particular upset Mr. Greer?"

Ms. Farley stopped in front of locker 403. "Here we are," she said.

The ski machine stood in the corner. Its custom-made handles were missing. Wally wasn't surprised. When interviewed, the maintenance men confirmed nothing had been disassembled or altered when Greer's effects were transported to storage. Wally believed them. Someone else had removed the handles and he was certain that someone would be the murderer.

"Ms. Farley are you sure Mr. Greer didn't complain more about one person than another? Could you possibly create a list?"

"Mr. Hendrig, with two hundred fifty people from all over the state in this residence there are bound to be disagreements and misunderstandings. There has never been a homicide and I cannot even recall anyone being charged with assault. Besides, I heard poor Mr. Greer died of heart failure. Do you really think there's more to it?"

"Unfortunately, I do. Now if I could just get a list of people..."

Wally and Ms. Farley returned to the front desk in silence. He waited at the counter; she disappeared into her office. The desk clerk was speaking with a student. Wally understood Ms. Farley's disbelief that evil could intrude into University territory, but facts were facts. He sighed.

The conversation between the student and the desk clerk was becoming more animated. Wally couldn't help but overhear.

"This is the second time you've misplaced your room key," the clerk was saying. "You know the rules. I can't waive the fee."

The student grumbled but eventually left with a key.

"Does that come up often?" Wally asked.

"More than you'd think," the clerk said. "The residents are

always losing keys. It's a pain because they pay for a key loan and have to return it within an hour. We log everything. If they're late with the return, another fee is charged. If we have to replace a key, there's a substantial charge."

"If it costs them money, why not just borrow the key from the residence don on their floor?"

"Oh, the residence dons only have keys to their own rooms," the clerk said. "We control access to keys."

"That's very interesting," Wally said. He looked at the clock. It read 2:15. "Please tell Ms. Farley I had to leave," he said to the clerk. "I'll pick up that list later."

"What are you doing here?" Arnie Gardiner asked.

Wally turned. The voice sounded brave but behind the bravado all Wally saw was a scared kid. He looked toward the desk and the residence don followed his gaze. Wally had spread the search warrant on its top. Arnie's shoulders slumped.

"I haven't been here long," Wally said, "But you could save me time. Want to show me where you hid them?"

Arnie hung his head. "How did you know?" he finally asked.

"I just bought a ski machine myself, so when I saw Mr. Greer's in his room those special hand grips caught my eye. Didn't think much of it at the time because I knew he worked out obsessively and figured he'd made the alteration to prevent blisters. But if the coroner's right, when I find them, and I will, tests will show they've been coated with hydrofluoric acid."

"So you figured out the mechanism, but why do you think I'm the culprit?"

"Whoever altered the grips had unrestricted access to Mr. Greer's room. You had a key. I found that out when you let me into his room after his death."

"What if I say you'll never find those grips?"

"I wouldn't believe you," Wally said. "I don't think you meant to murder him. Maybe you just wanted to scare him, warn him off from all the complaining. But when you found out he died, you wouldn't want to discard them in case someone else became poisoned."

"That's about right," Arnie said. "I guess I'll get them. I don't want you accidentally getting poisoned either."

"I gotta ask," Wally said as they walked down the corridor. "It wasn't just the complaints, was it?"

"No. There was more. If he hadn't cheated to win that Bowes sponsorship I could've let the complaining go, but it pissed me off. Bob Greer was a sanctimonious jerk."

Wally looked at his ski machine. The thought of skiing made his heart sink. Although unchanged, the metal machine looked dull and tarnished. Not because its twin had been used as a vehicle for murder, but because its function represented the expending of effort to get nowhere. He pulled his tools from the closet, disassembled the machine and wrestled its parts into the box. Then he left the apartment for a walk in the rain.

The Dead Of Winter

by Miriam Clavir

Miriam Clavir grew up in Toronto and her interest in museums began in her childhood during many visits to the Royal Ontario Museum. Today she is both a writer and a professional art and artifacts conservator. Miriam's first mystery novel, Insinuendo: Murder in the Museum, *was published in 2012 by Bayeux Arts. A second in the series,* Fate Accompli: The Golden Dog Murders, *is set on an archaeological dig and has just been completed. Miriam has also published a literary short story,* Knowing Home, *in* The Antigonish Review, No. 171, Fall, 2012. *A scholarly book,* Preserving What is Valued: Museums, Conservation, and First Nations, *was published in 2002 by UBC Press. Miriam divides her time between Vancouver, B.C. and Garter Lake, Ontario.*

The door yielded, and a musty odour of mothballs rushed out past Shirley Frankel. The suffocating, toxic smell was the worst part of opening up the old museum. Stepping into what had been the parlour of the 1860s farmhouse, Shirley quickly raised the wooden bar at the bottom of each storm window so the round holes the bar sealed off could let in the fresh outside air. Warm, new spring to displace the dead of winter trapped inside. Shirley called out to the sleeping artifacts, "Wake-y, wake-y, my little monsters. Mrs. Frankenstein's back," and glanced around the room. No leaks, no china on the floor tumbled by skittering mice. She sneezed. There was a smell of decay in the air mixed in with the mothballs. She'd be fine if she didn't draw too deep a breath until all the rooms in Tugston's Pioneer Museum were vented and cleaned.

The stench was stronger near the back bedroom. As she went to investigate, Shirley banged her cleaning bucket with the mop, holding the pole like a jousting lance. The mothballs would all have dissolved over the winter into the building's trapped air, but the decay? A dead snake like last year? A pooping raccoon in residence? There were no glistening eyes, though, and the floor and furniture were unsoiled. Everything had a winter's coat of dust, yes, but even the two costumed mannequins in the weaving diorama in the room still looked only as if interrupted in their spinning and carding.

A third figure slumped by the spinning wheel did not.

Shirley stared at the human form sliding out of the caned chair. Her curatorial brain raced through the artifact catalogue as her eyes swept over the armchair that should have been by the bedroom's fireplace. Quilts normally kept in the pine chest snuggled around the immobile figure. Shirley's museum mind observed that the displayed piecework patterns jarred where a bent head brought them in contact with a lurid bobble-topped acrylic tuque.

Shirley's body took over from her brain, shivering despite the sweat forming under her frizz of black hair that had worked its way out of her special cleaning-lady kerchief. The next instant she puked. And missed the bucket. It had spun with her mop to the ground. Shakily, she dialed 911, gasping, "There's a corpse in the museum!" Shirley hung up and dialed Al.

For twelve years she had been the museum's director, curator and collections manager while Al Smedley did everything else as maintenance man and groundskeeper. Running the town's museum had been burdensome but very satisfying. Tugston had been significant once, the village an easy wagon ride to market for the surrounding farmers. Families had contributed nine men to the First World War, and lost them all. The Spooner farm, its stone house already sixty years old, had given the money for the cenotaph. Now Shirley and Al waited together for the police to arrive as the farm marked new death.

The local paper would soon headline, "Police Investigate Museum's Mummy." The corpse had been female, and apparently somewhat desiccated from wintertime's dry cold. Shirley hadn't examined the body too closely, keeping her eyes glued to the quilts and the tuque, staring at the absurd knitting with its crocheted flowers, their stems like dreadlocks entwined around a turquoise bowl that was edged by sparse grey hair. The next day Shirley issued a general press statement and referred all interviews to the police.

It took the cops and Al together to confirm that there were no signs of forced entry into the building. Al said, "Sure, no broken windows, but these big old locks can be picked," and demonstrated on the front and back doors the kinds of mechanical skills for which he had been hired. "People here think we've got a whole darn alarm system, so what I'm showing you is secret, right? All these years this heavy old metal's been just fine."

Determined to get a quick resolution, the police redoubled their efforts and spread their net into the surrounding counties for missing elderly women. The only response they received was an offer to donate a specific in-law if the museum was still collecting.

Three weeks later, when the museum opened for the season, the director in Shirley took comfort in the record attendance. She had discreetly posted new directional signs to the museum's rooms and collections, including the now immaculate but pruriently thrilling back bedroom.

By the second month the crowds had diminished and the police had had no success with identification. The region's weeklies had published a computer-adjusted image of the elderly woman's face looking peacefully asleep, hair combed down as it might have been. No one stepped forward. There had been no papers with the body, no significant clothing labels, no local missing person calls, no leads to dentists, doctors, no bruising or signs of struggle that might have fed police forensics. The only people with keys to the museum— Shirley, Al and the chief of Tugston's volunteer fire department— had been interviewed to the point of denting the police station's coffee budget. But arriving at work now, Shirley liked it best when Al had gotten there first.

One morning in mid-June Al found Shirley in the pantry she called her office, head in hands, crying.

"I'm all right," she coughed into a tissue. "I'm the director, after all..." And she folded her arms on the desk and wept. Al laid his hand on the shoulder of her dark blouse, pulled a chair closer and quietly sat.

Shirley reached out and squeezed his hand.

"It's not just the cold case. It's... I need to know her name, Al. It's like she's still in residence. An invisible relative in the back bedroom. I hear visitors talking about her. I need..." her voice squeaked, "a proper funeral."

Shirley stopped, lowered her gaze and began to root around in the paper on her desk, using the time as well to take deep breaths and push the air back out in long huffs. She straightened. Scrutinizing a sheet, readjusting a comb holding back her mass of dark curls, Shirley fastened her eyes on Al.

"To business. The crowds we had in May are going to cost us $5,000 repairing the septic system. How can we afford that?"

"Shirl m' girl," Al said, his avuncular features serious. "Forget the toilets. And forget the repair on the mower, too." He took out a tobacco pouch and kept his eyes down, rolling a cigarette. "You've been dragging in here these last weeks like a pup with worms, if you don't mind my saying. The old lady died here but we didn't kill her. Somebody just stored her here for a while."

"Why?" Shirley almost shouted. She looked directly at his creased face and silvery hair and the stained, hardened hands nimbly lifting up the cigarette so he could lick the paper closed. "Al, what's your take? Tell me the truth. Why here?"

"That's what museums do," he replied with a poker face. "Store old things." Shirley groaned, and Al smiled. He'd dented her grim mood, and said, "Look, who's got something against us? Nobody I know."

"Seriously?" Shirley pushed out her breath again. "You were born in Tugston. Who don't you know here?"

Al shrugged. They sat in the tiny room with nothing more to say, and Al rolled another cigarette.

"Out on the Third Line, actually, not right in Tugston." Stuffing the two cigarettes into his shirt pocket, he met her eyes. "There's nothing for it but we gotta move on from this mess."

"Can't." Shirley was now the one looking at her lap. "Not without knowing why. Why us? I hate coming here now. Like I'm going to open that door and the death stink is waiting, another corpse."

"Not in summer." Al shook his head. "Too hot, too many people. Even cottagers aren't that dumb. But look here, no one is against us, Shirl. You've done wonders. For someone who came here twenty years ago looking like a hippie, no family to speak of, you're really part of the town."

Her lips crooked into a grin. Raking a loose curl back from her face, she said, "Al, we and the police have been asking the wrong question. Nobody's against us. The question we need to ask is, who's for us?"

To his puzzled face she said, "Who likes us so much they wanted to die here? There are easier places to dump a body. Who'd want to have their relative entombed in a museum?"

"Someone in the Friends of the Museum?"

"I'd laugh except the Friends have already been canvassed by the cops. Especially Friends who might inherit from sick relatives."

"The Spooners?"

The 1850s farmhouse and what was left of its 200 acres had been sold to Tugston in 1961 by Jimmy Spooner, a descendant of the original farmer, one Peter Spooner. Shirley had been fascinated that she could find no documents relating to the ancestor other than the land deed. No genealogical or military records, no letters, no name on ships' passenger lists from the right time. Maybe "Spooner" was a corruption bestowed at Immigration for a non-English name, or maybe Peter was hiding something in his background. There was a niece's letter from 1909, long after he'd died, mentioning a family bedtime story about the farm having been bought with stolen silver cutlery filched the night before he emigrated by a daring Peter, the younger son who, by the law, at least of English primogeniture, would have inherited nothing. Land went to the eldest boy. The letter also had a long passage about the evils of gambling and the hardship it brought to families.

No family or place name had been attached to the story. If true, though, Tugston as well as Peter's descendants had benefitted that he was never caught.

Jimmy Spooner and his siblings had inherited the farm when their parents died, and in the 1960s, being twenty-five, twenty, nineteen and sixteen, they had no use for a working farm and good use for money. Jimmy was determined to be a geologist and the first in his family to go to university. The twenty-five-year-old, a girl, had just wanted to get away. Shirley had found a diary entry that made it clearer. The brothers were demanding cooking and cleaning. A boy one year older than Jimmy had joined the military and soon after paid with his life for a stupid accident. The youngest girl was now estranged from the family, and the museum had been warned to deal either with Jimmy or with her, but not both.

Shirley had compiled as much of a family archive as she could find when she first joined the museum, and it was now easy to look up the contact information and find out whether there were currently any missing relatives.

"Jimmy Spooner's on summer vacation, like everybody else except us," Shirley said to Al, hanging up the phone. "In some remote mineralogical paradise, apparently. I'll send an email. He might just get it." She tapped out a pleasant summer greeting and her request about missing persons.

"Now for the big sister."

Al nodded, waiting.

"She's in a private long-term care facility in Montreal. Let's hope she's still got her mind. Here, I'll put us on speakerphone."

The voice answering Reception was clearly puzzled. "A Mrs. Spooner? I'm sorry, there's no resident here by that name."

"Mrs..." Shirley flipped the pages of her file. "Reilly. Mary Reilly, that was her married name."

There was a long pause on the line.

"Mary Elizabeth Reilly?" There was another pause. "I'm truly very sorry, it's just not possible to talk to her anymore. I can give you her brother's phone number."

Shirley made her polite good-byes and she and Al sat staring at each other until Al said, "The youngest sister. Since you never contacted Jimmy, it's okay. Today, anyways."

It took some digging, but a fluty welcoming voice on the other end of the line was not what Shirley had expected.

"No idea, luv, if someone's missing. Me? My dear, the story is short. I was a young sixteen when my parents died and Jimmy decided to sell our home. He and William were the executors. My parents were very old-fashioned that way. William died within months, you know, and Jimmy stowed me with an aunt out here in Dartmouth and that was that. We all went our separate ways. I did get some money for teachers' college, but whether the rest of my inheritance went to Aunt Inie for keeping me or what, I never received a cent more. And I haven't talked to my remaining siblings since."

"I'm sorry." Shirley was. Tugston had paid a modest price for the farmhouse back in '61, but it had not been stingy. "Did your siblings inherit?"

"I don't know. Inie said my share would come when I reached the age of majority. The day I turned twenty-one I phoned Jimmy. He'd had to pay back taxes, bills, the lawyers, he said, so there wasn't actually much cash, and he'd borrowed some for his geology fees but he was in a field that'd make a lot of money. I was not to worry. A few more conversations like that and I gave up."

"Your aunt Inie, is she still alive?"

"Afraid not."

Shirley's eyes fixed on Al and one hand pointed to a notepad. Al started scribbling down what he could hear of the conversation.

"I'm updating the family archives." Shirley was thinking fast. "Do you know of any relatives that are elderly?"

"My dear, as I've said, I'm not in contact with the family. Ask the man who is."

"Your Aunt Inie—do you mind if I just jot down the date of her death and where she's buried?"

"She's not buried."

"Where, then, is she, uh, resting?"

"God only knows, and I hope The Deity does."

206

Shirley said, "Yes, well, any hints? As next-of-kin you might have better luck asking than I would."

The laugh was melodious. "My dear, I scattered Aunt Inie's ashes to the Atlantic a quarter century ago. Bleak winter weather it was. That was my final act for the Spooner family. I do wish your museum well. Ta ta," and she hung up.

Al went outside to smoke. Shirley could not think of anyone who would choose to die in a museum. Maybe Tugston's corpse had just been on short-term deposit, so to speak, and something had prevented the depositor from coming back. According to the autopsy the woman had died of natural causes. The police were being polite but not entirely forthcoming. Was the implication still that staff at the museum might be involved?

Al was wiping his muddy work boots off at the back door when Shirley shouted out, "If people think this museum is just dead storage, I'll show. 'em. The police, too."

"You do that, Shirl m' girl," said Al from the doorway. "I've got my own ideas. Right now I've got errands to run." He took off.

Shirley didn't share what she was up to, just gave Al a knowing smile when she passed him during the workday. Al dropped in on her from time to time about maintenance, and always she had the Spooner files open beside her other jobs: new sticky-notes, lists of crossed-off items. Shirley figured they both were waiting for the pot to boil before tasting the other cook's stew.

She first saw Al's handiwork in a café. Shirley started hunting down his train of thought: the bus depot, truck stops and the pool hall. His posters reproduced a drawing and read, "Last winter did you see an older lady wearing this hat?" And after three weeks the driver of a long-haul rig phoned Al from a pay phone, saying he'd picked up this woman last December at a highway restaurant in Perth and dropped her off outside of Tugston at the gas station, but that's all he knew, and hung up.

It was enough. Shirley made two phone calls, and she and Al had a name for their body. They held a private celebration in Shirley's office. Al brought a six pack and Shirley laced her coffee with liqueur.

"What a gal," said Al. "Planned it all on her own."

"Let's talk about how we'll do the commemoration. Maybe in

September, when everyone in town can come."

The phone rang. Shirley winked at Al as if she had been expecting the call. Picking it up, smiling, she listened for a while to the caller and then mentioned the planned memorial event. Her face fell. Lips pursed, Shirley said, "We were all like that. Couldn't wait to get away, and a few decades later we'd be reminiscing about growing up." In a careful voice she added, "You too, Mr. Spooner, I hope you feel like you'll always have this place to come home to. Sorry to hear you'll be out of the country this fall."

Keeping the phone to her ear, Shirley took a quick slug of coffee and said more strongly, "I don't mean to make it sound like a Tugston family reunion, this commemoration, but there are people here for whom your family has, well, a lot of meaning. As director, I'd like to ask if you would consider perhaps a financial gift enabling the museum to commemorate the Spooners. Something we could put to a good purpose, like educational programming that's never been funded?"

After a minute Shirley grimaced. "Yes, of course, Mr. Spooner, we all have to honour existing debts. And your work does mean expensive travel. Certainly it does." She hung on for another thirty seconds before ending the call.

"Jimmy Spooner inherited, all right. He inherited Spooner DNA, including Peter's. The silver spoons are now in his mouth. And I think he stole as much of his sisters' money as he could get away with. He's just full of excuses for not donating. I bet he gambles, too, like in the family story."

She dabbed at her eye. "It would have been a small healing in this whole mess. I could've paid the Spooner sister in Nova Scotia to come and teach for a bit. Coax her into museum education. See if she would step inside here again and let us hear more of her story." Shirley poured liqueur on the coffee dregs in her cup. "Dammit, I'll raise those funds. And do something appropriate for the oldest girl, Mary Elizabeth Reilly. I hope she liked what she saw here."

"Our winter visitor wouldn't have stayed otherwise. No wonder that care place didn't fess up. They'd lost her. What did the police say when you told 'em you'd solved their case?

"They were pleased. The crime was no longer a cold case."

"Pleased? *You* solved it. And suicide's no crime if you do it by yourself."

"But a private care facility ignoring a missing resident? They hadn't said a word to the Montreal police either, not just us. So I think they'll get charged with neglect, not fulfilling the duty of care they're responsible for. Maybe more, depending on the history for their other residents. The cops in Quebec are still investigating."

Al shrugged, shook his head and twisted the cap off a second bottle. With a half-smile at Shirley he said, "What in your paperwork made you figure out it was her?"

"When the youngest sister mentioned not getting her inheritance. The museum, too, has more that should be coming to it from the estate, memorabilia family members kept. We're supposed to get the pieces when they die. I've archived the lists. The care facility confirmed Mary had a few things she treasured there, and I asked if they would give me some details. It was pretty clear to me she'd taken off with one of the listed mementos."

"That she must've tossed out after. A big old key?" Al grinned. "Remember the metal bits that wrecked the mower?"

"She knew she wouldn't want the key again once she was inside her own front door."

Forever Friends

by Ann R. Loverock

The dead girl typed another message. Her smiling picture sent a rippling fear through Mia. She sat frozen in front of her computer screen, unsure if she should answer.

"They never found my killer."

Mia had been looking forward to a quiet night. Her husband was out of town on business. Her baby, April, was fast asleep in her crib. Mia, with a glass of wine in one hand, was happily shopping online for new shoes when she heard her phone ping—notice of a new Facebook message.

"Mia, it's me, Jessica. How are you?"

The Facebook profile had the name Jessica Thornton next to the photo. Mia remembered when it was taken during a camping trip. They were both teenagers at the time. Jessica was wearing her favourite baseball cap with an Edmonton Oilers logo on the front, her sparkling blue eyes and blonde hair slightly obscured under the hat.

Reluctantly, Mia answered.

"Who is this?"

"Jessica"

"No it's not."

"It's Jessica. We're best friends forever, remember?"

"Jessica is dead."

"Are you so sure???"

Mia felt sick. She slammed the laptop shut. Jessica Thornton hadn't crossed her mind in a long time. They had been best friends

211

in high school. Inseparable. Then one night she was gone.

Mia drank the wine and went to the kitchen to pour herself some more.

"She's dead," she said aloud, reassuring herself. "She's been dead for twelve years."

She continued to drink until the bottle was empty.

The next morning was pretty routine. Despite a slight hangover. Mia got up with April around 6 a.m. She took two aspirins, made breakfast, got herself and the baby dressed and put her in the stroller. She decided ignoring the messages would be the best thing to do. This was obviously some sick pervert's idea of a joke. Jessica's family would have it shut down soon enough and that would be the end of it.

She walked around the neighbourhood admiring the manicured lawns and large homes. The six-bedroom, three-storey house she lived in now was a vast improvement from the tiny bungalow she grew up in.

Mia walked by children playing on the jungle gym in the park, their mothers watching from the nearby bench. She felt a great sense of pride in where she lived. She had moved up in life. Her husband was a doctor and, once their kids were in school, she would pursue a career in real estate.

She stopped for a moment to check on April. Mia watched her daughter sleeping, gently stroking her pink cheek. It occurred to her she had a lot to lose, a lot more than she did twelve years ago.

Mia arrived home intending to clean the bathrooms and feed April lunch. She was trying to manoeuver the stroller inside the front door when a brown car pulled up in front of the house. A familiar-looking man dressed in a suit got out of the vehicle.

Mia's blood ran cold.

"Hello Miss Hunter. It's been a long time."

"I'm Mrs. Burke now."

The last time Mia had seen Detective Archie Parker he was chubby-faced, soft-spoken, with a full head of dark hair. Here he had the look of a man weathered by a life of police work. He was balding. The hair he had left was salt-and-pepper. His skin was wrinkled and he was wearing glasses.

"Can I come in? I was hoping you may have a few minutes to chat," Parker said.

"The place is a real mess. I have to clean up, I have friends

212

coming over."

"I won't take long."

He came closer, onto the first step of her porch. April began to fuss, whimpering and thrashing inside the stroller. Mia took out a soother and stuck it in her mouth.

"It's really not a good time."

Mia pushed the stroller inside. She grabbed the door handle and began to shut it behind her.

"Miss Hunter," he called.

Mia paused.

"I'm sorry, I mean Mrs. Burke. Aren't you at all curious as to why I'm here?"

She took a deep breath and forced a smile.

"It was nice to see you again, Detective." Mia closed the door.

Once inside she pulled her phone from her purse. She had notifications of three new emails; one from her dentist, one from her mom, and another from her sister. The messages from her mom and sister both said almost exactly the same thing.

'Have you seen THIS?' with a link to a Twitter page. Mia had a sinking feeling it had something to do with Jessica. Despite her earlier decision to ignore the imposter, she opened the link.

"I was stabbed to death. Stabbed and left in the woods all alone. Can you help solve my murder?"

Mia felt dizzy. The messages weren't private anymore. They were out there for the world to see. Whoever was behind the accounts wasn't going to stop anytime soon.

"No wonder the police came calling today," she said to herself.

She looked at the Twitter feed again. It had eighty-five followers after just a few hours. The same profile picture was used; that one from the camping trip. Jessica playfully smiling. It was taken the same summer she vanished.

Mia frantically searched the news sites. She searched the name "Jessica Thornton" online for any new information. She needed to know if a body had been found. She scrolled through various news sites, both local and national. There was nothing. All the stories were from years ago. Mainly about the disappearance and subsequent search. Mia came across a picture of herself from the *Edmonton Journal*. She was at a candlelight vigil wearing a t-shirt with Jessica's face on it.

Mia sat in her kitchen, a room that usually felt so large, but today felt cramped and crowded. She breathed deeply. She barely registered her daughter's wails in the background. As much as she hated it, she knew she had to call the only person who could give her some answers.

April was seated in her highchair, tossing around her lunch of strained peas and mushed carrots. Mia searched through a cluttered drawer. It held years' worth of old pictures and junk, like ticket stubs and old address books. Nowadays that was all stored on smartphones or computers, Mia thought to herself.

She found an old phone number for Christina Gardner, a former classmate and friend. She figured it would be out-of-date by now, but called it anyway. The phone rang twice before a husky-voiced woman answered.

"Hello, I'm looking for Christina Gardner."

"Who's asking?"

"It's Mia Burke."

"Who?"

"I mean, it's Mia Hunter. I was Mia Hunter."

There was a long silence. Mia thought she had hung up.

"Hello?"

"Why are you calling me?"

"I know it's been a long time. I have been getting messages from someone pretending to be Jessica and I need to know if the same thing is happening to you."

The voice on the other end sighed.

"Yeah, a few days ago. I haven't checked my email since."

"Have the police been to see you?" Mia asked.

"No," the voice on the other end sounded alarmed. "Did they come to see you?"

"Can you meet me?"

The diner was in a busy section of town. It was frequented mostly by truckers, cops and construction workers. The coffee was decent. The food was greasy and cheap.

Christina Gardner sat alone in a booth. She twirled a knife around on the table as she nervously waited for her old friend.

Mia arrived fifteen minutes late, looking like she had come from a salon. Her brown hair was styled. Her make-up was perfect and her clothes looked expensive, aside from a few stains, which were pretty much unavoidable with a baby. She had gained a little weight, but other than that, looked just like she did in high school.

She scanned the diner, eventually resting on Christina. It was obvious she had not fared as well over the years. She was in her work uniform, clunky boots and a neon yellow vest. Her eyes looked tired and her teeth were dingy. She motioned for Mia to sit down

"I ordered you a coffee. It's about the only edible thing in this place," Christina said.

"Thanks."

Mia took a sip from the white mug in front of her. She swallowed hard. This was not coffee she considered "edible."

"How have you been?"

"I've been all right. Working construction on the new school they're building on Whyte Avenue. Keeping clean, you know. I've been sober for almost a year now."

Both women struggled to look each other in the eye.

"You've obviously been doing well," Christina said. She pointed to Mia's designer leather purse, sitting on the table. Mia shrugged, a little embarrassed.

"I guess, I can't complain."

She put her hands under the table, concealing the diamond ring on her left hand.

"So, I wanted to talk to you about this Jessica thing."

"There's a Twitter account now too. It's already got, like, two hundred followers. I'm not surprised. She was a popular girl. Seems like everybody in Edmonton still remembers her."

"The thing is Christina, this 'Jessica' person sent out a message about being stabbed to death."

Christina's eyes widened. "But they never found her body. No one could know that—except for—you know."

"You and me," Mia said softly, almost a whisper. "There hasn't been anything in the news, so that only leaves one other possibility."

Mia looked at Christina with a steely glare. The kind she used to give her back in high school. The kind of look that got Christina to do things her way.

"You think it's me?" Christina said. She shook her head. "Why would I do that? After all the time that's passed."

"I don't know. Maybe your conscience has gotten to you."

"Pfft. You're the one that did most of it. If anyone's conscience should be bothering anyone, it's not mine."

Christina sipped her disgusting coffee as Mia fumed. Her face turned red. She breathed heavily.

"That's not how I remember it, actually."

"Look, there really is no point in arguing about it. What's done is done. It was a long time ago," Christina said.

"I know that. I just want this to stop, OK?"

"I told you Mia, I'm *not* the one behind the messages."

Mia was convinced Christina was lying. She was the only person who knew what happened that night. What they did. Where they left her.

"Fine. As long as the accounts are shut down and the messages stop. That's all I want."

"Do you ever regret it?" Christina asked. She looked Mia in the eye. "Do you ever wish we didn't do it?"

A tear streamed down Christina's cheek. She wiped it away. Mia grabbed her hand and squeezed it, hard.

"You need to keep it together," Mia said in a hushed tone. Christina looked around noticing the waitress was giving her a worried look. "The cops don't know anything. They never found her body or the knife. We're fine as long as you keep your mouth shut."

The grip Mia had on Christina's hand began to hurt. Her nails dug into the skin. Christina pulled her hand free.

"You never told me what you did with the knife."

"Christina, let it go."

"How can I relax if I don't know for sure that it won't ever be found?"

"I threw it in a lake."

"A lake nearby?"

"No, one far from here. One my family and I used to go camping at when I was a kid. It's at the bottom of a lake far away. Now when I go home I expect all these social media accounts will be gone and you and I will never speak of any of this again."

Christina nodded in agreement.

Mia felt relieved. Christina would shut down the accounts and Mia would be free to get back to her life. Her husband would be home in a few hours and she was thinking of the meal she would cook for him when he arrived. She was halfway to her mother's house to pick up April when the cars with flashing lights passed her. She pulled over expecting the cars to continue. It was a shock when her car was blocked. Mia was yanked out, handcuffed and escorted into the back of a patrol car.

At the police station Mia sat across from Detective Parker. It was the same interrogation room they were in twelve years ago. Parker had questioned her at length when Jessica first disappeared.

"Would you like a glass of water?" Parker asked.

Mia didn't answer.

"I think you'll be surprised how good it will feel to tell the truth for once."

"Christina was wearing a wire," Mia said, more a statement than a question.

"Yes."

"And she was the one behind the Facebook messages."

"No, that was me," Parker said.

Mia appeared surprised.

"Christina told us the truth. After that I set up the accounts thinking it may put enough pressure on you to finally come clean."

"Clever. So what exactly did Christina tell you?"

"That the two of you picked up Jessica after sneaking out late at night. You drove to a secluded spot. On the count of three you and Christina, both holding onto a kitchen knife, stabbed Jessica to death. Then you buried her in a shallow grave. I just don't understand why."

Mia shrugged. She knew better than to talk to the cops. Besides, even if she told him, he wouldn't understand. The reason for killing Jessica sounded petty, but it was a major betrayal back in high school. Just like Christina had betrayed her today.

"All I can tell you was it was Christina's idea. I didn't really have much involvement. I mean I was there, but it was all her. She was very intimidating, even back then."

"It's her word against yours, Mia."

"So you think a jury is going to believe a former addict over a stay-at-home mom?"

"I think you might not get your way this time," Parker said.

He watched as Mia was led to a holding cell. She would soon trade in her designer clothes for an orange jump suit and her big house for a three-foot by nine-foot cell.

The Twitter feed and Facebook status of Jessica Thornton was updated one last time.

"A heartfelt thanks to everyone who has been keeping me in their thoughts and prayers all these years. This morning Christina Gardner and Mia Hunter Burke were charged with my murder."

The End of the World

by Catherine Astolfo

Catherine Astolfo is the author of The Emily Taylor Mysteries *and* Sweet Karoline, *published by Imajin Books. In 2012, she won the Arthur Ellis Award for Best Short Crime Story in Canada. Catherine is a member of Sisters in Crime. She's a Past President of, and Derrick Murdoch Award winner for service to, Crime Writers of Canada. For more info visit www.catherineastolfo.com.*

Grace says to Douglas, "This doesn't really feel like a crime, even though it *is* illegal. Perhaps in this case, the law is irrational, not the two of us."

They will commit their crime at the End of the World. With capitals.

Douglas, of course, is characteristically silent. As an introvert, he's always been shy and reserved. Since the stroke, he has had physical barriers as well. If he'd been a talkative husband, Grace might have noticed a huge difference. She has always done the yammering. Has happily continued to do so.

As she guides the car along the empty road, Grace notices that even now she appreciates the scenery. They haven't lived in Jasper long enough to be blasé. Ten years is a short time to a real westerner.

Ahead, the highway appears to narrow and disappear into a copse of trees. A yellow smudge pokes above the emerald triangles, a golden streak across the jade branches. She tries to think of the landscape in majestic descriptions, gives tribute to its grandeur with her words.

Her job as a newspaper reporter and, later, as a novelist, has left her with a dictionary and a thesaurus in her head. Words float by endlessly. Sometimes they leave impressions on her eyes and other times, she tastes them on her tongue. When she is with Douglas, she recites them to him, keeping him amused and entertained with her syntax.

Over the years of their marriage, they have been a nearly perfect pair. Part of their success, Grace thinks, is that they never had children.

"Offspring tend to suck the life out of you," she often declares.

Fortunately, Douglas agrees. They have spent their life on the go, following any newspaper or magazine that would give her a higher position. As a computer programmer, when such technicians were scarce, Douglas had a portable skill.

It's hard to believe they have been semi-retired for ten years. The time has, quite literally, flown past. It's also amazing that they have stayed in one place so long. Gazing up at the mountains just becoming tinged with white at this time of year, Grace knows that the topography has a lot to do with their contentment.

Another reason for their successful union is that they are complete opposites. Grace would usually explain it by saying, "You know the adage that opposites attract? In our case, it defines us. Douglas listens, I chatter. He cooks, I eat. He putters around the house; I go out to work. He is thoughtfully conservative. I am an emotional liberal."

She knows, however, that it's less superficial than that. Their partnership works because of her husband. Despite their differences, they never quarrel because Douglas thinks Grace is superwoman, capable of almost anything, someone to be admired.

He accepts everything she says and does without a whisper of protest.

It was she who initiated their first date, conversations at the coffee shop, long strolls through the park. Grace offered the first kiss, though Douglas became an enthusiastic participant very quickly. She arranged and executed their first sexual encounter too. He was the virgin. Despite strong urges, Douglas was never taught a single thing about physical love, other than admonitions to avoid it from his strict Presbyterian parents.

Yet the release and joy he found in intimacy were undeniable. With Grace, he was grateful, amazed and in love forever. He was an avid student, too, and more than able to keep his flighty, creative wife happy. In fact, their sex life was extremely active until the stroke.

Grace never wavers in thinking that Douglas has all the qualities she lacks and therefore cannot live happily without. What she adds to his life is excitement, fun, risk. Not qualities exactly, but she makes his life bigger, fuller. She thinks it's terribly unfair that he has been denied more years of pleasure.

"Remember when I went to work for the Northern Gazette and you got a job with the oil company, designing their first websites?" she asks him now.

She expertly guides the car around a bend in the road, past the spot that appears to end in forest, an optical illusion of curvature and density. Perhaps it's the wide expanse of blue river trailing along beside them that has made her remember the Fort, with its smudged northern lights and brisk water.

"You loved fishing up there, didn't you, darling? But those winters! I know the cold was hard for you. Wasn't that when I got the position in Toronto? We felt as though we'd gone to the tropics."

She laughs for both of them, knowing he loves to reminisce. Her words occupy them both, his forced silence giving her the burden of keeping them calm. In the past, Grace has provided the excitement, the rationale, the electric buzz in their lives. Douglas was the conduit, the base.

When Grace looks in the rear view mirror, she sees the Athabasca River winding its way from a glacial home. The blue is a clear robin's egg colour, dotted with rocks that can be seen clearly through the transparent water.

Next they cross the Miette River. Grace thinks about numerous picnics and leisure times watching the confluence of the two mighty streams as they tumble into and over one another. It was here that they nearly made a fatal error.

"Remember that time we almost got trampled by the elk?"

There is no response from Douglas, but she knows he recalls the moment vividly when the bull came out of the trees straight at them.

They were inadvertently between a male and female during rutting season, something the locals had warned them against incessantly. How easy it was to make a mistake that almost cost them their lives! The regal beast, antlers etching the sky behind him, looked as tall as the mountains in the background. He snorted and turned at the last moment, as Grace and Douglas scrambled away to stand breathless and frozen behind a corpulent old evergreen.

Nothing they did saved the day. Rather, it was the capricious female who lured him in another direction.

Grace points out various signs to Douglas. Whistlers Mountain, Mount Edith Cavell, the Marmot Basin. They climb over the Icefields Parkway and take the less travelled route, straight up the mountainside. They have camped and tramped on every trail, in every park, beside every river, that they could possibly visit in ten years. Some of those sites, such as the one only reached by paddling across Maligne Lake, they'd frequented often. No longer tourists, they are privy to views and experiences only Jasper-ites recognize. Allowed to absorb the End of the World in their blood.

Grace is amazed by how much they have accomplished. Before the stroke. Always before.

For a moment she feels the heat of anger take her breath and pump her heart. As only children, they had cared for both sets of parents. For the last few years of her employment, she had worked in Toronto, so they could spend all their free time care giving. Dementia, Alzheimers, Parkinsons and Arthritis became known diseases, as familiar as the veins in her hands, the ones that betray her own aging process. It wasn't easy watching parents die a small tear at a time, like ripping apart a favourite stuffed animal, bit by bit.

"Shoot me," Douglas made her promise, as they dabbed at drool and wiped up body fluids.

"Shoot me *up*," she replied, but she knew he wanted a more boisterous end, the kind of death that matched his life with Grace.

With love and forethought and kindness, the couple allowed their parents to die with some dignity. They made decisions, provided care themselves or purchased appropriate services. All four died within eighteen months of each other, just as Grace and Douglas were considering retirement. They suddenly felt quite bewildered.

For the first time, they wondered who would protect their dignity at the end. Who would guide them to the end of their worlds? Now that they were no longer responsible for or to anyone else, what should they do? Their first reaction was to simply *go* and see what happens, as they had so many times before.

"We decided Jasper was the place," Grace says aloud, as though Douglas has been privy to these private meanderings.

And Jasper *was* the place. A passionate, tiny, insular town, where locals quite readily accept people from "away," since tourists and transient workers are a regular part of life. Artistic, playful, loud, stunning Jasper. After purchasing the local newspaper company, she continues to publish enthusiastically once a week. Hires eager, creative people so she is free but involved.

Living in a Canadian National Park has given them a different perspective.

"Remember that time I was going to pick a flower on the trail? That man was extremely upset. 'Only take a picture as a souvenir,' he lectured. I was a tourist to him. He was so right, too, wasn't he, Douglas? I had a lot to learn."

They began to experience the joy of interaction, the fragility of relationships with animals and birds and landscape, the delicate balance of life. The give as well as the very careful take. She considered what they are about to do, and she has come to terms with it. Grace is not worried about the environment, despite what others may think. They will be giving, not taking.

The train of rage puffs through her once more. She is terribly angry at a universe that could strike her Douglas, especially in this way. To cut the cords of his beautiful body, his long gangly legs. To silence his deep reassuring voice, never used idly. Giving him a death he'd feared most seems revengeful and cruel.

Despite her name, Grace is not religious. She has been in awe of the world, appreciated its magnificence, tried to shepherd its resources. She has studied people, written thousands of words about their victories and trials, their stupidity, their brilliance. But she has never looked beyond, to the cavern of a church or the arch of the sky, and idolized a god. Since the stroke, she knows it is not possible to pay tribute to a puppet master who thoughtlessly cuts the strings.

"We're almost there," Grace says, trying to lighten her voice away from the dark emotions that have alighted on her chest. "Our favourite spot, Douglas. Just the ticket to make us feel better today."

She parks at the side of the road, opens the trunk and removes everything she needs. After she gets Douglas safely ensconced, Grace pushes and pulls him up the trail. It's a fairly flat pathway, carved into the curves of the mountain, although there are lots of rocks strewn across it. On both sides, the trees stare down at them, a seventy-five-year-old woman improbably lugging her beloved uphill.

She's not even sure Douglas approves, since he can't say yes or no to this last adventure. But she's committed now. She has to stop for breaths every few feet, so it's slow and somewhat torturous, but Grace is determined.

When they finally reach the summit—not of the mountain, just of a craggy fist the locals call the End of the World—she's joyful. She has made the right decision.

"Look, Douglas," she says, pointing. "Jasper."

There it is, below them, hugging the railroad track and the river. A string of treasures, homes and businesses and restaurants, threaded amid the soaring peaks, surrounded by sentries of rock, by turquoise water. Up here, at the End of the World, she and Douglas can always clearly see why they chose Jasper.

"Isn't it beautiful?" she breathes. "Aren't you glad we did this?"

Once she finds a good spot, Grace removes the trowel and shovel and begins. The sun is fairly strong for October, but she doesn't mind. There are no insects to shush. Birds provide hymns. The bears stay hidden. She isn't terribly comfortable crouched on the side of the mountain, but Douglas is here, and that's all that matters. Suddenly she feels that he approves of her actions.

When the hole is big enough, Grace pulls the lid from the urn. It gives with a pop of suction that surprises her. She laughs.

"Douglas, you scared me."

She upturns the ceramic vase into the hole, then replaces the soil. Next she rolls a neat round rock, whose face is wrinkled and lined with bright brown streaks, onto the grave. Grace takes the plaque from inside the wheelie and plants it beside the stone. Its shiny surface lights up in the sun.

Douglas Anderson, Beloved Husband and Friend, it reads.

The plaque was destined for a proper grave, far below. A few nights ago Douglas died in their bed, as though it was the possibility of speech that had kept him alive. Since then, their End of the World vista called to her.

Grace knows that it's against the law to bury ashes outside a cemetery in Jasper National Park. She can't even get permission, because they've been here less than twenty-five years. Irrational. She believes this interment doesn't harm the environment.

Behind this bundle of trees, on the side facing Jasper, she's certain no one will find him. If they do, she's even more certain that no one will tell.

She sits for a while beside him.

"I'm going to stay in Jasper, Douglas," Grace tells him. "As long as I can do it, I'll come up to visit often. But see, even when I'm not here..." She points in the distance. "I can see this spot from our windows."

Grace bundles the tools and the empty urn into the wheelie, gives one last look at the town.

"Coming back down," she says. "Not sure I can be happy without Douglas, but I'll try. He always said I could do just about anything when I put my mind to it."

Grace turns and ambles her way down the pathway toward home.

Women Who Wear Red

by Charlotte Morganti

Charlotte Morganti has been a burger flipper, beer slinger, lawyer and aficionado of the perfect tourtière. And, always, a stringer-together-of-words. She lives on the west coast of British Columbia with her husband and the quirky characters that populate her fiction.

My name is Philip Marlow. No relation.

Although, trouble *is* my business.

I own the only book joint in town that specializes in crime. That's where Candy entered my life.

She came through the door late one stormy afternoon, red shawl draped over her left shoulder, windblown Veronica Lake hair. A real knockout. I grabbed the counter to steady myself.

She requested the newest title in a popular series featuring a bail bondswoman and the two he-men in her life. I said, "If you were the heroine, which of the men would you choose?"

Candy smiled and said the bounty hunter, with his black-on-black wardrobe and mysterious origin, was the more interesting of the two male leads. I fingered the collar of my black shirt and returned the smile. I knew what she was getting at.

After I rang up her purchase, I told her about my email service. "It's a great way to find out about book signings and new titles."

She hesitated, cleared her throat.

"I don't sell the list. I respect privacy."

She signed up.

"Candace Wright. Nice name," I said. "I'm Philip Marlow. No relation."

She stared at me, expressionless. After a moment, she slid a glance toward the carousel of movies beside the counter.

"If you enjoy movies, this is the place to come," I said.

"Especially for film noir."

She had always heard that term, she said, and never really knew what it meant. Film noir.

There are days the gods smile on you.

"I'm closing up for the night," I said. "Come next door for a coffee and I'll tell you about Sam Spade and Bogie. They *are* film noir."

She acquiesced, and tilted her head so that a lock of blond hair covered her right eye. I knew then she was taken with me. Especially when you consider she was wearing red. Women wear red to attract men. It's a proven fact. There's been a study on it.

I settled my fedora on my head, pulled the brim down on the right, and led her to the java joint.

I ordered my usual: tall, dark, no room.

"And what does the lady desire, Candy?" I said.

Candace, she said. Tall-non-fat-mocha-no-whip. Thanks.

At our table I leaned toward her and said, "Don't people call you Candy?"

With a languid ease, reminiscent of Dietrich, she sat back in her chair. A frown, a moue. Only her mother, she said, and very, very special friends, were allowed to use the diminutive.

Our date was a complete success. Candy couldn't have chosen anyone better to teach her about film noir. I know the villains and heroes, the ditsy dames, and the falcons that populate those films like I know my mother's name. Sometimes people tell me they don't know where Bogie stops and I begin.

About an hour or so later—in the middle of my comparison of the plots of *The Big Sleep* and *The Big Combo*—she stifled a couple of yawns. "Long day?" I said.

She nodded, again allowing her hair to tumble downward à la Veronica. Tomorrow would be even longer. Most regrettably, she had to get going; she had to visit her ailing mother.

"How about dinner tomorrow?" I said.

Any other time, she would love to, but her mother was bedridden, recovering from a shoulder operation. There was no one else her mother could rely on. Candy needed to devote her time to caring for her mother.

Well.

Some things are sent to try us.

Her mother wouldn't be an invalid forever, so I resigned myself to simply having to be patient. No pun intended.

I invested my time wisely, and learned all about Candy. It's not hard these days to find out everything you need to know about a person. What with the Internet. And the diaries and keepsakes you find in bedroom drawers. And other means.

A week after our coffee date, I dressed in my new black-on-black sweater and pants, bought a bunch of pink dahlias, blue ones being impossible to find, and went to her office to take her for lunch. She questioned how I knew where she worked.

"Candy, you told me when we had coffee, don't you remember?" She shook her head.

It was innocent happenstance that I knew where she worked. Truly. I was in her neighbourhood one morning, just down the street from her house actually, and saw her come out. She didn't notice me. The newspaper I was reading shielded me from her view. I tagged along behind her and she led me right to her office building.

I digress. To continue:

"Let's go for lunch," I said. I donned my fedora, making certain it tilted at the correct angle over my right eyebrow.

Lunch was not possible. Candy was sorry. She had to work through lunch.

Working through lunch. One of the lines women use when they are pulling you in at the same time as they appear to be pushing you away. Wanting you to jump through the hoops.

I obliged—leaped through the hoops with finesse. I sent her copies of *Dead Reckoning* and *The Maltese Falcon*, two of Bogie's best. I signed the card, "Here's looking at you."

And I really was looking at her. She simply never noticed. It amazes me how unobservant women can be.

A few days later, I showed up at her house with a fistful of red dahlias and an invitation to dinner. The dahlias were appreciated, but dinner was impossible.

"I searched for blue dahlias, but the florist told me they only happen in the movies," I said.

Candy stared at me, wordless. "Candy, really," I said. "The Blue Dahlia? Veronica Lake?"

She drew herself back a smidge. Then she pushed her hair away from her face, and glanced up and down her street. Another petite moue. It's Candace, she said. She couldn't talk, she was expected at her mother's place and was running late. She had to take care of her mother all night, she said, as she pushed the door closed.

I was beginning to think her mother was that woman Bogie dreamed up out of a bottle of bad gin. Well, Candy and I just had to make the best of a bad situation. Eventually her mother would be back on her feet and we could get on with our life together. Candy was a devoted daughter. I was a lucky guy to have someone like her. Her sense of loyalty and obligation boded well for our future together.

Physical contact is optimum. However, there are other means of remaining close to a loved one. I called her daily, sometimes more often. She rarely picked up, so I left messages, filling her in on my day, inquiring about her wardrobe choices and lipstick preferences, and leaving best wishes for her mother's speedy recovery.

In truth though, I prefer email. You can't really put a telephone call into your scrapbook, and I knew Candy would treasure my notes. They were proof of how I felt about her.

I've kept all her emails, as you would expect. Printed out and safely stowed in a wooden box, nestled in my closet alongside my fedora, trench coat and a working replica of the gun the femme fatale used in *Blonde Ice*.

And as you'd expect, I memorized Candy's emails. Their words heartened me during our time of separation. *Philip, I'm sorry but I don't think a relationship is possible.* And *I am sorry, I am so busy taking care of mom.* And *Philip, it's time. You need to move on.*

She was torn up that we couldn't get on with our life together. It's all there. You don't even have to read between the lines to see it. She was willing to sacrifice her own happiness, and mine, in order to care for her mother.

Can you believe that? Bogie was right about the bad gin. What mother would expect so much from a daughter? To sacrifice her youth looking after an old woman. To pass up the opportunity for a happy-ever-after life.

I was not dissuaded. I sent more thoughtful notes. I suggested hiring a maid for her mother. A night nurse. Assisted living.

All to no avail. It was her problem, my devoted Candy replied every time, she would handle it.

Well.

It was my problem too.

Candy didn't seem to understand. We had starring roles in the reality version of *Double Indemnity*. We were destined to take this trip together. It was one way, no stops, no return.

My sweetheart deserved a life of her own. With me by her side. She would be free to enjoy our future only when her mother didn't require her help anymore.

Around midnight I arrived at her mother's house. I wore my standard black-on-black attire. I planned a tête-à-tête, a little persuasive moment. Late at night, everything is much more private.

228

Knowing her mother was bedridden, I didn't bother to ring the doorbell. The deadbolt posed a problem, so I set about finding another way in. I checked out the front windows but they were closed. And locked. I crept to the rear of the house. The back door had a simple thumb lock. When will people learn? I slipped a credit card in there, and, presto, the door was open.

I removed my shoes. It's simply good manners. Unfortunately, I bumped into a chair before my eyes became accustomed to the darkness. It screeched on the hardwood floor. How careless of Candy's mother not to use felt protectors on the chair legs.

When my eyes finally adjusted, I found the bedroom. Light showed beneath a door across the room. I heard water running. The en suite, I presumed. The bed was mussed but empty. I deduced Candy's mother was in the bathroom.

I tiptoed over, and stood facing the door, waiting for her to come out. Then we would have our little chat.

I heard a swishing sound behind me, like something brushing over the carpet. I turned my head slightly, and out of the corner of my eye I saw a figure. It's strange the things you think about in times of stress. I was sure it was one of the Yankees standing there. Maybe it was the striped outfit that did it. Or the baseball bat.

It gets fuzzy after that. I remember seeing bright fireworks explode. When I opened my eyes, my head pounded exactly like it does when I down a few tequila shots. Outside, sirens wailed and lights flashed red, blue, red, blue. A bunch of cops milled around the room.

My lawyer Jenny asked me later about the gun they found on the bedroom floor. Movie memorabilia, I explained. To show to my dear one's ailing mother.

I found out no one was in the bathroom. The running water was a ruse.

Candy's mother was lying in wait, in her closet. With that bat. I'll tell you what really steams me. As a cop strapped me onto the stretcher and clicked the handcuff to the side rail, I said, "What gives? I was merely paying a get-well visit to my girl's mother because she has a bad shoulder."

The cop boomed out a big guffaw.

"Judging from how she swung the bat, her shoulder's perfect," he told me.

Well.

It appears Candy lied to me about her mother's ailments. I love her but she really must work on being more honest and forthright with me. As soon as I get this all taken care of I'm going to have a private little chat with her about that.

Love. Promises everything, brings nothing but trouble, and packs a wallop. When I think of all I did for Candy. How I treasured her. Everything I did—watching her, tagging along in the shadows, checking her house in her absences, visiting her mother—was done out of love and concern for her. And look what it got me. Twenty-seven stitches, blurred vision and an itchy orange jumpsuit.

Jenny, my lawyer? There's a dame with potential.

Jennifer, she says Jennifer. But we're closer than that already. She wore a red scarf when she first interviewed me.

You know what they say about women who wear red.

CPSIA information can be obtained at www.ICGtesting.com
Printed in the USA
LVOW07s1632120215

426800LV00001B/269/P